IF I DREAM

(CORRUPTED LOVE #1)

K.M. SCOTT

Books by K.M. Scott

If I Dream (Corrupted Love #1)

Crash Into Me (Heart of Stone #1)

Fall Into Me (Heart of Stone #2)

Give In To Me (Heart of Stone #3)

Heart of Stone Volume One Box Set

Ever After (Heart of Stone #4)

A Heart of Stone Christmas (Heart of Stone #5)

Unforgettable (Heart of Stone #6)

Unbreakable (Heart of Stone #7)

Heart of Stone Volume Two Box Set

Temptation (Club X #1)

Surrender (Club X #2)

Possession (Club X #3)

Satisfaction (Club X #4)

Acceptance (Club X #5)

The Complete Club X Series Box Set

SILK Volume One

SILK Volume Two

SILK Volume Three

SILK Volume Four

The SILK Box Set

Books by K.M. Scott writing as Gabrielle Bisset

Blood Avenged (Sons of Navarus #1)

Blood Betrayed (Sons of Navarus #2)

Longing (A Sons of Navarus Short Story)

Blood Spirit (Sons of Navarus #3)

The Deepest Cut (A Sons of Navarus Short Story)

Blood Prophecy (Sons of Navarus #4)

Blood Craving (Sons of Navarus #5)

Blood Eclipse (Sons of Navarus #6)

The Sons of Navarus Box Set #1

The Sons of Navarus Box Set #2

Stolen Destiny (Destined Ones Duology #1)

Destiny Redeemed (Destined Ones Duology #2)

Love's Master

Masquerade

The Victorian Erotic Romance Trilogy

2017 Copper Key Media, LLC
Print Edition

Published in the United States
ISBN-10: 1-941594-52-2
ISBN-13: 978-1-941594-52-0

Cover Design: Natasha Snow Designs
www.natashasnowdesigns.com

Adult Content: Contains graphic sexual content

If I Dream

If I dream, will you dare?

All I wanted was my freedom. It's all I'd dreamed of from the first time I stood in the ring. Until I entered Robert Erickson's world. Until Serena. Cruelty and ugliness surrounded me, but she was beautiful and good. I wanted to protect her from her father's world, even though I knew being with her could mean the end of me.

I wanted for nothing as the daughter of one of the richest men in the world. But all my father's money couldn't buy what I truly craved. Until Ryder. I wanted all he was, all he brought out in me. All he made me desire.

Our love was forbidden by the one person who had the power to harm us. We dreamed of more than living in that world, though. We dreamed of having it all, but did we dare?

PART ONE

Chapter One

Ryder

A S USUAL, THE crowd at The Pit screamed its lust for the two of us to pound the fuck out of each other. Impatient bastards. I couldn't hear any one person's words clearly, but I'd done this enough times to know what the people who'd come to watch us wanted.

Blood. Pain. And one of us as close to death as possible. It thrilled them in some sick way almost as much as I suspected winning did when their fighter crushed another person.

My opponent tonight stood nearly as tall as I did at six foot three, but his body was smaller than mine. He looked older, like something in the way he carried himself said he'd seen more of life than I had. His angular face looked hard, and on either side of his perfectly straight nose were eyes staring me down like he thought squinting and grimacing would make me run for the nearest exit like some fucking scared little boy. He was fighting the wrong person if that's what he expected.

I'd never lost and for good reason. When you had nothing but the feel of your fists beating the hell out of someone and the sound of those rabid fucks cheering you on like you were some kind of hero for nearly killing another man, all you wanted was to win.

Fifteen times I'd won right here in this dank warehouse against guys bigger and stronger than me, and every time it seemed to surprise everyone. Even those who had bet on me.

If they only knew how unlikely it was anyone could match the rage inside me, they'd never bet against me again.

Some impatient bastard behind me barked, "Stop dancing around! Hit 'em!"

Mr. Grimace narrowed his eyes until he could barely see out of them and took a deep breath. Why did he bother with all this tough guy bullshit? That's not what these bloodthirsty fucks wanted.

Pain is what they wanted.

So that's what they'd get. His or mine. It didn't matter to them.

"Scared, motherfucker?" he grunted out in a deep voice I knew wasn't really how he talked. "I'm going to fuck you up."

I didn't bother answering.

He caught me in the face with a hard right that scrambled my brains for a second, and then his fist skidded along my jaw and ran square into my right shoulder. The last guy I fought had done a number on that one, so that hurt like a bitch.

I knew how this went, though. The people around us wanted a show as much as they wanted a fight. I could have just beat the fuck out of him and won, but that's not what this was. I'd been told that enough times to understand even if I could pound the piss out of a guy, I had to at least make it look like a fight and not just some sad beat down.

So that's what I did. I took a few hits, sometimes more than a few, and let it look like there was some chance I wouldn't win. The other guy got to feel pretty big in the shorts and the crowd got to feel like this was really a match between two fighters.

It wasn't, though.

He paraded around like a peacock, preening to the crowd while I gritted my teeth and pushed my shoulder back into place. I took a deep breath and waited for the moment I'd show him who he was dealing with.

Flush with the love of the crowd, he turned back to face me. A few shots into me had made him think he had a chance.

I stepped forward as he lunged at me and leveled my fist against his jaw. His head ricocheted back, sending him reeling for a second or two, but I didn't let up. My right hand zeroed in on his face again, this time connecting with his cheekbone. I felt it crack against my knuckles bulging out of my fist and saw him stagger back away from me.

But he would get no mercy from me. That wasn't what I was here for.

"Get him!" the crowd screamed as the guy cowered, hanging his head to protect his busted face.

That wouldn't help him, though. Not with me. I knew what my role was. I knew why all these people had come here tonight, and it wasn't to see mercy. Mercy was for suckers. Fuck mercy.

They wanted blood and pain, and blood and pain is what they'd get.

I walked toward him as a feeling of complete calm came over me. All the noise of the crowd around us faded away until all I heard were the words I told myself every time I stood to fight.

It's you or him. Nothing more. Either you win or he does, but if you lose, you'll have nothing.

He looked up and I saw the pleading in his eyes. I'd seen it fifteen times before. No matter how big and tough they'd been in the beginning, each one ended up giving me that same sad look that said they wanted me to be someone other than who they'd heard I was.

Someone other than who I had to be.

Maybe they fought for some reason that had nothing to do with their very survival. Maybe they thought it would be fun, or it would make them feel tough. Maybe they thought they had something to prove to some girl. Whatever their reasons for agreeing to fight, they weren't why I fought.

For me, every win put me one step closer to being free. I didn't fight for shits and giggles or because I wanted to impress some skirt. I fought for the chance that one day I would never have to step foot in this fucking shithole place again. I fought because deep in the back of my mind there existed the tiniest dream that one day I'd be normal and have a normal life.

That one day I wouldn't have to be the man I'd been forced to become in this fight.

I knew his weak spots and attacked them. My fists pummeled his face, and no matter how hard he tried to shield himself from the blows, it was no use. Over and over, I hit him until that pretty face of his looked like mangled hamburger. Blood, flesh, and bone mixed to make a horror show. The nose that had been so straight just a few minutes before now pointed down toward his mouth like some deranged compass.

As I stood up to my full height, I heard the crowd cheering, as if I'd done something worthy of praise. A man lay in a crumpled heap at my feet, defeated and broken, and these fuckers were thrilled about it.

Looking around, I saw some clapping and others pumping their fists in the air as my win filled them with some kind of messed up happiness. Who was I kidding? What it filled was their wallets. That's why they were so happy.

Floyd raised my right arm in the air to the delight of the rabid fans and said in my ear, "That's my boy. You done good, son."

I forced a smile and nodded my head. I wasn't his boy and he wasn't my father. I was his fighter and he was the scumbag who went out to find people for me to fight. Whatever else he thought we were was all in his mind.

He lowered my arm and slapped me on the back. "Go relax. You deserve it. You put on a good show. Just look at the way these people love you!"

I tore my stare from his greasy comb-over and beady eyes and looked over his head to see the people who loved me. Between the booze, the drugs, and the fight, they looked like wild animals.

Who was worse? Them or me?

"RYDER, THERE'S SOMEONE here to talk to you," Floyd yelled from the other side of the door.

I didn't want to talk to anyone. All I wanted to do was sit on my crappy metal folding chair in this dingy room and hope my shoulder started feeling better. I'd downed a few shots of Floyd's whisky about ten minutes ago, but so far, it hadn't helped ease the pain.

"Not now," I yelled back.

He'd only open the door anyway. I knew that. It still felt good to let him and whoever the hell was standing there with him know that I didn't want to talk.

The door opened a second later and I saw Floyd and some guy who looked far too well-dressed to be anywhere near the warehouse on any night standing in my shitty little room. He had a vibe that screamed money with his suit, expensive shoes, and slicked back grey hair that made him look what my mother used to call stately.

"This is Mr. Robert Erickson," Floyd said as the man walked into the room like he owned the place. "I'll leave you two to talk."

I'd never seen Floyd leave a scene that fast. As he closed the door, I looked at the man who stood in front of me and saw he was studying me as much as I was him. Not that I was all too curious about what he wanted. People dressed like he was coming into my world never brought anything good with them.

Never.

The intruder looked around the cinder block room I called mine and then looked down at me. "Ryder, as our mutual friend Floyd said, my name is Robert Erickson. Do you know who I am?"

Shaking my head, I shrugged. "Nope. Should I?"

His dark eyebrows drew in like angry black slashes and his eyes narrowed to slits, much like the way the guy I just beat to a pulp had looked at the beginning of our fight. "I'm the man who runs this show. You are sitting in my warehouse and fighting in my stable. So yes, maybe you should know who I am."

As much as I knew he thought I should be impressed by this, I wasn't. Folding my arms across my chest, I said, "Oh yeah? Nice to meet the big boss then. I hope you bet on me tonight."

His eyes opened wider as the corners of his mouth inched up into what reminded me of how a crocodile looked right before he ate his prey. "You're pretty sure of yourself, aren't you?"

I looked up at the ceiling for a moment, unsure how I should answer that. Fuck yeah, I was sure of myself. I may not have been wearing a thousand dollar suit and fine leather shoes like him, but I had gifts of my own that had made me a winner sixteen times already.

Pursing my lips, I shrugged again. "I haven't lost yet. Come see me when I do and I'll tell you how cocky I'm feeling then."

His crocodile smile spread even wider across his face. Nodding, he said, "I'll remember that. For now, I'm here to tell you I've bought your contract from

Floyd. So now you work for only me."

The words hit me like a fist to the face. I didn't have a contract with Floyd or anyone else. I fought to pay off money I owed him, and when that debt was paid off, I'd get to leave this shithole world of fighting. Now all that seemed like a pipe dream this fucker had dashed to pieces.

I stood from my rusted metal chair and stared at Robert Erickson. "What does that mean?"

Nearly the same height, he met my gaze with one so intense I thought about taking a step back. When he spoke, it sounded like his voice came from somewhere dark.

"It means I own you now. You fight for me and I expect you to win like you always have."

Left unsaid was the implicit threat that hung off every word. If you lose, you'll suffer. The only question was how.

My mind spun at the news that all I'd planned, all I'd worked for, was gone now. "So I guess my deal with Floyd to be released from fighting when I paid off what I owed him is gone too?"

"Yes."

"And if I don't agree to this new deal?" I asked, silently gauging my chances of not only getting past him but finding some way of surviving after I got away. He was big, and I had a sneaking suspicion even bigger guys stood outside waiting for him.

Robert Erickson looked like the type of man who got what he wanted, one way or another, whether the other person involved wanted it or not.

"You have no say in it, but let me assure you that you want to fight for me. For now, let's get you to your place so you can pack your things."

He turned to open the door as I explained this room was my place. "No need to go anywhere. You're already in it."

Erickson slowly looked back at me with confusion written all over his face. "You live here?"

I nodded. "Yeah. Short commute time to work and everything I need within arm's reach. What more could a guy ask for?"

Closing the door, he turned to face me. "How old are you?"

"Eighteen."

"And you live here, in my warehouse where Floyd holds fights for me?" he asked as he looked around my room again, this time with a look of disgust like the fact made him sick.

"Yep. Better than the street or jail. I might not get three hots, but I got a cot and a shower."

My answer didn't make the sickened expression leave his face, but he nodded anyway. "Well, gather your things. It's time to go."

I opened my mouth to ask where, but he walked out and left me standing there in that room I'd lived in for the past three months. As I stuffed the few clothes I owned, deodorant, and my toothbrush into a duffel bag, I thought wherever I was going had to be better than this place.

WE PULLED UP to a massive black gate between two even bigger rows of hedges and stopped momentarily as the driver got the go ahead to drive onto the property. I couldn't help but stare out the window as we drove up the long driveway past some kind of fountain that looked like something the Greek gods might swim in and a bunch of smaller hedges than the ones out front that looked like the gardener had cut them all into bird shapes. Robert Erickson was even richer than I'd first thought. Only insanely wealthy people lived in places like this.

The car stopped in front of a house so big I couldn't see all of it as I looked out the car window. Erickson tapped me on the arm as I stared out at the mansion and said, "Welcome home."

Home? This couldn't be my home. Instantly, the thought of what I'd have to do to live in a place like this raced through my mind. Fighting in The Pit wasn't going to be enough to live in a house like the one I saw in front of me.

I opened the car door and stepped out onto a stone driveway as I gaped at the house, which was even more impressive without the tinting of the car window getting in my way. Huge white columns towered above us to the second story of the gold colored home, and a glass front door so enormous I'd never seen one so big stood behind them.

"Follow me," was all Erickson said as he led the way to those doors. I couldn't imagine what waited inside after an outside this incredible.

I did as he ordered and caught up to him as he walked into an entryway so big the sound of our shoes hitting the white marble tile on the floor echoed off the matching marble tiled walls. He strode through like nothing around us was special toward the most spectacular curved wrought iron staircase I'd ever seen.

Not that I had seen many curved staircases with wrought iron in my life. I think I'd seen either a grand total of two times in a magazine some girl had in English class one time. I really didn't have much interest in reading architectural magazines, but she did and since I wanted to get in her pants, I sat next to her after school as she told me all about her dreams of having a huge house with a curved staircase and a wrought iron railing one day.

She would have loved Erickson's place. For me, it made me feel small, something very few people or things had achieved in a long time. Not small, actually. More like insignificant.

As my head swiveled left and right to look at the

artwork on the walls, Robert said, "Come in here to my office. I want you to meet some people."

My hand clutched the handle of my duffel bag tightly in my palm. Meet some people? I didn't even look like they'd let me on the property to be the goddamned gardener who made hedges into animal shapes and now he wanted to introduce me to some people?

That feeling of insignificance morphed into one of pure discomfort. I didn't belong there, no matter how much he wanted to parade me through the place, and whoever he wanted me to meet would know that as sure as I did.

He led me into his office, a room even bigger than the entryway and as dark as that was light. This room had dark green walls the color of a pool table and a dark wood floor. Floor to ceiling bookcases held books with names I'd never heard of and sculptures I guessed cost more than my life was worth.

"Wait here. I'll be right back," he announced before leaving as I continued to look around in awe.

Seconds later, he came back with two females and ordered them into his office. Neither one looked like him, but something about the way they acted told me they weren't servants or people he'd just basically bought, like me.

They stopped dead at the sight of me standing

there in my old gym pants and black t-shirt and the one I figured was older spun around to look at him in disgust.

"Who is this?"

"Girls, this is Ryder. He's going to be living here, so treat him like family."

Robert's proclamation infuriated her, and she shook her head angrily. "What, like a brother? You go out one night and get us a brother? Is that how it goes, Dad?"

He ignored her outburst and turned his two daughters to face me. "Ryder, the one who can't stop talking is Janelle. The other one is Serena."

"Hi," I mumbled, unsure if I should say anything.

They both stood staring at me like I was some foreign thing that needed to be removed and fast. The one named Janelle had short dark brown hair, and although I couldn't be sure since her eyes were flashing so much hatred, I thought they were brown too. Thin, she wore jeans and a tight blue shirt and heels that gave her at least three inches on her normal height.

The other one, Serena, had lighter brown hair that fell to below her shoulders in soft waves that reminded me of what mermaids looked like. Dressed in jean shorts and a white t-shirt that both showed off her tan and toned body, she stood barefoot next to her father and stared at me with big brown eyes that didn't have hatred but something else in them.

Disappointment?

As Janelle returned to complaining about my very existence, I heard Serena say in a pained voice, "You said you knew where she was. You promised you'd find her this time. Where is she?"

I imagined that's what that guy with the pleading eyes would have sounded like if he begged me not to beat the shit out of him. The way she said those words made my chest hurt, and I didn't even know who she was talking about.

But Robert was unmoved by her pleading. Waving off her questions, he said, "Maybe next time, honey. For now, I want you two to welcome Ryder to our home."

He put his arms around both of them, but Janelle slipped out of his hold and stormed off without another word. I didn't have to guess how she felt about me. Serena said nothing more about what was obviously so important to her and simply looked at me with that pleading in her eyes that hadn't worked on her father.

With a nudge from him, she finally said, "Welcome to our home. I hope you like it here."

And with that, she quietly left without another word to her father about whoever she wanted him to find.

Robert walked behind his desk and sat down in his chair as I watched her walk away, her sagging shoulders signaling how defeated she felt. Clearly, it didn't affect her father at all.

"They'll get used to you. Janelle is a little temperamental, but I guess that's to be expected from a girl, even one her age. She's a lot like me, though, so at least she has that going for her. Serena is the polar opposite. She's like her mother. Don't worry about her. She'll take to you like every stray she brings home."

Not that I didn't know I looked like some stray dog compared to them, but the way he said it brought the reality home for sure. In a hurry to get out of there and to wherever he kept the strays he brought home, I said, "Well, if you can just point me in the direction of where you want me to go, I'll get out of your hair."

He shook his head as that crocodile smile spread across his face again. "Not yet. First, I want you to know what I expect of you. So sit down and relax."

Dropping my duffel bag, I sat down in a chair in front of his desk as he'd ordered and listened to hear just what this whole arrangement would involve.

He steepled his fingers in front of him and began. "You'll continue to fight as you did tonight. As I said before, I expect you to continue to win. When you do, you'll get paid, despite the fact that you won't need money as long as you live here."

"I won't need money?" I asked, confused what kind of world this guy lived in that didn't require cash.

Lifting his chin, he shook his head. "No, you won't. Your room and board, along with all the food you want and clothes you need, will be provided. I have a state of the art workout center you're to use to make sure you're in the best shape possible. So you see, you won't need money."

I didn't know if I should question this whole situation that sounded too good to be true, but I asked, "And if I don't win a fight?"

His face grew dark. "Let's cross that bridge when we come to it. For now, I have very few rules, other than you performing in fights like I've seen. No drugs and no romantic attachments. I don't care who you fuck, but don't get involved. I remember being your age, so I don't expect you to live like a monk, but no relationships."

I wasn't a fan of having so much of my life dictated, but assuming I got a room even as big as a broom closet on his estate, maybe it wouldn't be too much of a tradeoff. I wasn't exactly looking for a relationship anyway and I didn't do drugs. Hoping he wasn't about to announce that I had to double as a stable boy or something like that, I smiled.

"Okay. I can live with those."

"And you aren't to tell anyone here what you do. Is that clear?"

"Sure. But if I'm not here as a fighter, what am I supposed to say if someone asks?"

"They won't," he said with a confidence I guessed came from being the boss.

"Got it."

"Good. I'll have my housekeeper take you to your room. For now, you'll have the spare bedroom on this floor."

A short, dark haired woman he called Josephine appeared a few seconds later, so I stood from my chair and grabbed my duffel bag to go with her. I felt like there were a lot more questions I should ask Robert, but he didn't seem interested in talking anymore and picked up the phone to call someone, so I smiled again and moved to leave.

Just before I reached the door, he said, "Oh, Ryder, one more thing."

There it was. The one thing that would make this whole situation unbearable. I slowly turned around and waited for the other shoe to drop.

"Don't even think of doing anything with either of the girls. In that respect, I do care who you fuck."

I thought back to how much Janelle hated me already and easily put the idea of fucking her out of my mind. And Serena? I wasn't sure if she was even legal, and I didn't need that dogging me. An angry father was one thing, but prison was an entirely different story.

She was beautiful, though. There was something about her I could definitely like, if things were different. But no matter how beautiful she was, I wasn't touching that.

"No problem," I answered with confidence, hoping that was the worst thing about living at Erickson's house.

If it was, this would be the best thing to ever happen to me, even if it meant I had to keep fighting. Maybe freedom wasn't all it was cracked up to be anyway.

Chapter Two

Serena

TURNING THE KNOB on Janelle's door, I found it locked, as usual, so I knocked hard to get her attention. I needed to talk to someone about the fact that our father had once again gone back on his promise to find our mother.

From inside her room, my sister barked, "Go away!"

"It's me, Janelle," I pleaded, hoping it would be enough to get her to let me in.

She said nothing, but a few seconds later I heard the familiar sound of the latch coming off the door. I opened it and saw her sitting on the bed cross-legged and smoking.

"You know what Dad said would happen if he found you doing that again."

"I don't care," she snapped as I closed the door behind me and made my way over to the window to open it.

Waving the smoke out, I said, "Do you think he even looked for her?"

Janelle took a long drag off her cigarette and shook her head as curls of smoke lifted from her lips. "No, I don't. What's the point anyway? She left and if she wanted to see us, she would have found a way, Serena. You have to give up this dream of her ever coming back. He doesn't want her back."

I turned away toward the window and inhaled a deep breath of warm night air into my lungs. "I don't think it's that simple. What if she wanted to come back but he didn't let her?"

"Then it's a waste of time to keep asking him to look for her."

My sister had a way of being able to end a conversation with just a few words. So much like my father, she seemed to have a heart of steel. She'd been nearly eight years old when my mother just disappeared from our lives one night, and it was like she'd never cared to know why she left us or where she went. To Janelle, she was just gone.

Out of sight, out of mind.

I wished I could be like that sometimes. Ever since that night, I'd wondered where my mother could be. Did she leave because of something I did? I'd replayed that night and the days preceding it a million times, and nothing seemed to make sense. We were happy, or at least I thought we were.

But then suddenly she was gone and all my father told us was she'd disappeared. No more details than those ever came. I didn't know if he looked for her or not. He said he did, and two years ago on my sixteenth birthday when I began to ask him to find out where she went, he claimed he would.

Two years later and still nothing.

I didn't want to talk to Janelle about this anymore. It served no purpose.

Turning back to face her as she snuffed out that horrible habit of hers in an aluminum pie plate that worked as a makeshift ashtray, I broached the other topic I knew was on her mind.

"What did you think of that guy Ryder?"

Her usually delicate features twisted into an angry look full of hate. "What do I think of the piece of shit our father has brought into our house clearly to marry one of us? Not much since he's at least two social classes below what we deserve."

Horrified by her idea, I sat down on the edge of her bed. "What? Marry one of us? No way, Janelle. You're way wrong on that one. There's no way he wants either of us to marry that guy."

My sister's brown eyes opened wide, like she couldn't believe I didn't understand how obvious my father's intentions were. "What other reason would he have to bring a man here? And don't kid yourself. He's a man, Serena. If our father wanted us to think of someone like a brother, he wouldn't have brought someone like him around. Did you see the size of him? He's like a fucking bull."

I thought back to seeing him standing in my father's office for the first time and had to agree. He wasn't like any of the guys I'd ever been around. He seemed rougher, like he'd had to deal with life more than they had. And he was definitely built better than any guy I'd ever known. He didn't look much older than me, but something in his green eyes told me he'd seen way more of the world than I had.

"That guy has one purpose. Stud."

"Stud?" I asked, knowing the meaning of the word but misunderstanding how he could be a better choice for either of us than someone who had money and status.

Janelle laughed in my face. "You're so naïve, Serena. He's here to marry one of us so our father can finally have boys to pass on his business to. He's here to breed one of us."

"We aren't farm animals, Janelle. Daddy isn't just going to throw one of us into bed with Ryder and want him to make a baby."

"Fine, then if it makes you feel better, he doesn't see us as farm animals. He sees us as sperm receptacles. Not that this is a surprise. I just can't believe he thinks someone like him would be what either one of us should end up with. We're Robert Erickson's daughters, for God's sake!"

Ignoring my sister's comments, I tried to focus on reality. "But I thought he was going to bring you into the business. He's always saying how similar you are to him. I just figured that meant when the time came you'd get the business and that would be that."

Rolling her eyes at my apparently ridiculous idea, she lit another cigarette. "I don't have the right stuff for the business. I don't give a damn about it, in the first place, and in the second place, I'm not a male. No, our father wants a man to take his place, so he's brought us a fine stud to give him grandsons."

I thought about what she said for a few moments and saw she could be right. "I'm sorry about that for you. I mean, he's not ugly or anything like that, but he's definitely not your type. You're not usually into muscles and tattoos."

"He's got both of those in spades too. I don't even think long sleeves would cover those tattoos. They go all the way onto the back of his hands," she said with a sneer.

"They weren't that bad. They looked sort of cool, actually."

She smiled that way my father did when he wasn't so much happy as pleased at something. A sinister smile that always made me feel uneasy. "What makes you think I'm the one who'll have to fuck him?"

"You're older and more like Daddy. Why would our father want him to be with me? I might give him a grandson like me. Then where would he be?"

Lifting the cigarette to her mouth as her smile faded away, she took a drag and let the smoke float out of her mouth as she said, "I'm not going to be some baby maker for our father, Serena. Not with the likes of that Ryder guy. The only way he gets with me is if he holds me down, and even then I'll be kicking and screaming."

As the thought of Ryder doing just that to her settled into my mind, I shook my head. "Well, it won't be me. I'm going to college and getting away from here."

She sneered at me. "I wouldn't count on that. I was supposed to be in school by now. You see how that worked out."

Janelle had planned to go to school in the northeast and escape my father and everything that made up the Erickson world that surrounded us. She applied to some great schools and got accepted, but once my father heard about it, he stopped everything and threatened to cut her off if she left. College was nothing compared to the money he gave her each month, so she never left.

Now she was twenty and spent her time shopping and drinking at her friends' places in the afternoons and out with guys who were bad news most nights. So much for dreams.

I stood from the bed, tired of this conversation. My father may have been able to bribe my sister into living a life entirely dependent on him and his money, but he wouldn't do that to me. I'd already been accepted to the University of Virginia, and come hell or high water, I was going to be a college freshman in a little over two months.

"Well, it seems like our father is going to be disappointed when it comes to his stud because I'm not sleeping with him either. It's been a long day, so I'm going to my room."

She shrugged like she didn't care what I said. I left her there sitting on her bed smoking and hoped she wouldn't burn the house down some night.

ON MY WAY to my room I changed my mind and instead headed down the stairs to find my father. Janelle might have been fine with sitting in her room, smoking and stewing about this new person my father had brought home, but I wanted some answers about my mother.

I found him sitting behind his desk in his office like usual. He wore a look that told me my timing wasn't terrific, but I didn't care. I needed to know the truth.

"Daddy, I'd like to talk to you," I said in my

sweetest voice.

He looked over toward the door where I stood, and for a second, my words didn't seem to register. "What, Serena?"

"I'd like to talk to you, if you have a few minutes. It's important."

His face seemed to fall and then he turned back to look at his computer. "This isn't about not finding your mother, is it? If so, I don't have time to talk right now."

I knew a dismissal when I heard it, but I also knew how to get my father to talk, so I walked into the room and sat down in one of the two chairs in front of his desk. If he didn't want to explain to me why he hadn't found my mother this time, maybe I'd be able to get him chatting about our new houseguest and then be able to slip in my real questions.

"No, it's about that guy, Ryder."

My father's head popped up. "What about him?"

"I'm just wondering what he's doing here."

"He's here because I want him to be. He works for me," he said with a smile I knew meant he wasn't telling me the whole truth.

"What does he do?"

His smile grew so it spread nearly across his face. Leaning back in his chair, he said, "I don't think you've ever been this curious about any part of my business, Serena. This is a change for you."

"A good change?"

My father remained silent for a moment studying me. "I'm not sure. Let's just say he's here for the benefit of you and your sister, in addition to me, and leave it at that."

"What do you know about him? He doesn't look like the kind of person you usually have to dinner parties, Daddy."

My questioning quickly irritated him, and I saw I'd overplayed my hand as his smile slid down into a frown. "I would never bring anyone dangerous into this house, Serena, so you don't have to worry. In fact, you don't even have to speak to him. Just pretend he's not here. Now I have to get back to work, so give me a kiss and scurry off."

My sister's warning that Ryder was there to be with one of us sounded pretty hollow as I listened to my father basically say I didn't have to even bother with the guy. Maybe he was to be a stud for Janelle. At least I wouldn't have to deal with that.

I did as my father commanded and kissed him goodnight before telling him I loved him. As he gave me one of those rare kind smiles of his, I asked, "Daddy, do you think you'll ever find my mother?"

As if my question had caught him off guard, he continued to smile sweetly and answered, "I promise

I will keep looking for her, honey. Now off you go."

It wasn't much, but then again, my father never gave me much in the way of the truth.

Chapter Three

Ryder

A S MUCH AS I thought not being able to be with either of Robert's daughters would be the easiest part of living at his house, it didn't take long for me to realize I'd been wrong. Janelle wanted nothing to do with me, but Serena appeared intensely interested in everything about me.

Or at least it seemed like that since every time I turned around she was somewhere nearby looking at me like I was some butterfly under glass. I liked that the sadness in her eyes that had been there the first night was gone, but it had been replaced by a look of curiosity I had a feeling would end up getting both of us in trouble at some point.

The first week at the Erickson house went by quickly since I preoccupied myself with getting a feel for the place and avoiding practically everyone, for the most part. My new boss informed me the day after bringing me here that my next fight would be nearly two weeks later, a luxury I'd never had before with Floyd, so that left me time on my hands.

My mother used to say idle hands were the Devil's workshop, which seemed to be truer than I'd ever known by the end of that first week as Serena dogged me practically everywhere I went in the house. I saw her peeking around corners outside the pool in the morning when I went for a swim, through the window of the door to the workout room as I lifted each afternoon, and even near my bedroom a few times as I returned from talking to Robert at night.

I had no idea what she wanted or if she thought she was being sly about it, but I couldn't deny I was curious. The problem was that was exactly what I shouldn't be.

Finally, the day before my next fight, I caught her right near my room after listening to her father repeatedly remind me of how important it was to win for him. Frustrated and a little nervous about going back to The Pit in less than twenty-four hours, I let my curiosity get the best of me and snuck up behind her as she spied on the door to my room.

"See anything interesting?"

Serena spun around and stared up at me with wide eyes full of fear. "I…I wasn't spying on you, if that's what you think."

"That's exactly what I think. Why have you been following me since I got here? Did your father ask you to keep an eye on me and report back to him?"

Whatever fear she felt evaporated, replaced by confusion at my questions. "No, my father would never ask me to do that. In fact, I think he'd rather if I never spoke to you at all."

She was right. It was better if that's exactly what happened. Moving around her to go into my room, I said, "Sounds like a good idea."

I opened the door but Serena stopped me with a touch of her hand on my arm. "I just want to know about you since you live in my house. That's it. My father said to think of you as family, so that's what I'm trying to do."

Looking down at where her fingers touched me, I felt my skin grow hot. I lifted my head to see her staring at me with that look of vulnerability she wore that first night when she asked her father about whoever he hadn't found for her and my chest tightened.

"So you want me to be your big brother?" I teased.

"You're not much older than I am, Ryder, so you wouldn't be my big anything, and it feels weird thinking of any grown man I just met a few days ago as my brother. Maybe we could just be friends."

I let my gaze wander up from her tanned bare feet and legs to her too-short cutoffs and had a feeling this was the moment I'd live to regret if I made the wrong choice.

And then I made it anyway.

"Friends, huh? Okay, but something tells me we have very little in common to be friends."

The obvious truth seemed to strike her as we stood in the doorway to my bedroom, but she just smiled in a way that made her dark eyes light up. "Maybe, but that doesn't mean we can't try, right?"

"Sure."

I wasn't sure at all that I should even be talking to her, much less discussing us being anything to one another there on the threshold of my bedroom.

Still smiling, Serena held out her hand to shake mine. "Hi, I'm Serena Erickson. I live here. Nice to meet you."

I took her hand in mine and shook it. "I'm Ryder. Nice to meet you too, Serena."

As her hand slid out of my hold, she looked around me. "Do you like your room? It can get a little noisy down here sometimes."

"It's okay. Probably the nicest room I've ever had, come to think of it."

She took a step toward me and then walked right into the room. I followed her and watched as she examined the place like she'd never been there before.

After looking into the bathroom, she turned around to face me. "Do you know this is the first time I've been in this room? I've lived in this house all my life and I've never once come in here. Weird, huh?"

I had a feeling she planned to stay for a while, so I sat down on the bed, hoping to reclaim some kind of ownership of the room. "Yeah, pretty weird."

My gaze slid down her body as she stood in the bathroom doorway. Like the first time I met her, she wore cut-off shorts that were too short, a t-shirt, and no shoes. "Do you always walk around barefoot?"

Serena nodded. "Always. I have a thing with shoes," she said in a quiet voice.

"That's different," I said as she slowly walked toward my bed and sat down on the edge. "Most girls can't get enough shoes."

She turned her body toward me and brought her feet up onto my bed in front of her. Slowly, she ran her hands down her legs until they touched her ankles, and I noticed how clean her feet were considering she never seemed to wear shoes.

I thought about saying something about that, but staring down at her feet, she said, "When I was seven, this guy kidnapped me to get ransom money from my father. He had this thing with shoes. He loved them. The whole time he had me, he made me wear these dresses like dolls wear and every dress had a different pair of shoes I had to wear."

Her voice grew smaller with each word as I sat horrified at what she said. "Oh. I didn't know."

Serena looked up from her feet and smiled. "I know. I just wanted to explain why I never wear shoes."

"Was it awful?" I asked, feeling more morbidly curious than anything else.

She shook her head. "He didn't do anything to me, if that's what you're asking. I was at his house for three days, and the whole time he waited for my father to pay the money he wanted, he treated me like I was a doll. But he didn't undress me or anything like that. He just kept me tied to a chair and every couple hours he'd bring a new outfit and shoes and walk me to the bathroom. Then he'd tie me up again in the new clothes and shoes and give me something to eat."

The way she talked about something that must have been terrifying for a little girl felt distant, like she hadn't actually lived through it or been affected by it. But the fact that she never wore shoes showed it had done something to her.

"Well, I wouldn't wear shoes after that either, I guess."

Her eyes opened wide, like she was surprised at what I said, and her body relaxed. "So how long are you staying here, Ryder?"

"I don't know. I guess that's up to your father."

I waited for her to ask me what I was doing there, even though Robert had said no one would, but she never did. As we began to talk about things like the shrubs trimmed into animal shapes and how much I liked the pool and workout room, I had a sense she didn't care why I was there.

She just seemed to like that I was. And as much as I knew I shouldn't, I liked that.

✧   ✧   ✧

ROBERT TAPPED ME on the arm as the car rolled to a stop outside the warehouse, tearing me out of my head. I preferred to be alone before fighting, but since he was for all intents and purposes my owner, I had little choice but to let him be around while I got my mind in the right place for the match.

"Are you ready?" he asked in a way that signaled impatience.

"I will be."

He stared at me with those dark eyes of his and nodded. "Good. You've had two weeks to get ready. I'm putting good money down on you tonight."

I wanted to ask if there was anything such as bad money, but now wasn't the time for being a smart ass. "You'll get what you want. I know how this goes."

That I'd spent the night before talking with one of the two people he'd explicitly forbidden me from being with said otherwise, but I wasn't going to think about that. Now I needed to get my head in the game before I got it crushed in by some superstar wannabe.

"Aren't you curious to know who you'll be fighting?" he asked as I leaned toward the door to get out.

Shaking my head, I looked back at him. "Nope. I'll know all I need to know about him the minute he's standing in front of me."

Robert let out a laugh like I'd said something funny. "You are one cocky son of a bitch, son. Well, I guess we'll see if that's true."

"I guess we will."

He followed behind me as I walked into the building I'd called home until two weeks before. That time away made the place seem different. The smells were the same, dirty and dank. It looked the same as it had when I left last time, all rusted metal and busted concrete. The sound of the crowd screaming as the two fighters in front of them did their thing sounded the same.

But it just felt different there now.

Robert slapped me hard on the back, pulling me out of my study of my old home. "I'll see you after you're done. One word of advice. Keep moving."

He left me standing outside the dressing room wondering what the hell he meant by that. I'd see soon enough, so I headed in and hung my hoodie and pants up on a nail barely clinging to the strip of plywood on the far wall. The toilet in the corner of the room was free, so I took a piss and got myself ready for when Floyd called my name.

Ten minutes later, he bellowed, "Ryder Rhodes and Luke Mason! You're up!"

I strode out to the center of the main room of The Pit and waited to see who I'd be fighting. After another couple minutes, he hadn't showed and the crowd began getting restless, so Floyd yelled his name again and we all waited as I wondered if tonight would be a bust. Then from the changing room came someone I'd never run into on the fight scene before.

Fuck, this guy was huge. Robert's advice to keep moving finally made real sense. The guy lumbered toward where I stood and came to a stop. Very few people lumbered, but that's exactly what it looked like when he walked, like his limbs weighed too much for his body to handle. Even a few yards away, he towered over me, but it wasn't just his height. This Luke guy looked like he belonged in some bizarre car pulling competition, not the Baltimore underground fighting circuit.

Floyd rattled off the basics that pretty much added up to there were no real rules and the one who gave up first lost and then he backed out of the ring to let us at it. Unlike Mr. Grimace a couple weeks before, this guy came right at me. No playacting tough from him.

I got past him and dodged the first shot, but his second came fast and connected square with my eye. He looked disappointed, so I guessed he'd been aiming to break my jaw or my nose. Either way, he hit hard and for a second I couldn't even get out of my own way as he pummeled me over and over in the face and my bum shoulder. I staggered back away from him hoping to catch my breath, and he turned toward the crowd to enjoy their love for his attack on me. Luckily, the cheers of the crowd distracted him long enough for me to get my wits back, so when he stopped preening for the fans, I was ready for him.

At least I thought I was.

He charged me like a fucking bull and I was holding a red cape. Fuck, the guy was jacked up! I caught him on the cheek like I had with the guy two weeks before, but this time I did no damage. He shook it off like it was nothing and hit me with a right and then a left, sending me flying to the ground. I landed hard on my ass and knew if I didn't get up right then, the fight was over. He'd jump on me and pound me into dust.

So I was the one who did the jumping and scrambled to my feet in time for him to connect with my right shoulder one more time. That nearly took my breath away he hit me so hard. Backing up, I tried to shake off the pain as I got my shit together. If I didn't start doing some damage now, he was going to beat me and fucking good.

Quickly, I figured out what his weakness could be. He was big, but that wasn't always as great as it sounded. Bigger often meant slower, so I had to use that to my advantage.

Time to get those feet of mine moving.

I didn't generally like to dance around since the crowd saw it as avoiding getting hit. They didn't care if I got the piss knocked out of me, but I did. He came at me again, but this time I zigged and zagged left and right and jammed my elbow into the back of his head as he passed me. My bone slammed into his skull, sending him to the ground.

And that was my chance.

While he struggled to get back up on his feet, I pummeled his sides with kidney blows. He doubled over, and I jumped on him. My fists crushed his jaw and anything else I could find to slam them into until he fell onto the ground and curled up to protect himself. I didn't stop my attack, but then I saw that familiar two fingers signal as he surrendered.

The deafening sound of the crowd roaring its delight at my win made adrenaline race through me, and I stood to raise my arms in victory as Floyd came toward me to officially pronounce me the winner. I'd fought harder guys before, but for some reason, this win felt better than any other one.

"Ryder Rhodes is the winner!" he yelled to the crowd, which cheered even louder.

Floyd smiled at me and in my ear said, "You must be living right with Mr. Erickson, son. Good job."

I thanked him and looked out to see my new boss giving me that crocodile smile from the back of the crowd. He had every reason to grin. If he'd put down the kind of money I thought he did, I'd just won him a shitload more.

Ten minutes later, I sat in the dressing room as other fighters congratulated me on my undefeated run while the pain in my shoulder made it feel as if someone was jackhammering into the bone. I was going to need more than two weeks to recover if I kept having to go up against behemoths.

Erickson appeared in the doorway and waved me out to leave. I did my best to hide how hurt I was, knowing I was only useful to him if I could win. Chuckling, he slapped me on the back and sent waves of pain tearing through my shoulder.

"You did good. I didn't think you'd be able to handle that guy."

"Yeah, he was something else," I mumbled as we walked toward his car.

Stopping, he turned to look at me and chuckled again. "Where did that trademark cockiness go? You won, remember?"

The pain radiating across my back and down my arm made celebrating my success difficult, but I didn't want him to know how hurt I was so I forced myself to smile. "I wasn't sure you liked that cockiness, so I figured I'd try to tone it down a bit."

Erickson opened the car door and stood waiting for me to get in. "No need. You have every right to be cocky. You were a junkyard dog out there tonight. You're as good as I heard you were and as good as you think you are. In fact, I think tonight you should treat yourself to something. What do you say to a little entertainment good enough for an undefeated champion?"

I had no idea what he meant by that, but all I wanted to do was soak in a hot bath for hours and then talk to Serena. When he closed the door and told the driver to take us to someplace called The Red Velvet Room, I had a feeling I'd get to enjoy neither.

Chapter Four

Serena

FOR THREE DAYS, Ryder avoided me. I waited by his room to see him, but he never seemed to come out. Not for a swim, or to work out, or even to talk to my father. I began to wonder if he'd disappeared into the night like my mother.

By the fourth day, I was bound and determined to find out why he suddenly wasn't around. When I heard my father leave the house just before midnight to go visit his current girlfriend, I tiptoed down to Ryder's room, and as my heart slammed against my ribs, I knocked on his door. While I waited, my mind conjured up a thousand reasons why he may have left the house not even a month after moving in, but whatever had caused him to change, I wanted to know why.

He didn't answer my first knock, so I knocked again, this time a little harder. When he didn't answer that time either, I thought about forgetting the whole thing. My curiosity got the better of me, though, and I turned the doorknob and found it unlocked. Whether or not it was a sign I should go inside, I took it as one and quietly opened the door to find Ryder's room empty.

What had happened to him?

From the bathroom, I heard a noise like a moan. It hit me like a bolt of lightning and made me freeze in place where I stood. Was he in there with someone?

I didn't know if I should continue, but I needed to know if he was in there and what he was doing, so I willed my feet to move and quietly walked over to the door to listen for any more noises. He moaned again, deeper than the first time, but it didn't seem like a sound of pleasure.

Was he hurt?

Slowly, I opened the door to see him lying in the bathtub, his eyes closed as the water filled in the space around him. His muscular body looked just as I'd imagined it—tanned and rugged, like every muscle strained against his skin—but his right shoulder looked swollen and his face had bruises all over it.

I didn't know if I should apologize for prying or offer to help him. He opened his eyes and turned to look at me as I stared at him, effectively eliminating my indecision as to what to do.

"I would ask what you're doing in my bathroom, but from what it looks like, you're back to studying me. See anything you like?"

Averting my gaze from traveling over the muscular and tanned peaks and valleys of his washboard abs to between his legs, I focused on his bruised face. "Was it your smart mouth that got you beaten up like that?"

He winced at my mention of his injuries and shook his head. "Nope. Why don't you give me a couple minutes and I'll come out seeing as you don't look like you intend on leaving?"

I agreed and closed the door as my heart began slamming into my chest again. If my father caught me in Ryder's room with him dressed or not, he'd go crazy. The man had tried to convince me to stay a virgin until I was married, sitting me down for a rare serious talking to when I was sixteen like I hadn't had sex yet. I admittedly hadn't had that many boyfriends, but I wasn't some virginal little girl, no matter how much he wished I was.

While all this raced through my mind, Ryder appeared wearing only a white towel slung low on his hips. God, his body was incredible! He looked like a statue carved out of granite. Hard and chiseled, every inch of him perfect, from his broad shoulders and muscular chest to his hip bones that formed a V shape guiding my eyes down to where that towel barely hung on to him, he stood in front of me and my mind scrambled to decide what I should focus on.

Those gorgeous muscles or all those tattoos that covered his skin.

For a moment, I stood dazed, but then I saw clearly how beaten he was. The bruises on his jaw and under his right eye were bad enough, but his shoulder looked terrible. Swollen and purple, it had to be agonizing for him.

The urge to help him washed over me, and I asked, "Would you like me to get you an ice pack for your shoulder? It looks very painful."

He winced again as he looked down at it. "It hurts like a son of a bitch, but no, thanks. How about you just turn around while I put some clothes on?"

I couldn't help myself. I let my gaze slide down his still damp body to where that towel barely clung to him as I nodded and said, "Okay."

Closing my eyes, I turned around as I listened to him open a drawer and then close it, all the while imagining what he looked like standing there naked.

"Okay. You can turn back around now. I'm decent," he said with a chuckle.

I turned around to see Ryder walk past me in just a pair of black basketball shorts and a red t-shirt to lie down on his bed. He put his arms behind his head before lowering them a second later, probably because as much as he wanted to appear cool, he was in real pain.

Unsure what to do or say, I slowly inched toward the bed as I asked, "What happened to you? Where have you been for the past three days?"

His deep green eyes stared up at me for a long moment before he said, "Right here."

"You haven't left this room for three days?" I asked, sure I'd never heard anything so bizarre.

"Nope."

Frustrated by his unwillingness to tell me anything, I snapped, "Is that all you can say? Nope?"

Slowly, the corners of his mouth rose into a sexy smile. "Why, Serena, I didn't realize you cared so much."

I sighed and sat down at the foot of his bed. "So you aren't going to tell me what happened to make you look like that?"

He started to answer nope but stopped. Still smiling, he said, "It's better you don't know. Just assume I pissed someone off. That sounds believable, doesn't it?"

Screwing my face into an expression that showed how frustrated he made me, I grumbled, "Yes."

"Well, then that's my answer. Now I have a question for you," he said with a twinkle in his eyes.

I turned to face him and crossed my legs. "What's that?"

"Why are you here in my bedroom at midnight? Shouldn't you be in bed?"

God, I hated the way he acted like he was so much older than I was!

My stomach tensed and I leaned forward toward him, my hands landing on the bed next to his legs. "I'm not a child, Ryder. We're about the same age, so why would I be in bed at midnight?"

"Then I'll rephrase the question. Why are you here in my bedroom?"

I didn't exactly know the answer to that. I'd missed spending time with him after we'd stayed up talking the other night, and I certainly was curious why he'd suddenly disappeared. But I didn't know how to explain all that.

So I blurted out the first thing that jumped into my mind. "I was in a talking mood and no one else is home."

Neither of those were exactly lies, but as far as excuses went, neither was the truth. The problem was I didn't really know how to express to him why I'd gone looking for him that night.

"It's just the two of us?" he asked with a curious look on his face. Was he concerned about that?

I nodded. "Yeah. Janelle is out for the night, and my father went to see his latest girlfriend. There are still staff around, but other than that, it's just us."

He processed what I said for a moment and nodded. "That sister of yours is a piece of work, isn't she? I don't think I've ever seen hate at first sight like she had for me."

"She's just unhappy because she's stuck here. Oh, and because she's sure our father brought you here to be a stud with her."

Ryder laughed and then winced as he cradled his shoulder. "Ow. A stud? As in I'm supposed to sleep with her kind of stud?"

"Is there any other kind?" I teased.

He shook his head. "I guess not. Well, you can tell her that's not why your father brought me here. In fact, he made a point of telling me I wasn't to be with either of you."

Relieved I'd been right, I moved up the bed toward him. "I told her that. She's just a little crazy sometimes."

"If crazy means bitchy, I guess."

We sat there silently for a minute before I asked, "Why did my father bring you here?"

I saw by the way his face stiffened that he wasn't going to tell me the truth. "I work for him. That's all I can say." His expression softened, and he added, "I promise I'm not working as his stud, though."

"Well, you aren't the gardener or the pool boy because we already have them. And you don't seem to cook or clean or drive his cars. So I'm not sure what you could be other than the obvious."

He chuckled. "Stud?"

"Nope. Son. You're here to make up for what

he's never had."

I hadn't intended on sounding so sad when I said that, but it was the truth. Janelle and I weren't males. Our father liked us well enough and may even have loved us, at least when we were smaller and less hassle, but the simple fact was we would never be what he wanted most of all.

Ryder shook his head. "And what's that mean?"

"An heir," I answered, forcing myself to smile. "Someone he can pass down the business to since he can't pass it down to Janelle or me."

"I hate to disappoint you, but he doesn't want me here to be his heir. I'm pretty sure of that."

He wasn't going to tell me why my father brought him to the house, but maybe it wasn't to take the place of the son he never had. I couldn't think of any other reason to bring him home, though.

It didn't matter. Ryder was like my father. I could ask until I was blue in the face, but I wasn't going to get the truth until he wanted to tell me.

Changing the subject, I jumped up from the bed and said, "I'll be right back. Don't go anywhere."

I ran to the kitchen for an ice pack and returned to the bedroom. "Whoever hit you did a number on your shoulder. You should put ice on it to bring down the swelling. You might even want to see a doctor about that."

Dismissing my offer, he said, "It'll be fine. I just need to keep it immobile."

"Move over," I ordered as I sat down next to him on the side with the hurt shoulder.

He looked surprised but did as I said, making room for me to sit next to him on the full-size bed. "You're pretty demanding when you want to be."

Pressing the ice to his shoulder, I held it there and said, "And when others don't want me to be."

We sat silently next to one another on his bed as I kept the ice on his shoulder until I worked up the nerve to ask him about the tattoos that covered both his arms from his wrists to his shoulders and half his chest.

"That's a lot of tattoos. Did it hurt to get so many?"

For a moment, he seemed surprised by my question. Or maybe he thought it was stupid. Whatever he thought, he smiled and looked down at his arms like he'd forgotten all about his tattoos until I mentioned them.

"No, not really. Maybe on some parts of my arms, but not really. Do you have any?"

I stared down at the myriad of images on his skin and shook my head. "No." Pointing at his left wrist, I asked, "What's that supposed to be? It looks like some animal or something."

"It's a dragon's eyes." He lifted his arm to show

me the underside where the rest of the creature hid. "There's the rest of him."

Leaning forward, I stared at the dragon with a long spikey tail that traveled up toward his elbow and looked like it practically came off his skin. "Why are all your tattoos black and white? You don't like color?"

Ryder shrugged. "I could lie and say I think black and grey are more artistic, but the truth is I didn't have a lot of money when I first started getting them so I skipped the color."

I looked up at him and wondered why he'd chosen to be so honest with me. Every guy I'd ever spent any time with would have gone with a much cooler lie.

"Oh. Well, they're nice even if they are black and grey," I said, correcting myself.

My compliment was met with silence. Unsure if I'd said something wrong, I waited for him to speak and when he didn't, I filled the empty space on my own.

"So some guy didn't like your smart mouth and beat you up?" I asked as I watched his expression to see if he'd get any closer to the truth when he answered this time.

A slow smile spread across his mouth, showing his straight teeth. "How do you know it was a guy? It could have been a girl."

His teasing made me chuckle. "No way. You're pretty big and I've never seen a girl who could do that kind of damage to someone your size. Nope, it was a guy, and I bet you did something like hit on his girlfriend to make him angry."

Ryder raised his eyebrows in surprise. "So that's what you think of me, huh? I'm just some guy who would try to steal another guy's girlfriend. Sounds pretty shitty."

Instantly, I felt bad for saying anything and my hand holding the ice pack slipped from his shoulder. He winced in pain, compounding the damage from what I'd said and making me feel even worse.

I quickly replaced the ice on his shoulder and apologized. "I'm sorry. I didn't mean to say you were shitty like that. I just...I guess I wasn't thinking. I'm sorry."

He stared at me as I spoke, his eyes slowly narrowing until he looked like he was studying me. When I finished, he remained silent for a long moment before saying, "You worry a lot about hurting other people's feelings, don't you?"

Something in the way he said that as he practically glared at me hurt my feelings. Turning my head, I looked away toward the door and shrugged. "I was just trying to apologize. Sorry."

I should have left at that moment since the conversation had clearly turned sour, but I didn't want to. I didn't know why, but Ryder intrigued me and I wanted to spend more time with him.

Even if he didn't feel the same about me.

After a few moments, he said, "So that sister of yours seems to hate me more every day. Is that going to be an issue with your father?"

Turning to look back at him, I shook my head. "I don't see why. If you're not here to stud with Janelle, he'd probably just as soon have you avoid her. Most people do since she's a little difficult."

"What about with you?"

I thought about my relationship with my sister and didn't know how to answer that question. Not exactly close, she wasn't as bad as she could be. "Well, she's like a typical big sister. Anyway, we're all we have since it's just us and our father."

Ryder grinned in a way that was nothing less than wicked. "And me. Now you have a brother."

Rolling my eyes, I said, "No, I don't, unless my father has decided to officially adopt a grown man now."

He chuckled. "You never know."

I pressed the ice pack to his shoulder to stop it from slipping again. "I guess I don't, but I still don't think I'll ever consider you a brother. I never wanted a brother anyway, so I'm sorry to say you can't be that."

My dismissal of the whole brother thing didn't

seem to bother him much. He simply continued to look at me like he was studying me, which quickly became unnerving. Turning away, I asked, "So do you have any brothers or sisters?"

"You mean other than you and Janelle?"

I looked back at him and shook my head. "Stop. You know what I meant. Real brothers or sisters."

For the first time since I'd intruded on him lying there in that tub, he looked truly unhappy. "No. It's just me."

"What about your mother and father?" I asked, needing to know what he meant by that answer.

"Dead," he answered in a clipped tone.

I wanted to ask how they'd died, but I didn't because the way he said that word told me he didn't want to talk about that. I could understand. Even thinking about my mother sometimes made me so unhappy I didn't want to talk either.

"So how long will your shoulder take to heal?" I asked, hoping my change of topic would bring back the person he'd been before.

He looked down where my hand held the ice pack to his skin and then up at me. "I don't know. A while, I guess. It's not the first time I've injured it."

Like with his parents' deaths, I wanted to ask about what kept hurting his shoulder, but I got the sense that he wouldn't give me any answers to that question either.

The ice pack began to feel warm against my palm, so I stood up and said, "You can get another cold one from the freezer in the kitchen. We have a bunch of them. Once the swelling goes down, you'll feel a little better."

"Time to go already?" he asked with a sly smile.

I had the sense that he didn't want to stop our talk so soon, but the whole time I'd been next to him holding that ice to his shoulder, all I could think about was how incredibly sexy he was. Between the muscles and the tattoos, his body was a distraction no matter which way I looked at it. Concentrating on what we were discussing became harder and harder with every minute. The urge to touch him, to run my fingertips over his skin and feel the softness of it over the hard muscles beneath nearly over-whelmed me, and I wasn't sure I'd be able to stop myself if I stayed much longer.

As I walked upstairs to my room, I knew the answer to why I'd gone to see him tonight. The only question was why did he want me to stay?

Chapter Five

Serena

THE STAFF BUZZED around the house setting up flower arrangements and checking food deliveries as I wondered why all this activity was going on. My father hadn't told me about any party, so why did the florist and caterer seem permanently stationed at our house at five o'clock on a Thursday?

Poking my head into his office, I saw him seated behind his desk staring at his laptop. He didn't look upset or angry, so I took a chance and knocked on the doorframe.

"Do you have a minute?"

He looked over at me and nodded. "What is it, Serena?"

As one of the housekeepers passed me with an enormous purple and white flower arrangement, I said, "I was wondering why we're getting all these deliveries, Daddy. You didn't mention a party, but it sure looks like something's going to happen here today."

His face lit up like something I said had turned

on a light inside his head, and he stood up quickly. "I forgot to tell you. We're having a little get-together here tonight. You, your sister, and Ryder are expected to be dressed and ready by seven."

"Ready for what in two hours?" I asked, mentally going through my closet for something to wear to my father's surprise party.

"Just a little get-together. I want you to make sure Ryder is dressed appropriately, so find him and make sure he's in good shape. I had some things brought to his room this afternoon."

I hadn't seen Ryder in two days, so I didn't mind checking up on him. "Is this a black tie affair?" I asked, suddenly dying to see him in a tux.

My father shook his head and waved away my question. "No, just a little cocktail party. I know you and your sister will be your usual charming selves, but I want to make sure Ryder is ready too, so be a sweetheart and make sure he's got things under control."

"Okay. I'll see what I can do."

"I knew you would, honey."

I didn't think an eighteen-year-old man would need help with a regular suit and tie, but since my father had ordered me to assist him, I'd check on him after I dressed and make sure he understood what would happen that night. I couldn't imagine he would be happy about this party, though. Since he'd arrived at the house, Ryder had done everything he could to remain as unobtrusive as possible, staying in his room more often than not. I suspected that was so he could avoid Janelle and her nastiness, so having to spend a night with her and my father's business associates who attended his parties probably didn't top his list of things he wanted to do.

AT QUARTER TO seven, I made my way down to Ryder's room. He opened his bedroom door just a crack and looked out suspiciously at me.

"What?"

My ego dinged from his curtness, I said, "My father asked me to check on you."

"Oh yeah? Why?"

I pushed against the door and saw he was already dressed in a dark grey suit and dark blue dress shirt. "I don't know. Maybe he's afraid you're going to come to the party buck naked, Ryder. Can I come in, please?"

He made me stand outside his door for another few moments before relenting and letting me in. Quickly closing the door, he stalked by me toward the bathroom, nearly knocking me over.

"What's this whole thing about anyway tonight?" he asked as he began to fumble with the ends of the grey and blue tie my father had gotten him.

I leaned against the doorway and watched as he struggled with what was supposed to be a Windsor knot. "My father likes to give parties sometimes. Janelle and I are trotted out like show horses for his friends, who are invariably impressed that we are poised and demure and not flinging our own feces at one another."

Ryder looked up from his tortured mishandling of his tie and stared at me in the bathroom mirror. A small smile crept onto his face. "I get the feeling that you don't like this kind of thing either."

"I don't mind it, to be honest, but sometimes my father's friends are a little grabby for my taste."

Narrowing his eyes, Ryder frowned and made a grunting noise. "Sounds like a nice crowd."

"And tonight you get to join the show horse crew. Do you feel special yet?"

He shook his head and returned to attempting the knot again. I watched him in the mirror for another minute before I stepped forward and tapped him on his good shoulder.

"Here, let me help."

Stepping around him, I took hold of the two ends of the tie and proceeded to work my magic on it. He stared down at me as my fingers deftly slid over the silk to create a perfect Windsor knot.

When I finished, I patted it down against his body and smiled up at him. "There. All set."

Instead of inspecting the fine job I'd done, he seemed more interested in looking down at my legs. Instantly self-conscious, I said, "Yeah, you're welcome, Ryder. Happy to help."

That got his attention, and he looked up at me. "Why is it you get to be barefoot and I have to wear these ridiculous shoes?"

"I have to wear them too. Don't feel bad. I just didn't bring them with me."

"Oh. That was a shitty thing to say. I'm sorry," he said quietly.

Suddenly, how close we were standing to one another became apparent, and I slid out from between him and the vanity. His gaze followed me, though, and he said, "You look nice. I don't think I've ever seen you in anything but shorts."

Turning toward the mirror, I checked myself out. The black silk dress I'd chosen looked more like a nightgown than a dress with its spaghetti straps and the way it draped over my body, but I didn't care. I hadn't been given enough lead time to get anything new to wear, so it would have to do.

I looked back at him and couldn't help but be impressed with how he looked too. Used to seeing him in shorts and t-shirts, I liked how he wore a suit. It made him look even more muscular than usual, and even though the tattoos on the backs of his hands poked out from underneath his white dress shirt, at first glance he could be mistaken for any one of the men who'd be at my father's get-together tonight.

Ryder tugged at the bottom of his suit coat sleeves as he caught me looking at those tattoos. "I don't know why your father wants me dressed up in this stupid thing. I look ridiculous."

His discomfort bothered me. I'd spent my life attending parties in my home, but for him, this clearly made him uneasy, likely because while my father liked to refer to him as his son, he wasn't that at all. I still didn't know why he'd brought Ryder to the house and wasn't sure I'd ever know, but I understood how it felt to feel out of place.

Turning toward him again, I took hold of his hands and brought them down to his sides. "Don't worry. You're going to be great. Remember, you're a show horse. No one wants to hear the show horses speak. We just need to prance around a bit and look nice. You've got that down pat, so you'll be fine."

My compliment fell on deaf ears, though, and Ryder's face twisted into a look of pain. "Prance around? What does that mean?"

"Well, other than standing for way too long listening to people you don't care about talk about subjects you care even less about, it means you might have to dance. My father loves dancing, oddly enough since he never dances, so he always has it at his parties. The weird thing is that they usually don't include too many females other than me and Janelle, so you'll probably get stuck dancing with one of us. I guess it could be worse. My father's friends are mostly old guys who've spent too many years in Washington, so a lot of their wives are old too. Be thankful you don't have to dance with some sixty-year-old woman."

None of what I said made him feel any better. "I don't dance. Ever. So your father is going to have to find something else for this show horse to do."

I knew my father. He'd make Ryder dance, likely just to see if he could. But was that the problem? Couldn't he dance?

He stood looking miserable and fiddling with his tie as he mumbled, "First I have to wear this and then dance? No way."

"Ryder, do you know how to dance?"

His fingers stilled on his tie, and then he simply marched past me out into his bedroom. So that was the problem. He didn't know how to dance. But I could help him with that. Years of dance classes and my father's parties had made me the resident expert.

I followed him out into his room and found him sitting on his bed wearing a deep frown. I stopped in front of him and held out my hands. Looking up at me, he asked, "What is that for?"

"I'll show you how to dance."

K.M. SCOTT

He shook his head as his frown deepened. "I don't need you to show me. I'm not going to be dancing."

I grabbed hold of his hands and tugged him up onto his feet. "Trust me, you're going to, so you might as well at least have an idea of what to do."

He winced in pain as I realized I'd forgotten about his shoulder injury. "Oh, I'm sorry. I didn't mean to hurt you."

"It's okay. I'm good."

Positioning his right hand on my lower back, I gingerly took hold of his left hand in mine and placed my left hand on his sore shoulder. He towered over me by more than half a foot, so I had to crane my neck to look up when we were this close.

Ryder stood stiffly, his palm barely touching my back like he didn't want to get too near me. We'd spent nearly every night for two weeks sitting on his bed together practically on top of one another, but now that we stood there as I prepared to teach him how to dance, he acted like I was a leper.

"Okay, normally the man leads, but since I'm teaching you, we'll have to switch roles. You won't have to do any fancy steps like the waltz or anything. Just move your feet like I do. Watch."

He looked down at my bare feet as I began to step right and then left and then right again. Not exactly my best moves, but he just needed to know how to move without looking like a robot or Frankenstein.

"Now you try."

A look of terror crossed his face, and after a moment of hesitation, he moved his left foot enough to step hard onto the top of my foot, making me cry out in pain. Instantly, he backed away as I hobbled toward the bed, trying to keep back the tears from how much my foot hurt.

"I'm sorry. I'm sorry, Serena."

The regret at what he'd done came through loud and clear in his voice, and I looked up to see him staring down at me in horror. He had enough to deal with tonight with my father putting him on display. He didn't need to think he'd done anything wrong in his first attempt at dancing too. So I took a deep breath and stood up to try again, even though the top of my foot throbbed like a toothache.

Taking his left hand in mine once again, I forced a smile and said, "Okay, put your hand on my lower back like before and we'll try this again, okay?"

This time he put his hand against my body almost possessively, like he needed to protect me, and we slowly moved our feet, doing little more than shuffling them back and forth as he stared down at the floor watching to make sure he didn't hurt me again and I forced myself not to look so he wouldn't think I didn't have faith in him.

I slid my hand up near his neck and gently touched where his hair hit near his collar, marveling at how soft it felt against my fingertips. "Ryder, you need to look at the person you're dancing with."

He stopped moving his feet and looked up at me. "I don't want to look at Janelle, to be honest, and I'm worried I'm going to step on your foot again. Either way, I think I'll keep my eyes on the floor."

"You can't. It's part of dancing. But how about this? When I'm wearing shoes, even if you do step on my feet, it won't really hurt. And as far as Janelle goes, she usually drinks too much at these parties and spends all night talking to people, so you might get to escape dancing at all with her."

A tiny smile lifted the corners of his mouth. "Good. Then I'll just dance with you."

"Or some sixty-year-old woman who will probably want to grab your ass. Here's to hoping none of the guests bring their wives like usual."

My teasing made his smile fade away. "Any chance your father has a thing for underage drinking?"

"Oh, definitely. Feel free to have whatever you want. As far as my father's concerned, that whole drinking age thing doesn't apply here at the house."

Ryder took a deep breath and let it out in a rush. "Good."

AFTER TWO HOURS of doing our best show horse act, Janelle flopped down into a chair at the far end of the enormous dining room where my father had his parties and began to chat up two men I believed might have been congressmen who had just begun to come out to the house within the past year. Ryder and I stood off to the side as my father and a small group of men talked about a bill in the House of Representatives involving some tax that would affect his mining interests.

Looking down the room toward where Janelle sat, Ryder whispered in my ear, "I think she's drunk. She hasn't been nasty to me in nearly a half hour."

I smiled and elbowed him in the side. "My sister is far nicer when there's alcohol involved. Maybe we should keep her drunk all the time."

"Good idea."

From behind us, I heard my father say something about his adopted son and turned to see him put his hand on Ryder's shoulder. So far he'd escaped any serious discussion with anyone in the room, but I had a sense that had come to an end, unfortunately.

"Serena, why don't you go sit with your sister for a few minutes while Ryder joins me and the other men?"

I saw by the pained look on Ryder's face that was the last thing he wanted, so quickly I suggested, "I was hoping you'd put some music on, Daddy. I'm sure he'd love to dance with me, and I know how much you love when we dance."

It wasn't fair, but between dancing with me or being stuck as a captive audience with my father and his friends, surely dancing had to be the better option. At that moment as Ryder appeared to be disgusted by both choices, I sensed it might not be until later that he'd thank me.

My father took the bait and happily announced the time for dancing had come. Taking Ryder's hand, I led him over to a small area near where Janelle sat and whispered in his ear, "I hope you don't hate me too much."

He didn't answer, but the look on his face told me he might hate me a little at that moment. The music began to play, some instrumental slow enough that actual dancing could occur, and I smiled up at him as he pressed his hand to the small of my back and took my right hand in his.

"Remember, look at me. I promise it won't be bad."

Before we could take even a step, I heard Janelle loudly announce, "Daddy, I don't think Serena should get to dance with our brother. She's definitely the better dancer, so she should dance with anyone else who wants to. I'll dance with Ryder since I bet the two of us are pretty bad at it anyway."

Horrified, I turned around to see her hurrying toward us and then saw my father nodding in agreement as some man with steel grey hair stepped forward to take me away from Ryder. In a flash, I'd been replaced in his arms by my sister and thrust into some old guy's arms. I looked over at Ryder and saw the same look of horror as when he'd stepped on my foot a few hours earlier, but even worse was how quickly Janelle moved him away toward her chair, leaving me alone with my father's friend.

For five minutes, I spent my time moving my partner's hand up from my ass over and over and prayed for the music to stop so I could escape. Whenever I tried to look at Ryder to see if he was okay, the man spun me around so my back was toward him. If I didn't know better, I would have thought he and Janelle were working together to ensure my misery.

All the while my father smiled and swayed to the music like nothing was wrong. When the piece ended, I wriggled out of the old man's hold to see Janelle and Ryder practically hanging on one another. He didn't seem bothered at all that he'd had to dance with her.

I hurriedly made an excuse to leave the room to go downstairs to the wine cellar and ran out before my emotions got the better of me. Janelle didn't even like Ryder, so why would she want to dance with him?

Alone and surrounded by my father's wine collection, I tried to convince myself that she hadn't done it on purpose, but no other answer made sense. What did it matter anyway? Even though Ryder and I spent night after night talking, whatever I felt for him wasn't reciprocated.

The sound of footsteps made me turn toward the stairs, and I saw Ryder coming down to join me. I took a deep breath and plastered a smile on my face so he wouldn't see my true feelings at what I'd seen him do.

"Why are you down here?" he asked as he walked to where I stood near the wall of wine bottles.

Pretending to look for a particular vintage, I pulled out a few bottles and acted like I was checking the labels. "Nothing. Just grabbing some more wine. A few of my father's friends love their wine."

"Yeah, they seem to love anything they can get drunk on."

I yanked one last wine bottle out of its home, and without even looking at the label, turned to leave. "They do like to have a good time. I better get back up there. I'm sure there's someone else who needs my dancing ability to get through this party."

Ryder gently grabbed my arm to stop me, and I looked up to see something strange in his eyes. Was he worried? About what I'd seen him do with

Janelle?

"Serena, that guy had his hands all over you. Maybe you shouldn't dance anymore tonight."

"So you noticed that while you and Janelle were busy doing your own thing, huh?" I asked, unable to hide my feelings of jealousy.

For a moment, Ryder looked confused, but then he smiled. "I'm not sure what I'd call her kind of dancing. It's more like drunken falling into people. Well, that and a little palming my dick, oddly enough. She's way friendlier when she's in the bag."

Furious at my sister and him for enjoying it, I yanked my arm from his hold. "Well, don't let me keep you from having someone grab your dick, Ryder. Have a good night. I'll see you around."

I didn't get two steps away from him before he grabbed me again and pulled me close against his body. Staring down at me, he placed his hand on my lower back like I'd taught him for dancing and held me to him.

Looking up into his intense green eyes as they practically glared down at me, I said, "Let me go. I have to get back with this wine."

"No. Not until you dance with me."

"I don't want to dance with you. Let me go," I said, looking away from him as my emotions swirled around inside me in a mix of desire, anger, and hurt.

"Yes, you do," he said defiantly as he roughly

moved my head so I had to face him.

"Stop this! I don't want to dance with you. Go find Janelle. She obviously wants to dance with you and a whole lot more."

Ryder pressed his hand harder into my lower back so the bottle pushed against our bodies. Reaching down, he took it out of my hold and placed it on a nearby table. Now nothing stood between us.

I pressed my palms against his chest, but it was no use. He was too strong and so much bigger than me.

His fingers slid over my shoulder as his other hand held me to him and he said, "You come to my room every night. You lay in my bed with me every night and fall asleep with your head on my shoulder. Don't tell me you don't want to dance with me, Serena."

Hurt coursed through me. Why did he say those things like my visits to him every night were an imposition?

"Fine. I won't come to see you anymore. Maybe Janelle can come down to see you every night. She won't ask as many questions about things you don't want to talk about, so you'll probably like it better."

His fingers slipped under the strap of my dress, and then he slowly let them drift down to just above my breast, all the while never breaking his gaze focused on my eyes. His touch thrilled me, and beneath the silk my nipples hardened to excited peaks that pressed against the fabric and showed him his effect on me.

As my body betrayed the reality of how I felt, it became harder to lie to him. I did want to dance with him, and just watching him with Janelle had made me more jealous than I'd ever been before in my life.

"I don't want Janelle to come see me. I want you to. You didn't come for the past two nights and I missed you."

His voice, low and seductive, hit me deep inside. "I figured I'd leave you alone for a few nights so you wouldn't get tired of hanging out."

"I get tired of a lot of things, but never being with you."

My emotions began to whirl around like spinning tops. "Why are you telling me this? Did Janelle say something to you? Did she put you up to this?"

Slowly, his hand slid down over my ass until he pushed under my dress and touched the top of my thigh. "Janelle has nothing to do with you and me, Serena."

At the top of the stairs, my father yelled down, "Serena, are you down there?"

"Yes, Daddy."

I stared up in terror at Ryder, but he didn't flinch, daring to keep his hand under my dress. If my father came down those steps and saw us standing there like that, he'd lose his mind, so I tried to push him away, but Ryder held me firm to him.

Terrified, I whispered, "Please let me go. If he finds us like this, he'll freak."

His response was to run his tongue over his bottom lip and shrug the shoulder that didn't hurt.

"Is Ryder down there with you?" my father asked.

"No, Daddy," I said as Ryder slid his finger up under my panties to touch the bare skin of my ass.

Leaning down, he whispered in my ear, "Are you down there with that stray, Serena? Is he making it difficult to answer these questions, Serena?"

"Okay, hurry up and get back up here," my father ordered from the top of the stairs before closing the cellar door behind him and leaving us alone again.

I didn't want to return to the party, though. I wanted to stay right there with Ryder and let him do whatever he wanted to.

But now that we were alone again, he seemed less interested in doing just that and slid his hand out from under my dress before gently moving me away from him. I looked up into his eyes and saw the intensity gone now.

"I better go back up there. I don't want you to get in trouble if he finds out I was down here."

I didn't get a chance to say anything before he hurried up the stairs, leaving me standing alone surrounded by wine bottles and wanting him so much it hurt.

Chapter Six

Ryder

I KNEW WHAT I did down in the wine cellar was shitty, even more because I wanted Serena more than I'd wanted anything ever before in my life. If it had been anyone else, I would have taken them right there in that basement, fucking them right against those walls of bottles, my cock slamming into them over and over until there was nothing left inside either of us to go on any longer.

But Serena wasn't just anyone. Every night she came to my room, and even though I wasn't sure why or if she wanted me as badly as I wanted her, I let her in every time, knowing if her father found out he'd probably kill me.

For five nights after what I did in that wine cellar, she didn't come, though. I waited every night to hear her gentle knocking on my door, but it never came.

She had every right to be angry with me. I shouldn't have teased her like that. I didn't know why I did, to be honest. Maybe it was her sister's stroking my cock as we danced and how I wished it had been Serena's hand on me. Maybe it was seeing that old guy grope her, each time lifting her dress higher and higher until I saw the bottom of her perfect ass right there as she danced.

Maybe I was just a dick who didn't deserve to have her anywhere near me and never seeing her again was my just desserts. I didn't know. All I knew was night after night I felt worse about what I'd done until she was all I could think about.

I knew she was avoiding me because I didn't see her during the day either. By the sixth night, I needed to talk to her, to say something to show her I wasn't the world's biggest dick. After an hour of waiting for her knock on my door, I couldn't wait any longer.

Flinging my door open, I stepped out into the hallway and saw her standing there barefoot in her usual shorts and t-shirt staring at me like she'd been waiting forever to see me come out of my room.

"Serena…" I didn't know what to say next. "I was just coming to see if you were around."

"I'm around," she said as that hurt I'd seen the first night I met her filled her dark eyes. "I live here, Ryder."

"I know. I mean, yeah. I just wondered where you've been."

She opened her mouth to say something and

then pressed her lips tightly together before saying, "I better go. Bye, Ryder."

"No, don't go," I said as I reached out to grab hold of her wrist. "I was hoping we could talk like we used to every night."

She slowly moved her head to look down at where my hand held her arm and then looked up at me, that sadness still in her eyes making my chest hurt like someone had it in a vice. "I don't think so. My father wouldn't like that. Whatever you're here for, it's not to be nice to me."

"Don't say that. Come in and we can just hang out for a little while."

Serena didn't answer, so I said, "I'm sorry. I didn't mean to do that the other night."

She winced at my mention of what happened. "Just tell me why you did it. That's all. Tell me why."

My hand slid from her wrist, and I shook my head. "I don't know. I'm a dick."

A look like what I said caused her pain crossed her face, and she frowned. "Don't say that. We're friends, and even when a friend does something awful, you forgive them."

I didn't want to be just friends, but I'd take it if it meant seeing her every night again. "So will you come in?"

She smiled and it went all the way up to her dark eyes. "Okay."

We sat down on the bed facing one another, but I didn't know what to say. I'd fucked up, and now I didn't know where we stood.

Serena hugged her knees tightly and looked at me. After a few minutes of silence, she said, "Remember when I told you about when I was seven?"

I nodded as my gut tightened into a knot just thinking of what she must have gone through for those three days. "Yeah."

"When I went back to school, I had problems because all I wanted to talk about was what happened. The teacher told my father I was scaring the other kids, so he brought me home and had me tutored until high school. Sometimes I think that might be why I'm a little awkward with people."

I knew what she was saying, and I couldn't let her continue to think what I'd done was because of her. "You're not awkward. You didn't do anything wrong either. Not then and not the other night."

Hanging her head, she said quietly, "A doctor once told my father that what happened made me want to please people too much. People don't like that."

"There's nothing wrong with being nice, Serena."

"I guess."

She looked up at me and in her eyes I saw how

hurt she still was from what I'd done. God, I was a dick. She'd never been anything but sweet to me, and I teased her like some arrogant asshole. And even worse, she blamed herself.

"I'm sorry for what I did. I like you just the way you are. Fuck that doctor and whoever else doesn't think you're fine."

She smiled and her eyes lit up. Letting go of her legs, she said, "Maybe we could watch a movie tonight? You know, instead of talking?"

I didn't care what she wanted to do. All I cared about was that she was back there with me.

EVERY NIGHT FOR the next six weeks, Serena knocked on my door after her father and sister left the house. She always wore shorts that made me want to touch her gorgeous legs and never wore shoes. And every night, we sat next to one another on my bed and talked about whatever was on her mind.

Her mother. How much she wanted to get away and live her own life. Why I was at her house.

We talked about her mother leaving and my folks dying in that car wreck. I told her about having to go live with my uncle, even though I didn't tell her the truth about my time with him because there was no way I could explain him selling me to Floyd without getting into what I did for her father.

I never told her the truth about my role in her father's world, and after that fight with the behemoth I didn't have to since the next three fights were basically cakewalks. I beat each of my opponents easily, getting barely a mark on me from each, so she never asked again about the beating I'd taken weeks before.

When she found out I'd lost my cell and didn't have one, she bought me a new phone so we began texting when she wasn't in my room late at night for our talks. While Janelle simply sneered at me when she passed me in the hallway and Robert treated me like one of his employees and nothing else, Serena became the most important thing in that house to me.

All the while I knew we were on borrowed time. Once her father found out, he'd likely send me away to do something far worse than fight for him. I knew the risk, yet every time I could I texted her and every night when she knocked on my door, I let her in.

I wanted her so much it hurt. Sometimes my hand would brush against her body and I'd wait to see if she noticed, wishing I hadn't been such a dick in the wine cellar that night so I could touch her and she wouldn't question it. I imagined the feel of her beneath me as I slid into her and those dark eyes looking up at me as I fucked her until her thighs

K . M . S C O T T

quivered against me.

"I have a surprise for you," she said with a smile as she sat down on my bed next to me one night.

A quick glance at her showed the surprise couldn't be anything too big. She wouldn't be able to hide much in her black shorts and pink t-shirt.

"Oh yeah? What's that?" I asked, charmed by how cute she was being.

From her back pocket, she pulled out two red foil wrapped pieces of candy and held them up in front of her. "Christmas chocolate."

Confused, I reached out for one. "It's the middle of August. Where did you get Christmas chocolate?"

She yanked the candy from my grasp and proudly explained, "I made it. I make it every year around this time. I saved us a piece each."

"Did you eat the rest?" I joked and waited for the look of irritation.

"No. Does this body look like I eat pounds of chocolate, Ryder?"

Serena busied herself with unwrapping the first piece of candy as my gaze slid over her body. Lean and toned, she definitely didn't look like she ate much chocolate at all. Her long legs that seemed to go on forever turned into ever so slightly rounded hips and an ass that I had fantasized about more than once. Nope, that body didn't look like she ate pounds of chocolate.

84

I watched her take a tiny bite off the corner of the candy square and smile like it was the best thing she'd ever tasted. After all the time we'd spent together, I knew she wasn't that innocent thing I thought she was that first night we met in her father's office, but at times, she had a sweetness about her that was nothing short of adorable.

"Mmmm, this is so good."

Reaching for a piece again, she yanked it away, so I asked, "Are you going to give me a taste or is this just about teasing me with it?"

She smiled and ran her tongue over her bottom lip to catch a stray piece of chocolate that had been left there. "You have to close your eyes. It's better the very first time if you close your eyes for the first bite. I'll put a little piece on your tongue and you'll see."

Normally, someone telling me to close my eyes so they could put something in my mouth sent red flags up all over the place, but I trusted her so I did as she wanted and waited to taste this incredible chocolate she'd made.

She did as she said she would and placed a piece on the tip of my tongue, and instantly my mouth watered. It was good, but even better was the feel of her fingertip grazing my lips. My cock sprang to life at her touch and threatened to tent in my grey gym shorts.

I licked my lip where her finger had just been

and smiled. "I want more."

"Keep your eyes closed and I'll give you another piece," she said sweetly.

As much as I wanted to see her expression, I kept them closed and she slipped another bite of candy onto my tongue. This time I closed my mouth around her fingers and sucked lightly as she pulled them over my lips.

I heard her make a tiny gasp, but she said nothing about what I'd done, instead asking, "Was the second piece as good as the first?"

Moaning, I nodded as the sweet taste of chocolate filled my mouth and my cock grew even harder. "Even better."

Her warm breath skimmed my cheek, and then I felt her straddle my hips. Opening my eyes, I saw her smiling down at me.

"What are you doing?" I asked, knowing I should push her away as my hands instinctively settled on her hips to keep her right where she was.

"Don't tell me you don't want me sitting here. I can feel how much you want me, Ryder."

There was no point in denying how much I wanted her in every way possible. My rock hard cock pressing against my belly told her that. But just because I wanted her more than my next breath at that moment didn't mean I should continue what we were doing. I hadn't forgotten Robert's rules, as much as I wished I could.

Avoiding her stare, I looked away and willed my mouth to say what no other part of me wanted to. "Serena, we shouldn't…"

"Why? Just because my father wants to play big daddy with you doesn't mean we're really related, so why not?"

I turned to face her and saw a look in her eyes I'd never seen in all the hours we'd spent together. It was a mixture of seduction and need that made her look sexier than ever before.

"Because it's not a good—"

Before I could get the words out, she pressed her lips to mine in a kiss that made my head swim. Her tongue teased mine, and all I could think of was how that tongue would feel when her mouth was sucking me off. One kiss and every reason I'd had for not touching her all those weeks evaporated into thin air.

My hands cupped her ass and squeezed as she slowly rolled her hips so her pussy slid over my cock. The thin fabric of her shorts did little to hide how wet she was. She moaned into my mouth as my finger touched the delicate skin between her legs, and it took every ounce of restraint I possessed to not dip it inside her.

Against my lips, she whispered breathlessly, "See? I knew you wouldn't say no."

Of all the things rambling around in my brain at

that moment, the word no wasn't among them. How much I wanted to bury my cock inside her and fuck her like she'd never been fucked before quickly became my singular thought. I wanted that like I'd never wanted anything else in my life and none of my excuses overpowered my need for her.

Her hands roamed over my chest and she stared down at wherever they touched, her eyes wide like the feel of me thrilled her. I buried my hand in her hair and pulled her to me to kiss her hard, needing to taste her mouth and the sweetness on her tongue again.

Pulling away, she trailed her fingertips down over my stomach to where a faint line of black hair disappeared beneath my shorts. My body ached with need as I prayed for her to follow that trail.

She stopped and looked at me almost as if she wasn't sure she wanted to go any further. But I did.

I pressed my fingers hard into her hips and pushed her down against my cock. "Tell me you don't want to feel me inside you. Tell me and I'll stop, but if you don't, I'm going to fuck you so good you'll beg for my cock after tonight."

Serena bit her lower lip and leaned forward while she rolled her hips slowly, grinding her cunt against the front of my shorts. In my ear, she moaned softly and said, "Don't make me beg, Ryder. Fuck me."

Dying to feel my cock inside her, I rolled her over onto her back and slid a single finger into her pussy. Damn, she was tight. Fucking her would be like having a virgin.

She arched her back and moaned with each thrust into her, but I wanted the real thing. She tugged at my shorts to release my cock while my fingers fucked her, and I fumbled with my free hand to unbutton her shorts.

"Hurry," she said in a faraway voice as I tore at the fabric to get it down her legs.

When those damn shorts were finally out of the way, I slipped my finger out of her and sat back on my heels to remove the last barrier to being inside her. As I tugged her cotton panties down over her hips, she wriggled her ass to help so cute that if it wasn't for the fact that every cell in my body was screaming to ram my cock into her, I might have laughed.

She pulled me down to kiss me hard on the mouth, thrusting her tongue in to meet my mine as she wrapped her legs around my waist and urged me into her. But before I could plunge into that tight pussy, Serena screamed something and pushed me away. I turned to see her father standing in my bedroom doorway with a look of rage in his eyes.

"Daddy, this isn't what you think!" she pleaded as the two of us quickly rushed to put our clothes back on.

"In my office, now, Serena! You too, Ryder!" he bellowed and then stormed away down the hallway.

Everything became a blur for the next few minutes. Serena straightened her shirt and shorts and ran out of my room without saying a word. I hurried to get a t-shirt on and followed her a few seconds later to where Robert waited for us in his office just down the hall from my room. Janelle stood next to him with her arms folded across her chest like she had some judgment on the events of the night.

Serena again told him it wasn't what he thought, even though he'd have to be blind to not understand what we were doing on my bed, but Robert waved her off.

"I'll deal with that in a minute. Now I want you to tell me the meaning of this."

He leaned over his desk to grab an oversized white envelope and held it up for her to see. I couldn't imagine what it could contain that would be more damning than seeing us half-naked and my cock out ready to fuck his daughter, but a glance over at Serena told me she knew.

"I was going to tell you. I was. I just never found the right time," she pleaded to no avail. Nothing in his stony expression said her lame excuses were helping.

"You know how I feel about this and still you went behind my back! You don't leave me any choice."

Robert dialed a number on his cell phone as Serena began to sob. "No, Daddy! Please don't do this! Janelle, tell him not to do this!"

Her sister let her usual sneer fall away and smiled. "No way. If I couldn't go, you can't either."

"Don't expect your sister to help. She's the one who did the right thing and told me about it."

Serena covered her face with her hands and cried as I listened to her father tell someone on the phone that she'd be coming to live with them. What the hell had she done?

I wanted to ask, but I didn't think she was in any condition to explain and her sister seemed to be enjoying her misery way too much. And Robert likely would be sending me packing at any moment.

"Daddy, please don't send me away," she begged after he put his phone back into his pocket. "I won't go to school. I'll stay right here like Janelle. I promise."

Robert just shook his head as his frown deepened. "No, you can't be trusted. You knew how I felt about this and still went behind my back. You knew what the punishment would be if I found out, so now you'll pay the price for your lying."

He turned to face me and narrowed his eyes to

angry squints. "Plus, after what I just saw, I think a year or two away is the only thing that will set you straight."

Janelle's smile broadened as Serena cried out, "A year or two? No! Please don't send me to Uncle Joseph's for that long. I won't do it again. I'll be the perfect daughter, Daddy. I promise. Just let me stay here."

"No. It's done. I'll have the plane ready to go tonight. Pack your things."

Serena collapsed into the chair behind her and cried harder, but Robert simply rolled his eyes. "For God's sake, it's not like you're being sent to military school. Do you know how many girls would kill to live in Italy? Damnit, I'd kill to spend a year or two there, so stop your crying and go get ready to leave."

She didn't say another word, but when she looked over at me before she left, I saw that same sadness in her eyes I'd seen the night I met her in that very room. I couldn't help feel bad for her. Her own sister had betrayed her, and her father didn't seem to care how what he was doing made her miserable.

I wanted to tell her something, but Robert shot me a nasty glare to let me know no matter what he'd said about me being family, this wasn't something I should get involved with.

Janelle followed her sister out looking incredibly

pleased with what had happened and I waited for Robert to tell me where I'd be shipped off to. It didn't matter. All that had been good about this house was leaving for Italy, and I'd probably never see Serena again.

So much for another of my pipe dreams.

PART TWO

Chapter Seven

Serena

I WAITED FOR the driver to stop the car in front of the house, my mind filled with the past and what had sent me away from there two years before. Janelle had been thrilled to tell me that Ryder ended up in the hospital for two weeks after getting beaten until he was unconscious right after I left. She didn't know who did it, but I guessed it had been my father as punishment for what he'd caught us doing.

Week after week, I sent Ryder texts, but he never answered back. I sent letters too but never received one back from him. I called him but got the message that his number was out of service. I knew better than to ask my sister about him, so in all my time away I hadn't heard a word from him.

Maybe it was for the best. Like he said, we didn't have a lot in common, and now that was truer than ever. Two years in Italy away from my family, friends, and the only home I'd ever known had made me a different person. I'd changed little on the outside, but who I was had changed. Gone was the sweet girl who had just wanted to go to school for social work and try to make the world a better place.

My father had made sure that person died the night he sent me away without a second thought. I hadn't spoken to him more than a handful of times in all the months I spent at his brother's. Not that I had any expectation of him calling to apologizing for sending me away where I knew not a soul except for my aunt and uncle. That wasn't my father's style. In his mind, I'd betrayed him and had to pay the price.

Nothing like fatherly devotion.

I walked up to the front of my home and marveled at the size of the glass doors leading into the grand entranceway. In all the years I'd live there before, never once had I noticed how big they were and how grand the house itself was. I'd always just seen it as my home.

The sound of my heels as I walked across the white marble tiles alone struck me as they echoed off the walls. I hadn't expected a formal welcoming party, but my father and Janelle knew I was coming home this evening. I'd thought at least they'd be around for my return.

Dropping my bags at the foot of the staircase, I balanced myself on the wrought iron railing and slipped my shoes off to be barefoot once again. I'd never felt right doing that at my uncle's house, but now that I was back in my own home, I intended to get comfortable.

I headed to my father's study, hoping to find someone home. Hearing noises like people were talking in there, I knocked on the doorframe and quietly said, "I'm home. Did anyone miss me?"

Both Janelle and my father turned to look at me and smiled like nothing had ever happened. "Serena, we were just talking about you. Come in!"

My father's excitement at seeing me threw me off a bit, and when my sister ran to me to give me a big hug, I immediately suspected something was wrong. Someone had surely died. That was the only explanation that sounded right as I reluctantly hugged my Judas.

"Daddy has great news he wants to share with you," she said as she backed away and grinned from ear to ear.

My sister's smile reminded me of my father's, and I'd never seen him smile like that for anything truly good. I braced myself for whatever the news was, hoping no one I knew would be harmed by it.

"Tell her!" Janelle said with a nudge to his arm, practically overflowing with excitement. "If you don't tell her, I will."

"Serena, you're home just in time for the celebration. Your sister's getting married," my father announced in a chipper voice.

I stood stunned as the news of my sister's

impending wedding sunk in. Never in all the times I'd asked for news of home had she even mentioned seeing anyone, much less being serious enough to be engaged.

"Really? To whom?"

"Charles Anderson IV," Janelle said, beaming her happiness. "He's the sole heir to a multi-million dollar fortune."

"Oh. Well, congratulations," I said in a voice that didn't sound very convincing.

That my sister and father were giddy over her marrying some guy who she described in terms of how much he was worth told me everything I needed to know about this coupling. If ever there was a marriage of convenience, this was it. The guy was probably old and decrepit with one foot in the grave and another on a banana peel my sister had happily thrown on the ground in front of him.

Janelle grabbed my arm and tugged me toward the door. "Come! We'll go upstairs and talk all about my upcoming wedding, your bridesmaid dress, and all sorts of good things that have happened since you've been gone."

My father waved us out with a smile and I followed my sister, my homecoming obviously over. I hadn't expected much, and I hadn't been disappointed.

I SAT DOWN on Janelle's bed and watched her bounce up and down with excitement to show me her wedding gown. White satin with enough lace to make it qualify as the world's biggest doily, it reminded me of something uptight Victorian women wore to their weddings. Since my sister was anything but uptight, it seemed like a strange choice for her.

"What do you think? It's gorgeous, isn't it?" she asked as she twirled around with it trailing behind her.

"It's very nice."

As I watched her dance around with her lacy dress, I had a horrifying thought. What would the bridesmaid dress look like if that was the wedding gown?

She hung it up and sat down on the bed in front of me. "Charles picked it out. He loved it from the second he saw it."

"Isn't it bad luck for the groom to see the bride in her wedding dress before the ceremony?" I asked, really wanting to ask what kind of man picked out his future wife's gown.

But she seemed disinterested in my concern for superstition. "Oh, I'm not worried. He's got great taste and it cost a fortune. How could I say no?"

"I guess you couldn't," I mumbled, feeling like I'd come home to the wrong house. Where had my bitchy older sister gone and who was this Stepford wife sitting on her bed with me?

Janelle touched my arm and squeezed it. "I'm so glad you're home in time for the wedding, Serena. It really does mean a lot to me."

That my return fit in with her schedule was a complete coincidence as far as I was concerned. I'd finished classes a few weeks earlier and my uncle informed me that my father had called to say he wanted me to come home. He never mentioned any impending wedding to anyone, and as far as my uncle was concerned, my father simply had decided the time was right to have his younger daughter back.

"Well, I'm just happy that you're happy."

Empty words and meaningless platitudes seemed to appease her because she gave my wrist another squeeze and continued going on about how blissfully happy this Charles guy made her. "I can't wait for you to meet him."

"How long have you two been dating? What's he like?" I asked, curious enough to wonder if this Charles was the reason my sister had experienced a total change of personality.

Janelle tilted her head to the side and scrunched up her face like she was trying to think of a good way to answer me. "We haven't really been dating, per se. I met him and we hit it off, so I said yes when Daddy made the deal for us to get married."

Just as I'd thought. This marriage was made well south of heaven.

"So this is an arranged thing because he wants you to marry someone who can help him?"

Shrugging, she nodded as if none of this bothered her. "It's not a big deal, Serena. Charles has money, he's not ugly, and I'll be taken care of for the rest of my life. All I have to do is be the kind of wife a wealthy man wants."

"I'm not even going to ask what that means."

She rolled her eyes at my judging her. "Life isn't about hearts and flowers, baby sister. I have no education and no job. I need to make sure that I get myself set up with a good man, and Charles is a good man. So he's a little older. So what? So he's not some hot stud. He'll take care of me, and when his father dies, he's set to inherit a lot of money. From where I stand, he's a good catch."

"How much older is he, Janelle?"

I had this image of some old geezer who was barely mobile standing all hunched over at the altar at their wedding. My sister wasn't a real prize, and I wasn't her fan by any means, but even she didn't deserve to shackle herself to some geriatric money machine just for security.

"He's ten years older than me. It's not a big deal at all. And he doesn't look like he's thirty-three, so it's all good."

Early thirties wasn't ancient, but it certainly wasn't what I'd want. Then again, my sister and I had always been like night and day, so maybe she'd be happy with this guy.

"Do you at least care for him, Janelle? I know you don't want to live here with our father for the rest of your life, but are you and Charles in love or is this just a business arrangement?"

Sighing, she shrugged again. "Love isn't always what it's cracked up to be. Anyway, I like him and we get along. That's better than most married couples can claim."

"I guess."

It all sounded so sterile. I couldn't imagine settling for something so lacking for the rest of my life. There was no way I'd ever be forced into some arranged marriage simply because it benefited my father's business interests. I'd sooner be thrown out into the streets and have to beg for every morsel of food I put in my mouth before I'd be used as a pawn like that.

Janelle patted my hand sympathetically like she was trying to make me feel better about her choices. "You'll see. It's all going to work out for the best. Charles and I will be happy, and Daddy's happy. It's a win-win situation."

"You know, you don't have to settle for this just

to make him happy. I know a life as a kept woman sounds good now, but what about ten or twenty years down the road? Daddy isn't going to live forever."

She jumped up off the bed and began pacing. "But that's the best reason to do this, Serena. What happens when our father dies and he leaves us nothing because we had the bad luck not to be born with dicks? He'll leave his businesses to one of his guys and we'll be left with this house, if we're lucky. I'm looking out for my future with this marriage. You should start to do the same for yourself before it's too late."

"I got to go to school while I was away. Whether Daddy likes it or not, I'm going to finish my degree and get a job. I'm not going to be saddled with the future he wants to force on me. I made sure of that the night I left this place two years ago."

Completely ignoring her part in my forced exile, she sat down next to me as a look of curiosity settled into her face. "He made that guy one of his guards, you know that? Ryder. He spent weeks in the hospital right after you left and when he came back to the house he was different. Now he lives in the apartments in the south wing with the other security guys."

I hadn't wanted to know about Ryder or what had happened to him. I'd promised myself I wouldn't try to find out since he'd never bothered to try to contact me in the entire two years I was gone. Hearing that he'd suffered because of what we did and then became one of my father's henchmen didn't make me happy.

Not that he ever had much of a future other than that once he walked through those glass front doors.

"Well, I better get to bed. I'm dealing with a case of jetlag, so sleep is calling."

I stood from the bed and forced a smile for Janelle. I'd expected to find the same bitchy person she was when I left, and I was happy she'd changed that part of her. But the woman she'd become was no more like me than that other version of her.

As it had always been, I was the odd one of the family. Janelle may not have been as nasty, but now she was more like my father than ever before.

"Okay, when you wake up we'll start on your gown and all that stuff because the wedding is next weekend."

I forced another smile at the thought of what that bridesmaid dress would look like and headed toward my room. If I was lucky, sleep would come fast so I didn't have to think about it or any of the things that had changed while I was gone.

Chapter Eight

Ryder

"HAND ME MY belt," I said as I stood next to the bed buttoning my shirt.

"If you want it, you'll have to come get it."

I didn't have time for Kitty's games tonight. Janelle and her fiancé's engagement party would be starting in less than an hour, and if I didn't get back to the estate in the next few minutes, Robert would start peppering my phone with nasty texts by the minute.

Leaning over the bed, I ripped the belt out of her hand, nearly slapping her in the face with the buckle as I yanked it toward me. Like always when I left, she sat staring at me with a pout on her lips.

"Why do you need to be at that stupid party for Robert's daughter anyway? It's not like you're the one marrying her," Kitty whined, twirling her blond hair around her finger.

I looked up as I slid the belt through the loops on my black dress pants and threw her a look even she'd understand. "Because it's my job. That's why.

Do I ask you why you have to go to the club when you're scheduled?"

Her lower lip jutted out into an even more pronounced pout. "But I'm not scheduled every day, twenty-four seven. He barely gives you time to have the tiniest bit of a social life, Ryder. For being his favorite, you don't seem to get treated very well."

"I have to go," I said flatly before turning toward the door.

"Don't you even want to give me a kiss?" she whined, and when I looked back she'd crawled across the bed near where I stood.

I didn't want to kiss her. I didn't want to do anything more than what I'd already done with her, which was likely too much. For almost two years, I'd come to this two-room apartment of hers once or twice a week for nothing more than to get laid. I wasn't proud of that fact, but there it was.

Kitty had always chosen to interpret what we were doing together as something far more than just sleeping together. At first, I'd just ignored her when she called me her boyfriend because I couldn't believe anyone could confuse what we did a couple times a week with a relationship. Fuck, we didn't even talk much before or after getting down to business. How could this be a relationship?

We were just two people escaping the loneliness of life with each other for a little while. Nothing more. I'd never wanted more. Hell, I never even wanted this much.

I'd helped her one night after her shift at one of Robert's clubs when her boyfriend slapped her around and left her bloody behind the building. I'd never meant to do anything other than take her home and help her clean herself up, but one thing lead to another and we ended up sleeping together.

As far as I was concerned, that was supposed to be the first and last time we got together, but somehow in those early days after Serena left for Italy, it didn't take much more than a call from Kitty asking for my help with some stupid thing to get me to her place, and from there we evolved into what we were now.

I would have ended it a long time ago, but it never seemed like the right time. So it continued, even though I couldn't honestly say I wanted it to.

"Ryder, did you hear me? I asked you if you're coming by tomorrow."

Shaking my head to clear my thoughts, I looked down at her kneeling naked on the bed. "I don't know. Robert's got me working overtime with this wedding business. I'll call you."

Her blue eyes opened wide, and she looked like she'd begin to cry at any moment. "Oh. I miss you when you can't come."

We went through this routine every time I left

after we slept together. I hated it.

"I'll talk to you later, Kitty."

I didn't kiss her before I left, throwing her a half-hearted smile instead.

BY THE TIME I returned to the estate, the sun had begun to go down and all the torches blazed out in the garden as the staff scurried around making the final preparations for the engagement party. I'd been to enough of Robert's get-togethers to know this one was different, and not just because Janelle was getting married.

A glance at the food told me he'd pulled out all the stops for tonight. Trays of lobster, shrimp, and crab filled an entire table, and the two chefs manning the grills that took up the far side of the enormous patio looked like they'd been brought here straight from some five-star restaurant with their white chefs' hats and uniforms.

I headed inside to Robert's office to ask if he had anything he'd like me to do special tonight, even though I already knew the answer. As part of his security detail, my job was to keep him safe.

Security detail wasn't exactly what I did for him. In the plainest terms, I was the muscle he used to get people to come around to his way of thinking. At least that was the way he liked to describe my job.

Whatever I was, I knew my role in this whole

thing Robert Erickson had going on. He said jump and I answered how high. Ownership was like that. I'd long ago worked off what he paid Floyd for me, and I technically was free, but he had a way of making a person realize they probably weren't going to find much better anywhere else.

Well, most people. Not Serena.

I hadn't seen her since that night two years ago, but I'd heard enough from her father's complaining that she'd gotten just what she wanted, even after he sent her away. She'd gone to school in Italy and done well.

He'd never said anything to me about what he'd seen the two of us doing in my room that night, but I knew how angry he was when he put me up against the biggest fighter ever seen on the underground circuit. I didn't last five minutes against that guy, and my reward for that defeat was two weeks in the hospital with a bruised kidney and spleen and a collapsed lung, in addition to a broken nose and cheekbone.

When they released me, Robert stood waiting for me at his car out at the curb. What choice did I have? I could have chosen homelessness and stealing like I'd done before I met Floyd, but I'd had a taste of more and didn't want to sleep in piss stinking alleyways with fucking drunks and drug addicts anymore.

So I took the ride back here to his house and accepted the security job he offered with his new detail he claimed to everyone he needed. I didn't have to fight anymore, at least not in The Pit, and when I did have to use my fists, I wasn't in danger of getting my head crushed in.

All in all, it was a decision I could live with.

Robert paced back and forth across his office with a glass of his favorite bourbon and branch in one hand and his phone in the other as someone on speaker begged him for more time paying off some debt they owed him. I could have told the guy it was a hopeless cause. Once you were into Robert for anything, he had you.

And he didn't let go, no matter how much you begged. Two years in his world had shown me that.

"Carlson, you know the terms. You have until next Friday. I wish I could do more, but I simply can't. Now if you'll excuse me, I have a party to attend for my daughter's wedding."

The man continued to plead his case, but Robert simply ended the call and stuffed the phone into his suitcoat pocket. Noticing me standing in the doorway, he waved me in.

"Just who I want to see. Your timing is perfect. Did you hear any of what that call was about?" he asked before downing the last of his drink.

"No," I lied, knowing how much he hated when

anyone eavesdropped on him.

"Well, when that man doesn't pay me what he owes me next Friday, you'll be paying him a visit."

I nodded my understanding. He'd kept me busier than usual the past few days with jobs like that, so much that I hadn't seen my own bed in three days. I wondered if the cost of Janelle's wedding had put a dent in his bank account and to pay for it he felt he needed to press his debtors a little harder than usual.

Whatever the reason, it didn't change what I had to do. I was just a messenger, although the news I had to deliver to the poor saps wasn't what they wanted to hear.

Robert stopped in mid-pass in front of me and studied what I wore. "You look ready for the party. Good." His mouth turned up in that terrifying crocodile smile I hated. "By the way, expect a surprise tonight."

Hearing a man who enjoyed hurting people for kicks say you should expect a surprise was never good, so instantly my senses went on high alert. I hadn't done anything to piss him off, so I was pretty sure I was in the clear.

"A surprise?" I asked, wishing he would just tell me what the hell was going on so I wouldn't have to wonder for the next few hours.

"Yes. It arrived two days ago."

His eyes practically danced this surprise made him so happy. That Robert Erickson could honestly be called a sadist meant his happiness might very well be my pain, so that sparkle in his eyes only made me more uneasy.

"Okay," I said, even though suddenly I felt nothing close to okay.

"Good. I'll see you out in the garden in a couple minutes. Make sure the staff hasn't fucked up anything."

His vague dismissal of me sent me on my way, and although I didn't have one clue as to what he wanted me to check up on concerning the staff, I headed out toward the party to scan the area for anything that could send him into a rage and ruin Janelle's night.

"RYDER, I WANT you to stay near me tonight."

I turned to face Robert and saw a strange look on his face. "Okay. Do you want me to tell the guys to position themselves anywhere particular?" I asked, unsure what he was up to.

He shook his head. "Whatever you think is right," he said as he scanned the garden.

Even though I knew I shouldn't ask, my curiosity got the best of me. "Any reason why you want me to stay close to you during a party? Are you expecting some potential problem?"

If I was actually security of any real sort, that kind of question would be something I'd ask, but since Robert either thought of me as some kind of adopted son or his hired muscle, my question verged on stepping over the line. I knew that and still asked because his threat of a surprise had me on edge.

His crocodile smile returned, and he patted me on the shoulder. "You tell me."

Robert generally didn't speak in riddles, so I had no idea what he meant. Following his gaze to the patio doors, I watched Janelle and her fiancé walk out of the house and then saw Robert's surprise.

Serena.

In the two years she'd been gone, she'd grown up from that pretty teenage girl into an even more beautiful woman. Her hair was longer now, but it still fell in those sexy waves around her face that made her look soft and touchable. Just seeing her made an ache form inside me I thought had gone forever.

My breath caught in my chest as I stared at her and thought of all the time we'd spent together. That last night before all hell broke loose wasn't all I remembered. Hours talking about things I'd never told another soul came flooding back now, and I couldn't help miss what we'd been to each other.

Her father had taken my phone while I was in the hospital, so I never knew if she tried to contact me from Italy. The night after she left I got my ass beaten in that fight and never had a chance to let her know how much I was going to miss her every night. I never got one card or letter or anything the whole time she was gone.

It was like she just moved on from everything that was part of this place, including me.

I didn't blame her. After how her father treated her just because she wanted to go to college and improve herself, I would have put this place and all of us in the rearview mirror and thrown it all the finger as I drove away.

As I reminisced about those sweet times so long ago, she left her sister and fiancé to mingle with guests. Swallowing hard, I pushed down those feelings that still remained inside me and forced myself to remember I had a job to do. It didn't serve any good purpose to live in the past.

"Are you going to just stand there or are you going to say hi?" Robert asked, tearing me out of my memories.

"I'm sure she wouldn't even remember me," I answered as casually as possible while I watched Serena follow her sister over to the bar.

Robert patted me on the shoulder. "You're probably right. Once a girl grows up, she leaves everything from the past behind. I think you should go join the other men on the grass."

His dismissal now that he'd gotten the exact reaction he'd hoped for from me stung. I knew as soon as I saw her that he'd be watching carefully to see what I'd do when I realized Serena's return was the surprise. His warning from the first night I arrived at this house echoed in my ears.

Don't even think of doing anything with either of the girls.

I'd dared to think of exactly that with her and we'd both paid the price. Then he'd made sure she stayed away, but now he wondered if our living so close to one another again would rekindle what we'd had between us.

I wanted him to believe her return meant nothing to me, even as every cell in my body craved to be near her again. I couldn't understand what power she had over me, but whatever it was, all it took was seeing her after all that time and I wanted to risk everything once more.

Chapter Nine

Serena

AFTER AN HOUR of forcing myself to smile for all of Janelle and her intended husband's party guests, I stole away inside the house to let the muscles in my face rest. I'd never been good with being fake, and standing around pretending my sister and her fiancé were anything close to being in love required a level of fake I couldn't achieve if I wanted to.

Which I didn't.

I'd been away long enough from this place that I knew there were people in the world like me who didn't want to spend their time pretending to be something they weren't. My father worked tirelessly to make the world think everything here was picture perfect, even as he paraded around with some woman who wasn't his wife and pretended like my mother didn't still exist somewhere.

And Janelle had practically perfected fake into an art form. Set to marry a man she barely knew just days from now, she beamed happiness like she'd found her soul mate.

Neither of them had anything real about them.

I walked through the house toward the front door, hoping to escape the noise of the party to find some peace and quiet. My time in Italy had been many things, some of them pretty awful, but one of the things I'd loved about living there was the quiet all around my uncle's villa. Now as I heard strains of dance music and people talking, I missed my former home.

Sneaking out, I made my way down the driveway to a tiny grove of Japanese maple trees my father had planted halfway between the main house and the front gate when I was eight. I used to pretend it made me invisible to be surrounded by them, and now as Janelle's engagement party raged on, I could think of nothing better than disappearing from this place.

Fireflies did their best to light up my special spot as I sat down on a concrete bench and struggled to push away the party just a few hundred yards away. I didn't want to think about Janelle and Charles. Nothing about them made me look forward to their wedding in just a few days. I had no idea why he wanted to marry my sister, but I knew all too well what her motivation was.

Money. Security. The continuation of the life my father had given her.

A life that had hobbled her in so many ways and made her so emotionally fucked up she actually believed marrying a man chosen by our father in this day and age could ever be okay.

My mind wrestled against such a horrible future, vacillating between disgust at her choices and pity for them. But only I worried about it. She and my father, always like two peas in a pod, walked around perfectly content with her willingness to be subjugated.

I'd only been back in this house for a few days, but everywhere I looked I saw people who'd had their choices stripped from them. It made me miss my time in Italy all the more.

One person I hadn't seen was Ryder. My sister mentioned him, but only to say he'd become one of my father's men. I tried to imagine what would have made him come back here at all after my father had him beaten for what we'd done, but in truth, for everything I knew of him, I guessed I never really knew him at all.

The person who'd sat with me all those nights talking about my mother's disappearance, his parents' deaths, and how much we both wanted more than what life at this estate offered would never have willingly stayed here if he had a chance to get away.

I choked back emotion as that reality settled into

my brain. He deserved more than being trapped here in my father's world.

The noise from the party filtered into my hidden area, breaking the peace I'd tried to find, so I stood to leave, not knowing where I'd go to find the quiet I so craved. All I knew was this place wasn't where I wanted to be anymore.

I turned to walk toward the house and saw a figure coming toward me in the dim light of dusk. Hoping they wouldn't see me, I stood perfectly still and watched as they walked straight at me and saw Ryder there in front of me.

His hair was no longer short anymore. Not exactly long, it skimmed his collar and looked as touchable as ever. He seemed bigger than when I'd last seen him, but his face with its sculptured cheekbones and strong jaw remained intensely masculine. And as always, his stunning green eyes next to his dark hair made him seem unlike anyone else I'd ever met.

He stopped a few feet away and stared at me with a pained look in his eyes. "Hi. I saw you had come back."

All at once, everything we'd shared seemed lost and we stood facing each other awkwardly.

"Yeah, I got back a couple days ago. I guess you aren't staying in that room near my father's office," I said, knowing full well where he lived now since

Janelle had told me.

He shook his head and appeared to wince, like the idea of that room hurt him somehow. "No, not anymore. Not since I stopped…not since I became one of your father's security guys."

"Oh. Security guy," I mumbled, hating how strange we felt around one another.

I wanted to ask why he never answered any of my letters or returned my calls. I wanted him to know I never wished for him to suffer because of me. I wanted to say so many things but didn't know how to begin.

"Are you going back to Italy after the wedding?" he asked, taking a step toward me, shrinking the space between us.

"No, I don't think so. My father seems to think I've paid enough penance for my sins, so I'm back here for good."

All I could think of when I said that was there was so little good about being back. Except for him. After just a few seconds being near him, I wanted to return to those moments we'd shared together in that room when it was just us in the house and we still had dreams of things we could do if only we got away from this world.

He smiled at my mention of staying but said nothing else. The awkwardness returned in the silence, and no matter how many words begged to be spoken, I couldn't ask those questions for fear I might hear he never cared enough to be bothered with thinking of me after I left.

"I better go," I said finally as the seconds of silence turned to a minute and then two of us just staring at one another like strangers.

I took one step and then another hoping he would stop me from leaving him once again, but he said nothing and with each step my heart sank. Finally, just before I left the grove, I felt his hand touch my arm and turned back to see him staring at me with a look of pure need like I'd never seen before in him.

"Why didn't you ever call? Did you decide after what happened that you needed to break free of everything in this place, including me?" he asked in a low voice tinged with hurt.

"I did call. I called every day for months, but your phone wasn't working. I wrote letters too, but you never wrote back. So I just assumed you moved on and you weren't here anymore."

Ryder shook his head sadly. "I never got any letters and your father took my phone while I was in the hospital. Why didn't you call the house?"

Looking into those green eyes so full of that beautiful intensity I loved, I saw the answer to all my questions I'd been afraid to ask. "I did call, Ryder. Every time I was told you weren't around."

He stepped toward me and brushed his hand against mine as he did. "I missed you."

Those three tiny words took my breath away. After all that time apart, he still had the same effect on me.

"I missed you too. You grew up, Ryder. That guy who looked so uncomfortable in a suit that night of the party—I remember him. He's gone now."

"You look as beautiful as ever," he said with the same smile that had always made my insides feel like they were melting.

He looked down at the ground and shook his head. "But no more bare feet?"

I looked down at my shoes and smiled. "Only for tonight. I'm still all about the barefoot thing."

Our gazes met, and he smiled again. "Good. There's something natural and real about that."

Another awkward silence crept into our conversation, but this time I didn't want to allow that strangeness to ruin things between us, so without a word, I wrapped my arms around him and hugged him tightly. His body felt so right against mine, like two years hadn't gone by since that night in his bedroom, and I loved how his arms enveloped me as we stood there in an embrace I'd wanted for so long.

I felt his hand gently stroke my hair down my back while the steady pounding of his heartbeat sounded in my ear as he held me to him. His strength washed over me, and I loved it.

"You feel so good, Serena. I've missed this so much," he whispered in my ear as he buried his hand in my hair.

I tilted my head back to look at him and wanted more than anything to believe he still cared for me like I cared for him. But what did it matter? My father would never allow us to be together.

"Nothing's changed here, Ryder."

He gently cradled my face in his hands and shook his head. "We've changed."

"You know what I mean. It doesn't matter how much I've changed or how you have. My father will never let us be together. You know that."

Instead of admitting the truth, he kissed me softly and whispered against my lips, "I don't care. I never did."

When he said things like that, it felt like butterflies had been let loose in my stomach. I wanted to think it didn't matter, but I knew how my father could be. Ryder knew that too. Why didn't he want to admit that?

"He's already hurt you for being with me. Who knows what he'll do if he finds out we're together again."

But nothing I said seemed to make a difference. He kissed me again, making all those memories of how much I loved just being with him rush back.

"Serena, I don't care. Whatever he does, it won't hurt as much as being without you."

I gently touched his cheek and felt the beginnings of a beard. "Janelle said you were in the hospital for two weeks last time."

He shook his head and brought my hand to his lips to kiss my fingertips. "I survived. I'll survive again too, but not if you're not with me."

"What if he sends me away again, Ryder? That's what will happen if he finds us together."

Tears welled in my eyes, and he pulled me close again. "He won't send you away again. We can leave if that happens. We'll figure it out. Just tell me you still care."

"Of course I do. There's been nobody since my father sent me away to Italy."

Something about how he looked away when I said that made me wonder if he'd been with anyone else in the time we'd been apart. "What about you? Do you still care?"

"Of course I do, Serena."

"Then why won't you look at me when you say it?" I asked as I gently turned his face toward me.

The intensity was gone from his eyes, replaced by a look so guilty I knew the answer before he spoke.

"Serena, whatever I did, it didn't matter because

I never stopped wanting you."

I stepped back from him as the whole world felt like it was falling away beneath my feet. "What do you mean?"

"I never stopped thinking about you. Every minute I laid in that hospital bed, all I could think about was how much I missed you. I didn't care about my broken bones or how much everything on me hurt. All I cared about was seeing you again."

"Then why do I see in your eyes that at some point you cared about something or someone else even more?"

He reached out to take my hand, but I stepped back even further. Why wouldn't he answer my questions?

"I never cared about anyone or anything more than you, Serena. You can trust me," he said, pleading with his eyes for me to believe him as he spoke those words.

I didn't want to believe what I saw in him. "You met someone? Are you still with her now?"

My stomach twisted into knots as I waited for him to answer, even though his hesitation to say anything told me all I needed to know. He had moved on, no matter what he said about how he never stopped caring for me.

"It's not like that. At least it's not for me," he finally admitted in a quiet voice.

"What's not like that? What does that mean?"

A look of pure pain settled into his eyes, and he said, "Her name is Kitty. I helped her when her boyfriend got rough with her, and we spent some time together."

"Kitty? Like kitty cat? What is she, a fucking stripper?" I asked, practically spitting the words out.

He didn't have to answer. The sheepish look on his face said it all.

"Kitty, the stripper, is the woman you started dating after I was sent away?"

Ryder shook his head. "It's not like that."

My disgust grew with each passing second. "Kitty. Who's named Kitty? Why don't you just call her pussy so you know what she's there for?"

He took a step toward me to hold my hand, but I pushed him away. His shoulders sagged, and he hung his head. "It isn't what you think. She was too young to be in that business and got herself into trouble, so I tried to help her. I guess she got attached."

I couldn't believe my ears! He'd helped this stripper because she got in trouble? That night in my father's office as he exiled me from the only home I'd ever known while Ryder stood by and watched him flashed through my mind, and my hands balled into tight fists at my sides.

"So I guess you are able to protect someone

when they need it most? Nice to know since you left me swinging in the wind when I needed you!"

He opened his mouth to speak but nothing came out. What could he say? He had the capacity to help this person named Kitty, but for me, he just watched as my father punished me and never said a word in my defense.

Finally, as the hurt spiraled through me, tearing all my memories apart, he said, "Serena, this doesn't change the fact that I never stopped caring about you."

As the tears began to roll down my cheeks, I turned to leave, unable to stand there and listen to any more lame excuses. "No. It just changes everything I thought about all that time I was away. That's all."

He didn't say anything else. He didn't have to. There was nothing more to say.

Chapter Ten

Ryder

A KNOCK AT my door signaled it was show time, so I downed the last gulp of my whisky. Dressed in my usual black suit, white shirt, and black tie as Robert demanded all his security detail wore, I looked like a pallbearer instead of one of the guys who had the job of making sure nobody got too close to him.

My job today as he watched his older daughter marry someone he'd handpicked for her was to make him look important. He didn't need security to guard him at his own house any more than I did, but by having men like me around him, he appeared to be far more impressive.

At least that's what it seemed like. I knew he had his hands in much of the seedier parts of what went on in Baltimore, so maybe he was in danger of being attacked here. He certainly traveled in a rough crowd compared to the people who'd be mingling with him to celebrate Janelle's marriage. Underground fighting, strip clubs, and other illegal businesses that involved everything from drugs to escorts brought with them ugliness most wouldn't suspect someone who looked like him would have anything to do with.

One last check of my look in the bathroom mirror and I headed out to the garden where the ceremony was to be held. The three other men who were part of his security detail stood watching as Robert barked out orders to the caterers and florist.

One of the men, a guy named Jesse who was a few years older than me and a former cop in some small town upstate, pointed at the hundred or so chairs set up and said, "That many guests and all he has is us?"

The two other men who were older and had been with Robert for years simply shrugged as if they'd seen things like this before at the Erickson estate and none of it concerned them.

"Like anyone's going to get over the walls or past the guard at the gate," Gannett said, raising his bushy old guy eyebrows up into his forehead to show his disbelief that either could happen.

"I think we're meant to be more ceremonial than anything else," I said to Jesse as I took my position next to him. "You know, show for the crowd."

Show horses.

He rolled his pale blue eyes and shook his head so his blond hair moved left and right around his face. "All this for a girl's wedding. I think if I ever have a daughter I want her to elope. Look at Robert. He looks like he's about to go out of his mind with those goddamned flower people."

Jesse wasn't the brightest bulb in the box, so I wasn't surprised he didn't know those flower people were called florists. I looked over to where Robert stood lecturing some poor guy half his size with thick black birth control glasses about some problem with the garland around the altar and saw his face get redder by the second. Maybe Jesse had something with that whole eloping idea.

Turning on his heels, Robert waved his arms in the air as he made a beeline toward us. Instinctively, the four of us straightened our backs and stood tall as he approached. To Robert, everything was about appearances, and to have your security detail standing like some group of scumbags on a street corner wouldn't do.

"Gannett! Pike! I want you two out here with me during the ceremony. Jesse and Ryder, you two will be at the front door as people come in. I don't need you to pat them down or anything like that, but keep an eye for any problems. Understand? When the ceremony begins, come back out here."

We all nodded and then Jesse and I headed toward the house to take our posts. Watching the front door like some goddamned bouncer wasn't much, but I was thankful I didn't have Gannett or Pike's job standing out in the sun at one o'clock on an August afternoon tagging along with Robert while he stressed out over every little detail of his little girl's big day. Let them have to deal with the garland problems and issues with the wrong champagne on the waiters' trays.

Standing on either side of the front door in the entryway that still impressed me every time I walked through it, Jesse and I did exactly as we were commanded and watched each guest as they arrived. None looked dangerous or even suspicious in the least. All they seemed to be were wealthy people like Robert dressed to the nines for a wedding.

The first notes of the wedding march floated through the house, and Jesse motioned for us to head back out to the party. "I think that's our cue. You coming?"

I wanted to stand out in the heat and watch someone I didn't particularly like get married as much as I wanted to cut off my own arm. "I think I'll stay here to catch any stragglers. I'll be out in a few minutes."

A worried look came over his face. "What do you want me to tell Robert if he asks where you are?"

As much as I liked Jesse, he really wasn't very smart. The guy was definitely all muscle. "Tell him I stayed behind just in case anyone showed up late and needed to be checked out."

"Oh, okay. Will do."

A few guests did arrive late, so I did my job and then enjoyed the relative quiet of the house since it was just me and the usual staff inside. When the ceremony was over, I made my way to the back doors that led out to the garden and I saw her.

Standing next to her sister as the wedding party posed for pictures, Serena smiled on cue as I watched in amazement how beautiful she'd become in the last two years. Even dressed in an ugly dark pink bridesmaid's gown, she stood out against everyone around her.

JANELLE'S RECEPTION WENT on well after its planned ending, so by the time Robert told us we could quit for the day, it was nearly eight o'clock. I turned down an offer from Jesse to go drinking at a little bar some girl he wanted bartended at and made my way toward my apartment in the south wing.

Turning the corner out of the garden, I saw Serena sitting on a bench alone far away from the party. Her shoulders were hunched over and her head was lowered. As much as I knew she might not want anything to do with me, I couldn't ignore her.

I walked over to where she sat and stopped, but she didn't seem to notice I was even there. Clearing my throat, I asked, "Too much celebrating?"

She turned to face me with a look of surprise in her eyes. "Celebrating. Yeah. That's it."

The edge in her voice said she didn't think much of the big party raging nearby.

"So Janelle's married now," I mumbled awkwardly, unsure if I should even continue the conversation. This Serena seemed different than the girl I'd know back then. Harder. Angrier.

She sighed and shook her head. "Yeah, to some guy she barely knows because it makes my father happy. Sounds like a sham to me."

With the old Serena I would have joined in and commented on what really did sound like a sham marriage, but I didn't know where I stood with this version of her. "Well, love comes in all forms, I guess."

Rolling her eyes at me, she snapped, "Really, Ryder? Is it the suit that makes you Robert Erickson's perfect employee or do you really believe that load of shit you just dumped on our conversation?"

"Whoa, okay. Maybe I should go. It sounds like you've had a few to drink and I'm not sure getting into an argument with my boss's daughter is a good career move for me."

This Serena and I mixed like oil and water, so I turned to leave, disappointed at how much she'd changed.

"Wait, don't go. I'm sorry, Ryder. I didn't mean to sound like such a bitch. That was the alcohol talking."

I turned to see her waving me back toward her and smiling. Maybe things weren't all that different.

Taking a seat on the bench next to her, I took a good look at her and saw that sadness in her eyes I'd seen before.

"I hope I'm more than just your boss's daughter, Ryder," she said, the sadness in her eyes morphing into hurt.

Hanging my head, I said, "I don't know why I said it like that. You're more than that. You know that."

"I don't know what I am anymore. At my uncle's house, I got to go to school and be a student. I got to live on my own pretty much. Now that I'm back, I don't know what I am here to you or anyone else."

I didn't say anything. I wanted to tell her that whatever I'd done with Kitty all this time meant nothing. That seeing her made me happier than I thought I'd ever be again.

"You look different, Ryder. I saw it the other night. You grew up in the time I've been gone. Now you're one of my father's suit guys. You're moving up in the world."

At the moment, it didn't feel like it as I sat there while she judged me for the choice I'd made. "It's a living."

She smiled and loosened the knot of my tie. "I never liked any of my father's henchmen. They've always been colorless thugs. You make me think maybe my father has changed his ways if he has you working for him like this."

I wanted to tell her whatever changes Robert Erickson had made in the past two years weren't for the better, but like always, I said nothing about my work for her father. A small part of me was ashamed, but another part wanted to shield her from the ugliness that came with what I did for him.

Her hand lingered near my neck, making memories of our time together come rushing back. Unsure what she felt for me after the other night, I changed the subject.

"So you're not a fan of your new brother-in-law?"

She frowned and let her fingers fall away from my collar. "I only met him twice, so I really don't have any opinion on him as a person. My problem is with my father arranging a marriage for Janelle because it benefits him."

"She seemed okay with it today, unless it was all a show."

Serena blew the air out of her lungs in a loud huff of frustration. "No, she seems perfectly happy, actually. I tried to convince her that she didn't have to go through with it, but she likes the idea of my father picking some guy out for her simply because he works for whatever business plans he has. As long as he's wealthy, it's all good, I guess."

"Some people aren't looking for love, I guess. She must be getting something out of it, though, right?"

Twisting her face into an expression of disgust, she said, "Yeah, security. Like being treated like chattel to be traded as my father pleases is anything close to security. What if Charles does to her what my father did to my mother? Then where will she be?"

I remembered the two of us talking about her mother's leaving, but she'd never accused her father of being responsible for that. Curious why she did now, I said, "I thought your mother just left one night."

"No. I thought that too because that's what he always told me, but I overheard my aunt and uncle talking about it one night and she didn't leave. My father sent her away. She became a hassle to him, so she had to go. That's what my uncle said. Do you know my mother wasn't here today to see her daughter get married? Even if it was a sham, she still should have been a part of it. Her own daughter's wedding!"

"I'm sorry. I didn't know."

My attempt at making her feel better failed, and she continued to complain about her father and my boss. "Did you see that woman my father had hanging off him today? He fucks around like he's a single guy who should be doing that kind of thing, but he's not. He's the husband of a woman he sent away. I don't know which is worse, thinking she just left one night and never wanted to come back or knowing that he was the reason she was forced to abandon us."

Her emotions bubbled to the surface, but she stopped herself from crying. "I'm sorry. It's just really hard to come back here."

I didn't know what to say to that because even just seeing her again made everything for me better. "It's getting late. I need to head toward my rooms. Do you want me to walk you up to the house?"

Serena shook her head. "I won't let this happen to me like Janelle let it happen to her."

"I can't imagine that would ever happen to you," I said as she stood from the bench.

She looked down at me with rage in her eyes. "I'd rather be dead than end up like my mother and sister. Disposable human beings who go away when my father decides he's got no better use for them. Not me."

I watched her storm off toward the house and thought even though so much about her had changed from the girl I'd spent all those hours with, I may have liked this Serena even more. Her time away had made her stronger.

Robert was sadly mistaken if he thought he was going to dictate her life like he did everyone else's.

Chapter Eleven

Serena

INSTEAD OF HEADING off on their honeymoon immediately after the wedding, Janelle and her new husband spent the week at the estate. During the day, she slept until noon or later while Charles and my father met to discuss business matters, and I had to believe all three of them couldn't have been happier.

For me, being back in my father's world made me miserable. I missed Italy and the independence I'd achieved there, and as it quickly faded into the past, I wished I'd never left there when my father beckoned me home. Nothing in this place had changed in the two years I'd been gone. If anything, it had all stayed exactly the same.

My father ruled like some despot over everyone, and they all seemed willing to accept their lots in life. Janelle finally had what she'd always wanted in life. Security. That it could be taken away at any moment by either of the men who ruled her life didn't seem to concern her in the least.

Italy had given me the chance to fulfill my dream of a life more than that, and now that I'd returned, I intended to do whatever it took to make sure I didn't lose it. Ryder had been part of that dream, but of all the things that had stayed the same while I was gone, he had to be the one that changed.

My stomach twisted into knots at the thought of him with that Kitty. I didn't know a thing about her, other than she had a part of him I'd never gotten the chance to, but I hated her. I didn't know if she was blonde or brunette, if she had long hair or short. I didn't know if she was taller than I was or shorter. Did he look at her and see someone so beautiful he couldn't do without her?

I didn't know, but from the first moment he said her name, I'd been consumed with jealousy. For two years, I wished for nothing more than to see him again, and then when the time finally came, he hadn't waited.

My brain filled with every conceivable insecurity, tormenting me. If only I'd asked to come home sooner or found a way to contact him while I was gone, maybe he wouldn't have ever looked at her.

I couldn't think about it anymore, so I walked out to the garden to find some quiet and peace of mind in the only place on the estate that could possibly offer it in the middle of the day on a

Thursday. As I made my way, I inhaled the sweet fragrance of the late summer blooms that filled the air. Something in the honeysuckle on the estate always smelled sweeter than anywhere else.

One of the gardeners worked assiduously trimming the hedges near the three-tiered cement fountain flanked by three white lions with heads proudly tilted high that was the showpiece of the estate's grounds. My father's garden had very few flowers, in fact, and was designed to be a carefully constructed and maintained work of art more than any celebration of nature. Some jasmine and rose bushes still lived on along with the honeysuckle from when my mother had a say in what would be grown, but now green hedges sharply manicured into straight-lined geometric shapes and animal forms were the focus.

All in all, little of it felt natural or wild, and it had the effect of making a nice walk in the garden inevitably feel like a trip through a maze.

I wound along the pathway to a spot where pink roses grew almost unrestricted, except for the trellises that kept them from truly following their nature. An old wooden bench that didn't match anything else in the garden sat alone near the bushes, so I hid there and tried to push away the hurt and anger that had stayed with me on my stroll through the garden.

This place wasn't good for me, and now that the only person I'd truly missed had moved on, maybe it was time I did the same. In less than a year, I'd finish school with my degree in social work, and until then I could work while I attended classes so I wouldn't have to stay at the estate.

It wouldn't be a life like my sister had enjoyed all these years, but it would be the kind of life I wanted. She could have her modern day slavery. I'd take poverty over that any day.

Closing my eyes, I let the sun warm my face as I silently condemned her choices even as I thought about my mother. Now that I knew she wasn't gone but had been kept from us, I wondered where she was at that moment. What had my father done to force her to stay away?

"Hiding out?"

I looked up and saw Ryder blocking the sun as he stood in front of me in the black suit that had become his uniform now. "Maybe. Just looking for some quiet."

He sat down and took a deep breath in. "I never come back here, you know? I've lived here for over two years and this might be the first time I've ever been in this part of the estate."

For a long moment, I studied the man next to me. The clothes he wore made him look older, but in the light of day I still saw that cockiness in his expression when he wasn't trying to be one of my father's henchmen.

"What are you doing here, Ryder?" I asked, wishing he'd say the words I'd waited years to hear.

He turned to look at me and forced a smile. "Your father sent me to look for you. I caught a glimpse of you as you headed toward the garden, so I followed you here."

Hearing he was doing my father's handiwork was the last thing I wanted to hear. Disgusted, I said, "Nice. Stalking the boss's daughter. Great job you have there. What's he want me for?"

My words hurt him, and his green eyes narrowed to slits when he winced. "I think he's planning on having one of his get-togethers and wants to make sure you'll be there."

I turned away from him and closed my eyes, letting the sun warm the apples of my cheeks. "You can tell him his show horse will be there."

Ryder didn't answer, but he didn't leave either. He just sat silently at my side as I tried not to focus on the fact that he was staring at me. Finally, I opened my eyes and looked over at him, unable to ignore him anymore.

"You don't think you should run off to report back to him?" I asked, hating how sharp my words sounded.

He stared at me, those green eyes focused

intently on my eyes. "I never cared about her, Serena."

His mention of her felt like someone had my heart in their hand and were squeezing hard. I didn't want to talk about what he felt for someone else.

"Don't. Just don't, Ryder. I get it. You moved on and I didn't. Too bad for me, right?"

I stood to leave, but he caught my arm as I turned away. I looked down at him and saw he had more to say.

"I need you to believe me. I never thought I'd see you again. I thought you got away from here, and I didn't blame you for wanting to forget everything about this place, including me. But I never forgot about you. Never."

"Yeah. You told me. Even while you were fucking pussy or whatever her name is, your stripper girlfriend."

My answer made him grimace, and he let go of my arm. "What else do you want from me, Serena? What can I say to make you believe me?"

His questions made me want to hit someone. What did I want from him? What I'd been willing to give him ever since all those nights we spent together in his room.

"Two years. Two years I wanted the person I'd fallen in love with all those times we sat on your bed and talked. I wanted you, but you turned into this stripper fucking, company man of my father's!" I screamed.

He practically jumped up from the bench, furious at my indictment of who he'd become. Looking down at me, his eyes flashed hurt even while he snapped back at me, "Grow up! Not all of us had the chance to escape this place and spend two years in Italy living in a villa. I'm sorry who I am is such a disappointment to you. Some of us don't get a choice in what happens to us."

I opened my mouth to tell him I thought that was bullshit, that everyone had a choice, but he didn't give me a chance to say anything before he stormed away, leaving me in that spot surrounded by nature's beauty and feeling worse than when I'd arrived.

Fuck him. I didn't run off to Italy like some spoiled little rich girl. I was exiled for the crime of wanting to make my life something more than a future as mere chattel. And his claim that he didn't have a choice but to become one of my father's thugs was crap. He always had a choice.

He just made the wrong one.

PEEKING MY HEAD around the corner into my father's office, I saw him sitting behind his desk and Ryder standing near the bookcases on the far wall like a statue staring straight ahead with no feeling or emotion or even a thought.

Nice choice of a life there.

"Did you want to see me, Dad?" I asked, pretending to be chipper after what had just happened in the garden.

He turned toward Ryder and smiled. "See? I knew you'd have better luck than anyone else getting her to come in. And you thought she'd disobey me."

I flashed Ryder a look of disgust that he would have said that about me and then looked over at my father with a big smile. "Of course not. What's up?"

He stood from his chair and came over to the doorway to pull me into the room. "I'm having a party tonight, sort of a send-off for your sister and Charles as they begin their life together. Just a few friends and their wives. I expect you to be there with bells on at seven and your usual gracious self."

"Of course," I said with all the enthusiasm I could possibly muster. "Anything else?"

My father stared at me for a moment with a look of suspicion but then shook his head. "No. I look forward to having you there tonight, Serena. It hasn't been the same without you these past two years. Ask Ryder. He'll tell you."

I nodded and turned to look over toward the bookcase at him. "Oh, he's told me all about how things aren't the same anymore."

My jab got no response, and Ryder simply

trained his gaze on a spot on the wall above my head to avoid looking directly at me. He could ignore me all he wanted. That didn't mean a damn thing to me.

AT SEVEN O'CLOCK sharp, I appeared in the formal dining room my father used for his parties and saw the small gathering of twenty or so people fawning over Janelle and Charles, much to my relief since I genuinely didn't want to have to entertain my father and his friends again. I'd done it countless times growing up, from when I was a little girl and was expected to charm them with how adorable I could be around adults to when I got older and was expected to tolerate his friends' inappropriate drunken advances on me as a teenager.

Tonight I hoped being gracious meant being silent and smiling while everyone ignored me in favor of my sister and her new husband.

I scanned the room for any sign of Ryder but didn't see him. Probably all the better since our fight earlier had left me a little shaken. As much as I wanted to hate him for what he said, I couldn't, even though I still thought he was dead wrong.

I had grown up. I just hadn't left what I felt for him behind, even if I should have.

Lost in thought, I didn't see Janelle next to me until she shook me by the shoulder. "Hey, what's going on with you, Serena? I just asked you what you thought of my dress."

"It's very nice," I said as I pretended to care about the form fitting black designer dress with purple and green floral print across her breasts.

"It's going to be just you now, little sister. Do you think you can handle our father alone?" she said with a sly smile, as if she'd ever done anything to help me with him.

Looking around the room for some escape, I said, "I'll be fine. I won't be here very long, so it won't be an issue."

Next to me, she continued to talk. "Why? Where are you going?"

I turned to see her wearing a curious expression, knowing she likely was pumping me for information for our father. "I only have a year left in school, Janelle. After that, there would be no reason to continue living here. Time to get out into the world and work."

That those concepts were entirely foreign to my sister was obvious by the confused look she gave me as she answered, "Oh. Well, I guess if you want that kind of life."

Thankfully, her husband walking toward us gave me a reprieve from her, and I quickly excused myself to get a drink at the bar. Maybe if I drank enough, I could make it through my father's little get-together.

Two glasses of merlot later, I didn't hate being at

the party so much but wondered why Ryder wasn't there. Then it dawned on me.

He was probably at his girlfriend's house. Kitty. Fucking Kitty.

Pushing my glass toward the bartender, I faked a smile and said, "Another glass of wine, please."

The last thing I wanted to think about as I was stuck at my father's party celebrating my sister's willing entry into a life of indentured servitude was Ryder together with some woman whose name was synonymous with vagina. There wasn't enough alcohol in the world to make that good.

From behind me, I heard my father announce it was time to dance and my heart sank. Who would he pair me up with this time? I imagined when I turned around I'd see some old man with roaming hands and bad breath all set to dance with me.

"Serena, it's been a long time since we all had the pleasure of seeing you dance. You can do the honors," my father announced.

Cringing, I silently prayed to God my partner wouldn't be too old or smell like death and turned around to see him grinning that crocodile smile of his. Knowing my entire job tonight involved being gracious, I plastered a smile on my face and joined him in the center of the room.

"Of course, Dad," I said as I took his hand and waited to find out my fate.

He swiveled his head left and right like he was looking for someone. "Where is he?"

As I stood there filled with dread at all the old men in that room, I saw Ryder step out from behind a group of couples and walk toward us. Stopping in front of me, he smiled at my father. "Sorry, I was just finishing my drink."

Dressed in a tux, he was nothing less than stunning. I pressed my lips together so my mouth wouldn't drop open in shock at what he looked like. If I didn't know better, I would have said he was any one of the movers and shakers my father liked to have attend his parties.

"Everyone, you all know my adopted son Ryder. It's been two years since he saw Serena, so I thought it would be nice to let them have the first dance."

The crowd clapped as he left us standing there together to turn the music on. Never before in my life had I been terrified to dance in that room, but now as Ryder stood there putting his hand against my back and taking my hand in his, I worried I wouldn't be able to move without melting into the floor.

He stared down at me when I didn't move and whispered, "They expect us to dance, Serena. I know you know how."

I positioned my hand on his shoulder and looked up at him. "So no more yelling at me?"

We began to move our feet, and it became obvious in our time apart Ryder had learned to dance. Gently gliding me across the floor, he moved even better than I did.

"No more yelling. At least not now," he said quietly in my ear.

All I heard was the not now part and couldn't help frowning. As if he read my mind, he added, "I'm sorry for before."

"I'm not disappointed in who you are," I said as he turned me.

He smiled like hearing that meant the world to him. "Good. I think I clean up pretty nice, don't you agree?"

Nodding, I tried not to think of how incredibly hot he looked in that tux. I'd always wanted to see him dressed in one, and now as he held me while we danced for the first time together, the last thing I could think of was being disappointed in him.

The music stopped all too soon, but he didn't let me go even as my father called for me to come meet some friend of his. I didn't want Ryder's hand to leave my back. I loved the feel of him holding me like pressed against his body was where I belonged.

"Your father wants to talk to you, I think," he said as we stood still in each other's hold, our gazes fixed on one another.

"I'm ignoring him hoping he'll go away," I said

with a smile.

But he yelled my name again, and I knew I didn't have a choice. Reluctantly, I slid my hand off Ryder's shoulder and my other hand from his hold, but he didn't let me go. Instead, he leaned down and whispered in my ear, "I enjoyed our first dance together."

The sound of his deep voice as his lips softly grazed the shell of my ear made my legs go weak and an ache formed in my core. I grudgingly left him to go speak to my father and whatever old guy he thought I needed to meet, wishing all these people could disappear and it could be just Ryder and me again.

"Serena, I want you to meet Oliver Landon. He's part owner of Landon Auction House," my father said in a tone that indicated I should be impressed by this.

Oliver Landon certainly wasn't an old man, but he looked old before his time for a young man I guessed couldn't be more than in his late twenties. He had light hair cut respectably short and blue eyes that didn't seem to hide anything deeper behind them. His smile appeared genuine when my father introduced us, but knowing the people Robert Erickson liked to surround himself with, it wasn't a stretch to think that smile was fake.

"It's nice to meet you, Oliver," I said politely,

extending my hand to shake his. "I hope you're having a nice time here tonight."

"I am. Your father's been a very gracious host."

"That's nice," I said as I scanned the room for Ryder.

"Serena, I thought you and Oliver would get along since he's very much into the arts."

I looked at my father and nodded without giving his idea any thought. "Okay. If you'll excuse me, I have to go freshen up a bit after my dance."

Quickly, I left and headed toward the first-floor powder room. I saw Ryder turn the corner toward the kitchen. Just before he made it there, he vanished into the stairway down to the wine cellar.

I slowly descended the stairs and saw him leaning against the table with his arms folded and wearing that sexy grin that never failed to make my insides feel like they were turning to molten lava.

"Why did you leave the party?" I asked as I slowly walked toward him.

"Too many people and they aren't really my crowd, no matter how much your father wants to say I'm his adopted son."

I couldn't help but laugh. My father's insistence on calling Ryder that verged on the ridiculous, but he continued to do it anyway. "I don't know why he does that. I certainly hope you're getting some benefit from being his supposed son, not that being his child comes with a lot of perks."

"Who was the guy he wanted you to talk to?" Ryder asked with a hint of jealousy in his voice.

Shrugging, I tried to remember anything about him but drew a blank. "I don't know. I can't even think of his name right now."

"A real memorable type, huh?" he said, still grinning in that way that made him look so sexy.

"I guess. I didn't really care, but maybe if I made some effort I could remember at least his name."

He stood up to his full height and stepped toward me. "Don't."

"Don't what?" I asked, acutely conscious of how close he stood near me.

In a low voice that hit me deep inside, he said, "I don't want you to make any effort to think of him while you're down here with me." He lifted his hand to touch my hair and said, "In fact, I want you to think of only one thing while you're with me."

My breath caught in my chest and I could barely speak, but I squeaked out, "What's that?"

Ryder slowly slid the tip of his tongue across his bottom lip and said, "How fucking bad I want to be inside you."

I swallowed hard and watched his eyes as they stared down at me full of desire. I'd waited so long for this moment, but now that it had arrived, I stood frozen to the spot.

He slid his arm around my waist and roughly pulled me to him so I felt his hard cock pressing against my belly. I closed my eyes and slid my hand over the front of his pants, and he moaned above me.

Thrusting his hand into my hair, he tugged my head back and said, "Look at me, Serena."

Slowly, my eyelids fluttered open as I nervously did as he commanded and saw that intensity in his green eyes that never failed to thrill me.

"I want you. Only you."

"But what about…?"

He interrupted my question with a kiss that took my breath away. "Don't say anything. Only you, Serena. It's always been only you."

Cradling his face in my hands, I said, "I'm sorry about what I said out in the garden. I'm not disappointed. I'm not."

His hands slid under my dress to cup my ass. "I don't want to wait any longer. Right here, Serena."

Right there where he touched me for the first time.

Suddenly, a noise upstairs frightened me, and I shook my head. If my father caught us down there together, I didn't want to think about what he'd do to us.

"Not here. Someone might see us."

Ryder slid a finger along the inside of my panties

as my head swam from how much I wanted him inside me. Leaning down, he whispered in my ear, "I don't care who sees us. No more waiting. I regretted not fucking you the last time I had a chance in this very cellar, and I'm not going to make that mistake again."

Lifting me off the floor, he brought me up to waist level, and I wrapped my legs around his body as my fear was overpowered by how much I wanted him. I felt his hands moving beneath me and then his cock pressed against the front of my damp panties. Thick and long and hard, just the feel of him against my needy clit made me wish I hadn't worn anything under my dress.

"Pull them aside," I said breathlessly, dying to finally feel him slide inside me.

His fingers fumbled with the fabric for a moment before he simply tore them in half and tugged them down my left leg before thrusting into me in one hard push that filled me completely.

In his ear, I moaned as my mind began to whirl out of control. "Oh, God…"

"You feel so fucking good," he said hoarsely as he began to thrust his hips, sliding his cock out of me and then ramming it back inside until there was nothing separating our bodies.

My hands clung to his neck as we fucked, neither of us aware of anything but how sublime it felt to finally give in to the desires we'd shared since those nights two summers ago in that guest bedroom one floor up. I watched him, enthralled by how he focused completely on me as he fucked me like no one had ever before.

"I want to feel you with my hands. Let me feel you," I begged as I slid my palms over his chest, needing to touch his body hidden under that tux.

He turned toward the table and gently lay me down, sliding out of me and leaving my body feeling empty. I tugged his shirt out of his pants, and he quickly unbuttoned it before untying his tie and shrugging out of his shirt and tux jacket.

I craved his body and desperately ran my hands up over his hard abs and chest, loving the feel of his smooth tanned skin against my fingertips. Every fantasy I'd ever had about being with him came alive there, and as he pushed his hips forward and eased his cock back into me, I felt like I was burning up.

Sliding up my body, he cradled my face and dragged his thumb over my mouth before he kissed me long and deep, his tongue teasing mine as he pushed into my pussy.

"God, I want this to go on forever," he moaned, pressing his forehead to mine and staring down at me with a look full of need in his eyes.

The feel of his cock touching a spot deep inside me made it hard not to let my eyes roll back into my head, but I wanted to watch every second of our fucking to remember the very moment when he owned my body and soul like he'd owned my heart for so long.

The muscles in his neck strained against his skin with every push of his hips. His intensity captivated me, taking me with him as we raced toward release. My heels pushed hard into his sweat drenched back, and he began making shallow stabs into me instead of the smooth thrusts he'd begun with as he moved closer to coming.

I wanted everything he was, every last delicious inch of him on me and every last perfect drop of him inside me. Clinging to his shoulders, I whispered, "Don't stop."

His eyes narrowed as he winced slightly, and I felt the first tendrils of my orgasm uncoil inside me. Raking my fingernails down his back, I cried out and he pressed his palm over my mouth to keep me from screaming. I clamped my lips around his thumb and sucked hard as my release washed over me, taking my breath away.

With one final thrust, Ryder stilled inside me and came, every muscle in his body stiffening as he flooded my insides. We lay there panting as sweat covered our skin and the evidence of our fucking dripped down my trembling thighs.

"You are so beautiful," he said and sighed. "I

never want to forget how you look right now."

I looked up into his deep green eyes and saw love in them. "I wish we didn't have to wait so long, Ryder."

He shook his head and kissed me softly. "I love you, Serena. Then and now."

"I love you, Ryder. Promise me no matter what happens that you'll still love me."

His expression grew dark. "Nothing's going to happen, so don't worry."

I knew how unlikely that was, though. Something always happened to make good things go bad. I'd lived long enough in this world to know that.

Chapter Twelve

Ryder

THE SUN SET a few minutes before I left my rooms to head to that tiny place at the back of the garden. I knew I should have waited a little longer before going to where I'd meet Serena because at least then I'd be hidden by the dark of night, but I didn't want to wait. I hadn't seen her alone since last night, and my body yearned to feel her again.

We knew we had to hide our being together from everyone on the estate. Not that I thought we actually could. We might get away with it now or for a few weeks, but someone would find out and then it would just be a matter of time.

I didn't want to think about that, though. I just wanted to enjoy being with the one person in the world who made me happy.

That wasn't too much to ask, was it?

I knew the answer to that. Yes, it was, if you lived in Robert Erickson's world.

A rustling in the hedges ahead of me put my

body on high alert, and I squinted in the dim light of dusk to see who was there. The figure ran toward where I was headed, so I followed them, breaking into a run to catch up.

Just as I turned the corner to that little spot surrounded by rose bushes, I felt a hand touch my sleeve. I spun around, my arm cocked back and ready, and saw Serena standing in front of me dressed in a white t-shirt that came down to the middle of her tanned thighs.

She raised her hands in surrender and backed away from me. "It's me, Ryder. It's just me."

The fear in her voice stopped me dead. I lowered my arm and opened my fist, hating the terror in her eyes because of me.

"Sorry. I guess I'm a little jumpy. I would never hit you. You know that, right?" I asked, taking a step toward her and pulling her to me.

She melted into my arms and hugged me tightly to her. "I never thought you would. I know you."

The truth was she didn't. She knew the man who adored her, the man who couldn't think of anything else most of the time because he wanted to be with the woman he loved. But she didn't know me. The Ryder she knew could never hurt someone, but that's exactly what my entire job involved on a daily basis.

I couldn't tell her who I had to be for her father, though. I couldn't bear to see the look of disappointment in her eyes like I saw when I told her that I'd been too weak to wait for her. I never wanted to see her look at me like that again.

"Did anyone see you?" I asked as I pulled her into our hidden spot.

She sat down on the bench and took my hands in hers. "No. I made sure."

"Good, although maybe you should have worn something darker," I teased, tugging on the bottom of her bright white shirt.

Giggling, she stood and wrapped her arms around my waist. "Sit down on the ground," she said as she smiled up at me.

I lowered myself to the grass and stretched my legs out in front of me. Looking up at her, I watched her slowly lift that t-shirt up, revealing her naked body. God, she was beautiful!

"Come here," I said, my cock growing harder by the second as I looked at her standing there on display just for me.

She straddled my hips and playfully tossed her t-shirt off to the side. I slid my hands over her breasts, cupping her perfect tits in my palms and lightly pinching her nipples.

"You feel so fucking good. You're all I could think about all day, Serena."

Rocking back and forth over my cock, she kissed me long and deep. "Me too. At one point today it was all I could do not to play with myself because I wanted you so bad."

I pulled her up and sucked a nipple into my mouth, teasing it with my teeth. Serena tightened her fist in my hair and held me fast to her while she moaned sweetly above me.

Moments like these were what I fantasized about all day. If only there was a way we could be together like regular people and not have to sneak around to find happiness in dark corners and hidden places.

Her nipple popped out of my mouth, and I tilted my head to look up at Serena smiling down at me. Every miserable moment away from her faded into nonexistence when I saw her looking at me like I was everything in the world to her.

"I love it when you use your mouth like that. Is there anything you'd like me to suck on?" she asked in the sexiest yet most innocent voice as she dragged her hand over the front of my pants like a fallen angel all my own.

"Mmmm…"

When I didn't make a move to take out my cock for her, she leaned down and kissed me softly on the lips. "Is something wrong? I thought you would like that."

I cradled her face and kissed her before I dared to speak something I'd been thinking about since finding out she had come back. "What if we left this place?"

Serena's dark eyes opened wide. "What do you mean? Where would we go?"

"Anywhere we wanted to. We could go away from here and start a life, just the two of us."

The excitement bubbled up inside me as I watched her nod at my suggestion. "Oh, Ryder, I want to. I don't know how much money I'll have, but I don't care if you don't. Do you care?"

"I would live like a beggar as long as you were with me. Tell me you'll go."

I eagerly waited to hear her answer, desperate to know that our future might not be dictated by her father and his world. For a moment, she just stared into my eyes and my heart sank. I could never give her what she had at this place—the money, the security, the comfort.

But I would give her everything I was to make her happy.

Pressing her forehead to mine, she whispered, "You tell me when and I'll go anywhere with you. When can we leave?"

I slid my palms down her back over her silky skin and drew her to me. "Give me a couple days and we'll go away from this place forever, Serena."

"Do we have to wait that long, Ryder? Can't we go tonight?"

As much as I wished we could, I needed that time to make sure when we did leave that her father wouldn't be able to find us. If he did, the rest of her life would be pure misery, and I suspected the best thing about the rest of my life would be that it was short.

To Robert Erickson, betrayal trumped all other crimes. His revenge would be swift and painful. I couldn't let that happen to Serena.

"We need to be smart about this. We can't let your father find out what we're doing. It might mean we'll have to stay away from one another until we leave, though. We don't want to give him anything to be suspicious about."

She buried her head in my shoulder and held me tight. "I can't stay away. Don't make me. There has to be some other way. You're the only thing that makes living here bearable."

"I know, but we have to be smart or we'll get caught. Give me two days. We'll leave on Sunday night when he goes out. It'll just be us in the house then since Janelle and Charles are gone. We'll be safe that way."

Lifting her head, she nodded, but her mouth turned down into a pout. "I don't want to wait or be away from you even for two days, but if you say so."

"I promise it will be worth it. Once we're away from here, we can go anywhere we want. The mountains, the shore. It doesn't matter because we'll be free."

She smiled and kissed me. "We'll find a little house and every night we'll fall asleep in each other's arms, right?"

I didn't know what we'd find to live in, but it didn't matter because every night we'd be together, and that's all that counted.

"It'll be just you and me," I said, cradling her face. "And you'll fall asleep with your head on my shoulder like you used to in my room when I first came here."

"I loved when I'd wake up and I'd look up and see you sleeping there with me. You know that?" she asked as she traced the outline of my lips with her fingertips. "I never wanted to leave."

Sadness crept into her voice, and I knew she meant more than each night when she snuck out of my room and up the stairs to hers. "That doesn't matter now. All that matters is we're together and in a few days we'll be away from this place."

"I love you, Ryder, and when we're far away from here, I'm going to make you the happiest person on earth. I promise."

Sliding my hands down her naked body, they came to rest on her waist. She rolled her hips over my cock, and I dug my fingertips into her skin to keep her right where she was at. "I can't wait for the day when I can be with you whenever I damn well want."

"Well, for now, let me give you a sneak preview of the way I plan to wake you up every single day," she said with a devilish smile.

Serena slid down my legs and unzipped my pants to release my cock. Already rock hard, it was ready for whatever she wanted to do. Expecting her to straddle my hips and ride me, I watched in delight when she lowered her head and sucked me into her mouth, teasing the top of my cock with her tongue and nearly sending me into orbit.

She took the base in her hand and stroked with each time she slid her perfect mouth down my shaft. I held her hair back so I could watch, loving the sight of her slowly sucking me off. I could have spent hours looking at her like that, but I wanted more, so I gently lifted her head and pulled her up on my lap.

"Why'd you stop me? Didn't you like that?" she asked with a hint of disappointment.

Stuffing my hand into her hair, I pulled her mouth to mine and kissed her hard. "I want to see you ride me."

She rolled her hips, gliding her wet pussy over my cock until it slid in and filled her. "Mmmm…like this?"

I loved the feel of her snug cunt around my cock, and watching her writhe in ecstasy as she fucked me always thrilled me. I held her hips in place and lifted her off me before pushing her back down hard onto me, stretching her to take every inch.

Her hands pressed down on my shoulders as she rode me, and she bit her lip each time I hit that spot deep inside her. A tiny moan escaped from her just before she whimpered, "Right there. Oh, God…don't stop…"

I felt her cunt squeeze my cock and then she closed her eyes and came hard on me. She stilled her body, and her thighs trembled against my hips as each wave of release raced over her. More beautiful than I'd ever seen her, she finally collapsed on top of me as I began to come.

Holding her body to mine, I filled her until there was nothing left in me. Exhausted but content, I listened to her breathe and couldn't imagine being happier than I was at that very moment.

"Promise me it will only be a couple days, Ryder," she whispered in my ear. "I don't want to wait for us to be together."

I tilted her head back and kissed her on the lips. "Two days and then we'll leave here and never look back."

She gave me a smile that filled my heart with joy that in just forty-eight hours we'd be finally together. Even more, we'd be free.

Chapter Thirteen

Serena

JUST DAYS AFTER my sister and her husband left on their honeymoon, I had a sense my father was feeling lonely without her. He'd granted her wish for her and Charles to live away from the estate, and since then, he'd wanted to spend more time with me than ever before. To my father, the past ceased to exist once he decided he wanted it to, no matter how the other person felt.

No matter how much I still resented him for making me leave my home for two long years.

As I hurried past his office one night before Ryder and I planned to leave forever, he called out my name. "Serena, come in here. I want to talk to you."

Not fast enough.

Resigned to my fate, I took a deep breath and plastered my best fake smile on my face as I entered the room. "Yes, Dad? I was just going to my room for the night."

At eight o'clock. Actually, I had planned on

going out to get some last minute things Ryder and I would need, so I hoped whatever he had to say didn't take long.

"Sit down. We have to talk."

Nothing good could come from any conversation that began with those words. In just seconds, he'd gone from I want to talk to you to we have to talk.

Every muscle in my body tensed as I looked around the room to see Ryder and the other young guy who worked security for my father. The last thing I wanted to do was have some serious conversation in front of them.

"You look busy, Dad. We can talk later or tomorrow."

He looked over toward them and shook his head. "No need. They're used to being around when I have business conversations. Sit."

So this was going to be a business conversation. Since I had no part whatsoever in anything even remotely connected to my father's businesses, I couldn't imagine what he wanted to talk about with me. Maybe he wanted my opinion on some acquisition he was considering.

Left without any choice, I did as he ordered and sat down in one of the chairs in front of his desk. "Sure, Dad. What's up?"

I didn't know if he believed the chipper tone of

my voice. I wouldn't have if I were him. Then again, if I had been a bastard to someone and basically banished them from their home for two years, I probably wouldn't have expected them to want to ever speak to me again.

He looked across his desk at me and smiled that broad grin that never failed to make my stomach knot up. It always made me feel like he saw me as prey.

"Your sister's wedding got me to thinking. It's time you make some decisions about your life, Serena."

"Some decisions about my life?" I repeated, feeling my stomach cramp even tighter.

"Yes. Janelle is only two years older than you and she's already married. If you ask me, she waited too long. I don't want to see you make that mistake."

"I'm only twenty, Dad. It's the twenty-first century. Females don't need to get married right out of puberty. In fact, they don't have to get married at all."

My comment about not marrying anyone made him sit up straight in his chair. Shaking his head, he looked horrified by the mere thought that a woman would choose to remain single.

"That's absurd. Of course you'll marry. It's the way things are done. I don't care what century it is. A woman needs to be married."

"Why?"

I felt Ryder's gaze on me from the side of the room, and I turned to see him staring at me with a look of panic in his eyes. I had no idea if he knew what was coming next or if the mere mention of me marrying someone terrified him as much as it did me.

Now that he had joined the ranks of my father's henchmen, he couldn't do a thing but stand there and stay silent or risk having my father know we were together. But I didn't need him to fight my battles for me. I had no interest in marrying anyone my father chose for me, and I had no problem telling him that.

"Because it's the role she's most prepared for in life," my father explained, sounding like some caveman fast forwarded in time.

"I will have my degree in social work next May, so I'll have far more roles open to me in life. If I do ever get married, it will be once I'm established and am my own woman."

My father's face screwed into a look of pure confusion. I truly believed he had no idea what I was talking about.

"Regardless, you'll be married this fall. His name is Oliver Landon, the man you met the other night and so rudely walked away from that I had to make my apologies just to keep him interested."

I couldn't believe my ears. Had he just announced that he'd picked a husband for me, even after I'd just told him how I felt about marriage?

Standing to leave, I smiled. "We've had this conversation, Daddy. I'm not getting married to anyone, and especially not in a couple months. And I'm not marrying anyone I just met and didn't even like enough to remember his name."

His expression hardened, and his mouth set into a tight line across his face. "Yes, you will. It's been arranged."

My eyes narrowed into angry squints. "No, I won't. I'm not Janelle. I'm not going to be traded for whatever this Oliver person has to offer you. Good night, Daddy."

I didn't take two steps before he slammed his hand down on his enormous oak desk. Too frightened to turn around, I froze and stood facing the door as he began to bark orders at me.

"You will do this, Serena. I will not take any disobedience on this. You remember the last time you disobeyed?"

My blood began to boil at his thinly veiled threats, and I spun around to go toe-to-toe with him. "Are you threatening to throw me out of my house again, Daddy? Because if that's it, I can be gone tonight and you'll never see me again. Is that what you want?"

Nobody ever threatened my father. I had never done it before, and as his eyes flashed the purest look of rage I'd ever encountered, I knew why. I quickly glanced over toward Ryder on the other side of the room to gauge if he'd help me if he attacked me and saw him standing there shocked. For his part, Ryder appeared ready to move, but I wasn't sure he could defend me this time any more than he did the last time.

"Serena, you're on thin ice with me, and I would suggest you watch your mouth. I won't be disobeyed in this matter. Oliver is coming here tonight to spend time with you, and you will be your charming self. Do you understand?"

My emotions began to spin out of control as tears welled in my eyes. I wouldn't be sold off to the highest bidder as if I was some piece of contraband at my father's disposal. I wouldn't! If it meant I had to go live on the streets instead of marrying some strange man, then I'd do that. Anything to keep my freedom.

"No! I am not yours to do with as you see fit. I will not marry anyone and that's final."

My father looked stunned at my declaration of independence, but I knew he wouldn't let me go that easily. He'd threaten me with something, probably disinheritance or something else awful that had to do with money, but I was ready for that.

I wasn't afraid of poverty. I was afraid of enslavement.

He took a deep breath and slowly let it out before he said in a voice full of iciness, "So you've given up on ever seeing your mother again? Is that what I'm hearing?"

Stunned by his words, my mind whirled. What a monster he was! He knew he couldn't control me with threats of taking money away like with Janelle, so he went for the one thing in my life he knew full well I cared about.

But I wasn't as naïve as he thought. Leveling my gaze on him, I answered, "So now you're claiming you know where she is after years of saying you couldn't find her? Maybe that's because it was you who sent her away, not her who left us?"

His mouth hitched up into a terrifying grin I knew signaled how enraged he truly was under that cool façade he liked me and his employees to see. "If you ever want to see your mother again, Serena, you will do as I tell you regarding this marriage. And if you choose to disobey me, I cannot promise you others won't suffer for your actions. Keep that in mind as you choose what course to take."

My uncle had said my father would do anything to keep control over me. I hadn't been one hundred percent sure of it until that very moment, but now I knew he'd willingly led me to believe he didn't know her whereabouts for all those years when he had been the one to force her out of our lives.

My chest tightened at the thought that he'd hurt my mother because of me. Or maybe he knew about how I felt about Ryder and would hurt him. How could I risk him taking out his rage on either of them? There had to be some way to make him see how wrong forcing me to marry someone I didn't love was.

Reaching out, I softly touched his hand as tears filled my eyes. "Please don't do this, Daddy. I'm only twenty years old. I'm too young to marry someone, but even more than that, I want to be with someone I love. I don't love this Oliver person. Please don't make me do this."

His expression remained stony as he listened to my pleas and obviously felt nothing in response. "Your actions have consequences, Serena. You've never wanted to understand that, but you will now. Choose wisely."

I'd overestimated my power and he'd taken advantage of my weakness. I didn't have a choice. I couldn't live with the knowledge that he'd hurt someone because of me. Hanging my head, I sat down in the chair again and mumbled, "Fine. I'll meet with him."

Oliver arrived a few minutes later and although he was certainly pleasant enough, all I saw in him was a jailer. As my father talked up my accomplishments like he actually felt any pride in anything I'd ever done, I silently pleaded for him to change his mind to no avail.

As he and Oliver talked like old friends, I looked around the room and saw Ryder simply staring straight ahead like a statue, his expression unfeeling and emotionless as I sat there in that room for yet another time and saw my father take my world away.

Chapter Fourteen

Ryder

I STOOD AT the edge of Robert's desk as he explained that we'd have yet another wedding in just a few weeks and ran through a list of things he wanted to do differently for Serena's ceremony. Meticulous with every detail, he didn't seem to notice his daughter didn't want to marry this Oliver person.

As I watched him torture her with the threat of hurting her mother the night before, I wanted to speak up, to defend her. I wanted to do what I couldn't do that night two years ago, but I didn't.

I stood there sickened by what he did to her and did nothing. And a few hours later when I'd drunk myself into a stupor so I couldn't think anymore, I thought about going to her and telling her how sorry I was that I, of all people, hadn't defended her.

I didn't do that either.

"...so I think that this time I'll have you outside with me because that asshole Maddox ended up boring the hell out of me for nearly a half hour at

Janelle's reception. I don't know where Gannett and Pike were while the whole damn thing was going on. They're lucky I didn't have their heads after that."

A knock on Robert's office door brought me back as he rambled on about some guy he had wanted to avoid at Janelle's wedding. Looking up, I saw Serena standing in the doorway, her eyes tentative and hopeful, so I backed up away from the desk, not wanting to even be within earshot for their conversation.

"I'm going to find Jesse and bring him up to speed on your plans," I said quickly and got the hell out of that room in a hurry.

As I headed down the hall, I heard Serena begin to speak. "Please, Daddy. Please don't make me go through with this marriage. I'm begging you."

I didn't want to hear anymore.

Instead of trying to find Jesse, I made my way out onto the grounds to take a walk and clear my head. Never before had fighting bothered me. Hell, I spent nearly a year beating the shit out of other guys and in some ways I liked it. Being forced to do it wasn't top on my list of things I ever wanted to do again, but when I was one on one with some guy and had him at the point that I knew all it would take would be one more hit and he'd fall to the ground in defeat, I liked the way that made me feel.

But the way Robert and Serena fought gave me

no pleasure at all. He was cruel, bordering on vicious when he made up his mind about her, and she was stubborn. Not that she shouldn't be. I wouldn't just roll over and take it if someone was going to force me to marry someone I barely knew.

It was just that I didn't know how much more she could take, and that made being around them when they fought feel like a ticking time bomb. I didn't think Robert saw it, but I had a sense one of these days she'd explode and all that resentment she held inside would finally be let out and turn his world upside down.

The fucker had it coming. He treated everyone around him like pawns on a chessboard, moving them around whenever he saw fit and without even the slightest interest in what they wanted. Janelle never seemed to mind, but that didn't surprise me. She wasn't much better than a parasite, as far as I'd ever noticed.

A wealthy brat who would do whatever necessary to make sure her cushy life wasn't disrupted by those nasty realities of the world like work and bills.

Robert saw everyone as an employee, there for him to do his bidding. If you did as he wanted, you survived to see another day and another ugly demand. If you didn't, then you found out how quickly you became meaningless in his world.

And Serena was no different. He'd shown her the consequences of disobeying him two years ago, and now I had no doubt he'd show her them again if she didn't marry this Oliver guy.

As I thought about the possibility I'd lose her again, the sky grew dark as a storm rolled in. Caught a few hundred yards from the house, I realized too late I'd walked to the secret spot she and I met at. The first drops of rain began to fall, so I turned back and began to run, but it was a useless effort and by the time I reached the house, I was drenched.

I heard Robert screaming as soon as I opened the doors from the garden, so I immediately made my way to my rooms to change. Peeling off my wet clothes, I imagined Serena standing in front of him as he bellowed his orders at her, those brown eyes of hers pleading with him and getting nowhere.

He wasn't going to change his mind. To him, she was a tool to help him achieve a goal. Nothing else. Merely a means to an end.

She had no power, like the rest of us, and he relished showing her that as often as he could.

And just like the last time, he wanted to take her away from me again.

Dressed in dry clothes, I slowly walked toward the main house and hoped whatever had happened between them was over and she'd left because I couldn't bear to see that look in her eyes again. It wasn't just sadness. It was like she was begging someone, anyone for help. When she looked at me like that, I felt like a knife was being twisted into my chest.

I didn't get my wish, though. As I turned into the main hallway, I heard him bark, "You will do as I say, Serena, or I promise you you'll regret it."

His words made me stop dead, and I waited to hear her speak, but she said nothing and left his office in tears. I stood there watching her as she broke down and buried her face in her hands and wished I could take her away from this place at that moment.

Her shoulders shuddered as she sobbed quietly, not knowing I was there. I wanted to tell her to run away. That I'd distract him for the rest of the day and she could escape from this place. She had to have friends who could help her. Someone who wasn't under her father's control.

Lifting her head, she dried her eyes and saw me there. She opened her mouth but nothing came out. Finally, after a few moments, she said quietly, "I'm not going to let him do this to me. I'm not."

I checked to make sure Robert wasn't anywhere nearby and pulled her into the side hallway to the south wing. "We can go tonight and never look back. I just need an hour or so."

Choking back tears, she shook her head. "I can't.

You heard what he said about my mother last night. I can't be the reason she's hurt. I just can't."

Her mention of what happened the night before made me feel guilty for not standing up for her. "I'm sorry I didn't do anything last night. If I did, I was worried he'd figure out about us."

Fuck, that sounded lame.

Serena's expression hardened, and she looked away. "I don't expect anyone to fight my battles for me, Ryder. No one has ever done it before, so why would they start now?"

I winced at her thinly veiled reference to that night I stood by and watched without saying a single word as her father sent her away from the only home she'd ever known. She had every right to blame me. I blamed me.

Cupping her shoulders, I turned her to look at me. "He's going to make you marry that guy. Do you honestly think he'll do anything to your mother? Do you think he even knows where she is? Just leave with me like we planned. It can work."

Serena hung her head and slowly fell back against the wall. "I don't know what he'll do. I do think he knows where she is. I can't be why he does something to her, Ryder. I wouldn't be able to live with that. I'm just going to have to find another way to stop this wedding."

"If you'd just get away from him, he might find

something else to care about, Serena. While you were in Italy, he didn't bother you, did he?"

"It doesn't matter anymore. As long as there's the chance he could do something to my mother, I can't leave."

I let my hands fall away from her body and shrugged. "There has to be something we can do."

She forced a smile. "You're not my savior, Ryder. In many ways, you're just as trapped as I am, I'm guessing. If you weren't, you wouldn't still be here, would you?"

"I'm thinking the only person who would be is Janelle. She seems to be the only one who wants the life your father dictates for her."

"That's because she's just like him. She doesn't care about anyone else but herself, just like him."

Someone's footsteps on the marble floor of the entryway made me look around the corner and I saw Pike going to Robert's office. Knowing I had to get back, I said, "I love you, Serena. Come with me. We can do this. We'll go away and be happy, just like we wanted to."

I couldn't imagine any other way around doing what her father wanted, and my stomach tightened at the thought of her being forced to marry another man. She was mine, and I was hers. I couldn't let Robert take her away.

With a strength that seemed to come out of

nowhere, she straightened her shoulders and shook her head. "I love you, but I can't go with you anymore. At least not now. But I'm going to find a way out of this."

She smiled up at me and left as I headed back to Robert's office. I didn't know what she planned to do, but I didn't blame her for whatever she ended up deciding on. He'd backed her into a corner. Now when she came at him fighting, he had it coming.

But somehow I had to convince her to leave this place.

AFTER A FEW more hours at Robert's beck and call, I returned to my rooms with the singular goal of getting as fucked up as humanly possible. I didn't want to think about his world and all the ugliness that came with it. Being told to beat the hell out of some guy had never bothered me much, but watching what he was doing to Serena made my stomach turn with rage.

He acted like he got some perverted pleasure from making her miserable. I wasn't even sure he saw how desperate she'd become. I saw it, though. I'd seen the look of desperation before in fights. Desperate people did crazy things. They had no reason not to. They had nothing left to lose.

By the time I'd downed half a bottle of whisky, Serena was all I could think about. I'd been such a fucking coward when she needed me most. She practically begged me to save her with the look in her eyes as she stood in her father's office, and I did nothing.

I stood there watching her get tortured by her father and did my best company man act like a good employee should. Would it have changed anything for her if he saw I loved her? Probably not. Robert was hell bent on her marrying this fucking Oliver, but at least it would have shown her she wasn't alone.

That she had someone in her corner, and the man she loved would do anything for her.

Sitting there in the dark, I finished another glass and closed my eyes, praying to God I'd had enough so I could just pass out and forget. The problem was my mind wouldn't shut off. That look in her eyes— that same look I'd seen the night her father sent her away—was burned into my brain. I'd have given anything to stop remembering how hurt she looked as her father imposed his will on her, but it was no use.

If only I could have convinced her to leave with me we'd be far away by now and free.

From the couch, I looked out my window and saw the lights were off in Robert's office. Maybe if I tried once more to make her go, she'd finally see I was right. I pulled myself up and headed toward the garage to see if he had left for the night. If he had, now was our chance.

A quick look told me he'd taken the Mercedes, so I hurried up to her room. He'd be gone for at least an hour, assuming his latest girlfriend didn't give him a hard time about leaving, so the window was small but possible.

I knocked on Serena's door but got no answer. Looking left and right down the hallway to make sure I was alone, I tried the doorknob and found it unlocked, so I quietly went in, ready to take her away from this place forever.

But the room was empty. The lights were on and I saw her purse next to the bed, but she wasn't there.

Had she left without me? Had she found her mother somehow and gone to her?

I hoped more than anything she had found her. I knew how much losing her meant to Serena.

Taking a deep breath, I choked back my emotions at the thought of life without her again. As I turned to leave, I saw the light under the bathroom door on the far wall and something told me to look in there. Opening the door, I saw she hadn't left at all.

There, in the bathtub, she sat with her back to me but said nothing as I walked in. Quietly, I whispered, "Serena, he's gone. We can leave now and get away before he even realizes we've left."

She didn't answer, and then I saw the water had turned a strange color. In a split second, I knew what she'd done.

Rushing over to the bathtub, I saw the blood streaming from her wrist into the water, making it a horrifying pink color staining the white porcelain. Serena's eyes were closed and her head rested on the back of the tub. Her left arm lay in the water bleeding out, and I saw the razor blade still in her right hand.

Terrified I'd gotten there too late, I yanked the white bath towel off the rack nearby and raised her left arm. I wrapped the towel around her wrist and pressed hard in the hope that I could slow the blood flow.

My mind spun wildly as all I could think to do was save her. Dialing 911, I told a woman with a soft voice what had happened and the address before dropping my phone onto the floor. I lifted Serena out of the water and grabbed the other two towels hanging on the rack to cover her. I didn't want her lying there all exposed when the EMTs came.

Her eyes remained closed, but I held her to me and whispered, "Don't go. Don't do this. I need you to stay with me, Serena. I love you. Stay with me and I promise I won't let anything hurt you ever again. I'll take you away from this place and we'll find that little house and every night I'll watch you fall asleep with your head on my shoulder."

She lay motionless in my arms as the white towel around her wrist turned red, soaked with her blood. In the distance, I heard the whine of the ambulance siren and squeezed her to me, afraid if I let her go that she'd be lost forever.

"They're coming. I need you to hold on until they get here and fix you up." Pressing my lips to her forehead, I kissed her and whispered against her skin, "I'm sorry. I'm sorry I didn't say anything when he did that shit to you. I'm sorry, Serena. I made a mistake. Please don't die. I promise I'll protect you from now on. Just stay with me. Stay and I swear I'll find a way to get you away from here."

I heard a commotion downstairs and yelled out to them. "Up here in the second to last bedroom on the right. Hurry! She's bleeding!"

The next few minutes were a blur. Two men rushed in and took her from my arms, and I stumbled back in shock as they quickly took her away. I stood with my back pressed hard against the white tile wall staring at the bloody water and red trail of liquid that ran down the side of the tub and onto the white marble floor.

My mind raced, a jumbled mess of dread and fear and confusion. I couldn't move from that spot against that cool tile wall. I pushed my shoulders back against it even as my head hung. Looking down at my hands, I saw them covered in blood.

Her blood.

I'd seen dozens of people bleed. I'd made dozens of people bleed with my own hands pounding their flesh. Never had I felt as sickened as I did at that moment staring at my blood stained palms and fingers.

Pushing down the bile that inched up from my stomach, I suddenly realized I had to call Robert and then go to the hospital. I reached into my pants to get my phone and found it wasn't there. Had I left it back at my rooms?

No, I must have had it with me because I called 911. I had called, hadn't I? Or had someone else called the ambulance?

My eyes darted around the bathroom and I saw my phone lying on the floor near the bathtub. I bent down to pick it up and saw the razor blade she'd used on the side of the tub, the edge covered in Serena's blood.

I needed to get the hell out of there. Dialing Robert's number, I heard him answer and said, "Serena's at the hospital. She slit her wrist."

The words came out of my mouth without the slightest emotion. Flat and monotone, my voice didn't sound like it ever had. He asked something about how this could have happened, and I stared at the bloody water in the tub in shock that he'd even ask such a fucking question.

"Who found her?" he asked like it mattered.

"I did."

He said something else that got lost once the words entered my head, and I said, "I have to go."

BY THE TIME I reached the hospital, Robert had already arrived. His eyes flashed a wildness I'd never seen in them when he came toward me as I walked through the emergency room doors. If I didn't know better, I'd have said he looked scared.

"They think she's going to survive. From what they say, I have you to thank for that."

I didn't want thanks from him for saving his daughter after what he'd done to push her to attempt suicide. "Is she awake?"

He frowned and shook his head. "Not yet."

"Okay. I'm going to wait around for a while, if you don't mind."

He clapped me on the shoulder and nodded. "I owe you, Ryder. You saved my little girl. That's a debt I won't soon be forgetting."

A nurse announced that he could go in to see Serena and he hurried away with her as I stood stunned at how much he seemed to actually care that she'd hurt herself. He'd made living unbearable for her, and now he acted like seeing her hurt pained him.

I followed them to her hospital room and took my place outside, standing guard not for him but for her. As I looked through the narrow window in the door, I saw her lying there in that bed and wondered if he'd give up on making her marry that man now. Maybe he'd needed nearly losing her to see how wrong he was.

God, I hoped so.

Chapter Fifteen

Ryder

A FEW DAYS later, Robert called me into his office at nearly midnight. I found him sitting behind his desk wearing a deep frown. He told me earlier in the day that Serena's condition was improving, so I couldn't imagine why he looked so unhappy. Like with most tyrants, his moods ruled everything around him, and I braced myself for something terrible to come out of his mouth.

My stomach tense, I sat down in front of him and in my most casual voice asked, "What's up, boss?"

"Serena comes home tomorrow, and I want to make sure she's safe. I've had Josephine search her room top to bottom for anything she can use to hurt herself, but I don't think that will be enough."

His concern seemed genuine, so I asked, "Has she said anything about why she did it?"

I had to believe he knew why she'd tried to kill herself, but all he did was shake his head. "She hasn't said much of anything. The doctors say she's angry and depressed. They want me to put her in a mental hospital, but I told them that wasn't an option. So she'll be coming home tomorrow, but I'm going to need your help with this."

"My help?" I asked, unsure what I could do since he'd decided to ignore the obvious blame he had for what she'd done.

"Yes." Standing from his chair, he walked over to the bar and poured himself his usual bourbon drink. Offering me a glass, he said, "My father used to drink bourbon and branch when he had a lot on his mind. I guess I'm like him in that way. Want one?"

Robert had never mentioned anything about his father or any other family member other than Serena and Janelle. I had no idea what the hell branch was, but at that moment, I didn't care. All I wanted to know was what he intended me to do to keep Serena safe.

"No, thanks. Do you think maybe she should have a nurse or someone like that with her for a little while? She did try to…" I let my sentence trail off, unable to say the words.

He swallowed a gulp of his drink and seemed to consider my idea. Walking back to his chair, he sat down and frowned again. "No, that wouldn't do. It might make her look sickly. I can't have anyone thinking she's not okay. Only you and I know, other than the hospital personnel, and I want to keep it that way. No, we're going to keep the issue in house."

Without thinking, I asked, "Why?"

Robert took a sip of his drink and stared across the desk at me as I realized what I'd done. No one ever questioned him on anything. He was the boss and everyone else was an underling. To question him meant I didn't understand my position in his world.

I waited for the inevitable explosion of his temper, but instead he just sighed and took another drink of bourbon and branch. "Because there's not a man on this earth that's going to want to marry a woman with mental problems. Not if he has any sense in his head. Trust me. I know from experience."

She doesn't have mental problems. She wants to be happy and loved. That's not fucking mental.

The shock at hearing him refer to Serena's marriage must have shown on my face because there was no way I could hide it. He really had no fucking idea marrying her off to someone she didn't love was the very reason she'd tried to kill herself.

Oblivious to my surprise, he continued. "So I'm going to need you to watch over her. I know I can trust you. You've been with me long enough that you're almost like a son to me, so I need you to make sure she doesn't hurt herself again before the wedding."

Unable to do anything else, I let my curiosity control me and asked, "When is it?"

"The doctors say it will take a few weeks for her injury to heal, so I think a month will do. I'll just tell Oliver it needs to be rescheduled due to a business issue."

I sat there trying to imagine a worse monster in the world. His daughter had just tried to take her life and all he could think of was getting her married off to this guy no one had ever seen before a month ago.

"Why the hurry to get her married to him?" I asked, feeling like I had some leeway to talk now.

So matter of fact was his answer that he didn't even take a moment to consider the question. "He and his brother own Landon Auction House, and I want to get into that business. The pre-nup will give me that in."

So it was all business. Serena's happiness had played no part in his calculations. That worried father act I'd seen in the hospital that night wasn't because he feared for his daughter's life but because he didn't want his business deal to fall apart.

There was nothing more to say. Serena's injury, as he called it, was merely a setback to his plans. Since he wanted me to watch over her, I knew what I had to do.

I had to convince her to get the hell away from

that house and never look back.

✧   ✧   ✧

SERENA PASSED ME as I stood at the bottom of the staircase and said nothing as she began to walk up to her room. Except for the bandages on her wrist, she looked like she always had.

Gentle and sweet, like that girl who came to my room all those nights. Except now her face was expressionless, a void.

I followed her as she walked down the hallway to her bedroom, all the while wanting to ask how she was feeling and if she needed anything, and to tell her I loved her, but I didn't. Her silence felt like a barrier she put up between us. I didn't understand why, though.

At her bedroom door, she turned around to face me. The pain in her eyes stopped me dead, and then she spoke for the first time.

"My father says you're the one who found me, Ryder," she said flatly.

I smiled. "I'm just glad I got there in time."

She narrowed her eyes and stepped toward me. "I'm not. I found a way to escape and you took that away from me. I won't ever forgive you for that."

My breath caught in my throat at her words, and I stared down at her knowing she meant what she'd said. I didn't know what I'd expected, but knowing she didn't want to be saved made my chest hurt.

"I couldn't let you go like that. I love you," I said, not caring who might hear me.

"I hate you. I hate that you took that away from me. I hate that you're the one who gets to babysit me to make sure I don't try it again so I can be married off to some man I don't even know. Anything I ever felt for you is gone. I hate you, Ryder."

The last thing I saw before she slammed the door in my face was that familiar sad look of pain in her eyes that never failed to make my heart feel like it was being squeezed in a vice.

I stood staring at her bedroom door wondering what to do next. Robert had insisted that I had to stay in the room with her, but I didn't need to try the doorknob to know she'd locked me out. Knowing what he'd do if I disobeyed his direct order, I knocked and hoped to God she wouldn't look at me in that devastated way anymore.

She didn't answer, so I knocked again and quietly said, "Serena, please don't make this more difficult than it has to be."

Flinging the door open, she glared up at me. "For who? You? Why should I make this easy on you, Ryder? You make sure I lose the one chance to do the right thing, and you want me to make your job easier? Fuck you."

She began to slam the door in my face again, but

I caught it just in time and held it open enough that I could squeeze my face into the space between it and the doorjamb. "I don't have a lot of choices here, Serena. Your father wants me to make sure you're safe. So that's what I have to do."

That I said those things for the benefit of anyone in the house listening meant nothing as I saw her fight back tears. She slowly backed away from the door and sat down on the bed while I closed the door behind me. Never before had I seen anyone as defeated as she looked at that moment.

"So now I'm a prisoner?" she asked in a voice barely above a whisper. "And you're my jailer?"

"It's not like that," I answered weakly, knowing it was exactly as she'd put it.

And in a month's time, if I didn't get her away from here, she'd trade one jailer for another.

Serena closed her eyes and sighed, making her whole body fold until she sat hunched over. "Why would you, of all people, do this to me? I found a way out, and you took it from me. Why?"

I pressed my back against the door as the memory of her bleeding to death in that bathtub rushed over me. "I couldn't let you die. I couldn't. I love you, Serena."

Looking over at me, she began to cry. "I did this because I love you. I couldn't bear marrying another man, but I couldn't leave knowing he'd hurt my mother. So now you've consigned me to a life no one would want."

If I wanted to convince her to leave this place, now was the moment. I walked over to the side of the bed and crouched down in front of her, taking her hands in mine. She didn't pull away or even move when I touched her, but she avoided my gaze and turned her head as her tears began to stream down her cheeks.

"Serena, leave this house. Do it tonight. Come with me and we'll never look back. It's the only way."

Shaking her head, she wiped her tear-stained cheeks. "I can't. He'll hurt my mother, and I can't live with knowing that."

"You were willing to kill yourself to get away. Why is this any different? Either way, I have a feeling your father was going to hurt her. He's a monster. That's what they do."

"Because I wouldn't know about it if I was dead."

As crazy as that sounded, I understood what she meant. "Are you going to try again?"

I held my breath as I waited for her to answer, not sure what I'd do if she said yes. I knew I should be saying I'd get her help, that she needed to talk to someone who could show her suicide wasn't the answer, but Robert would never let a doctor see her.

She pressed her lips together and winced in pain before she answered, "No. I knew I only had one chance to get it right, and that's gone now."

It was the saddest promise to live anyone had ever spoken.

Standing, I moved to leave, but Serena stopped me by grabbing my hand. "Please don't go. Sit with me like we used to when you were staying in the spare bedroom downstairs."

I knew when Robert ordered me to guard her that me staying with her hadn't been what he meant. He wanted me to be that jailer, someone to watch over Serena to make sure she didn't do anything to endanger his well-laid business plans.

But as I looked at her sitting on the edge of her bed so lost, like some broken bird whose wings had been clipped, I didn't care what he thought. If she couldn't see a doctor, then all she had was me.

I sat down next to her, the two of us still holding hands, and she leaned over and put her head on my shoulder. "I'm sorry, Ryder."

"You can't marry him, Serena. You can't."

She hugged me tightly and sighed. "I didn't know what else to do. At least if I was gone, you'd be free. You wouldn't have to stay here anymore."

Leaning back, I pushed her away and shook my head. "How could you think I'd ever be free? I was the one who found you. I held you in my arms as the blood ran out of your body and you nearly died. How could you think I'd ever be free after that?"

Her expression contorted like my question hurt her. As tears welled in her eyes, she stood from the bed and walked toward the bathroom. "I didn't know that would happen. All I knew—"

I cut her off and followed her. Pointing at the tub, I said, "Do you have any idea what it's like to find the one person in the world you love nearly dead in a pool of her own blood?"

Pulling her into the bathroom, I pushed her in front of me and forced her to stand where I had that night. "Right there," I said as I pointed at the edge of the tub. "That's where the razor blade was when the EMTs left with you and I was left standing here covered in your blood. Free? I'm never going to be free of that ever, Serena."

She shook her head and ran out into the bedroom. Once again, I followed her, unable to stop my emotions now.

With her back to me, she whispered, "I didn't see any other way. You have to believe that."

Even from the across the room, I felt her sadness. It mixed with mine, twisting my gut into knots. "I have to believe you didn't see another way other than killing yourself? Well, I don't believe that. What would make you think that was the answer?"

She spun around and shook her head. "I can't tell you how many times I've thought about killing myself. Then you came into my life, and I didn't want to die anymore. Even in Italy those first few nights when all I could think of was just doing it, I didn't because I believed I'd see you again and we'd have a chance to be happy together."

Slowly, I walked over to her. Cradling her face, I looked down into her sad eyes and asked, "Then why would you do it now when you know how much I love you, Serena? How could you think I'd be able to go on after you killed yourself?"

As tears streamed down over her cheeks, she said, "I couldn't think of anything but him hurting my mother if I didn't marry Oliver and how much it will hurt you if I do. No matter what I did, I couldn't think of a way out other than taking me out of the picture."

I pulled her to me and held her close as she sobbed against my chest. "You leaving this world is never the answer. We'll figure this out. I swear, Serena."

"Promise me something?"

"Anything," I said as I looked down into her watery dark eyes.

"If we don't figure out a way, promise me you won't hate me for what I'll have to do."

Tilting her head back, I kissed her as tears began to roll down her cheeks again. "I can't hate the one person who makes me happy in this world."

I took her hand and led her to the bed, and like

we had all those nights in that spare bedroom downstairs, she fell asleep with her head on my shoulder as I watched over her. Every ounce of my being screamed for me to take her away from that place, but I knew she'd never be able to live with herself if Robert followed through on his threats about her mother.

She had no choice.

Neither one of us did.

Chapter Sixteen

Serena

E VERY DAY RYDER stayed with me became more
bittersweet than the last because I knew one day
soon he wouldn't be able to come to my room
anymore and I'd be given to Oliver like some kind of
prized pig from my father. No matter how hard I
tried to forget these realities, each night as I fell
asleep I silently crossed off another day of freedom.

That being watched by someone twenty-four-
seven had become some sick sort of freedom didn't
escape me. I knew how twisted my life was. It didn't
matter. For the rest of it, I'd be just as watched. Just
not by someone I actually cared about.

I knew so little about my future husband that I
might have been wrong to indict him like that.
Maybe I would care in the least about him someday.
Right now, he was practically a stranger to me.
Someone chosen by my father for his strategic worth
to his business interests and nothing more. If I liked
him or loathed him was of no concern to anyone.

Well, almost anyone. Although we never spoke

about my impending marriage, I knew Ryder cared. He just never said anything about it after that first night, like if he didn't speak the words everything we'd planned could still happen.

But we knew the truth. All the plans we'd made just went away.

My father visited me once each day like some long lost relative checking to make sure I was still among the living. His wide smile he flashed every time he walked into my room appeared forced, but I couldn't imagine who he was pretending for. He didn't care about my feelings on anything, and Ryder was simply one of his employees.

Neither of our opinions mattered, so why take the time to feign concern?

And so it went every day for weeks as I pretended not to hate being trapped like some breakable creature who needed to be watched every moment and Ryder and I pretended that what would happen at the end of this wouldn't break both our hearts.

Maybe hate was a strong word. I truly hated my father for what he was doing to me. There was no denying that. Sometimes I silently prayed for him to disappear so I'd be set free. I didn't care if he just vanished into thin air or went away by other more violent means.

I just wanted him gone so I wouldn't be a pawn

anymore.

But I didn't hate every second of my time my father referred to as my recuperation period. When he wasn't terrifying me with that horrible fake smile and forced sympathy I knew he didn't feel and when my sister wasn't dropping in unannounced to pretend to play nursemaid, it was just Ryder and me and I could pretend we'd escaped and found that life together, just the two of us.

By the third week, we'd settled into a daily routine. I'd wake up around eight to find him sitting next to me in bed wide awake and wonder when he actually slept. He'd smile down at me and my day would start. Then I'd shower and get ready as he waited for me. After that, we'd have breakfast in the kitchen or out on the patio and talk about things occurring in the world, as if everything we were doing was normal. Then I'd swim while he watched me, likely to make sure I didn't drown myself, and lay out in the sun until lunch.

My life had become something similar to a Hollywood starlet's, except I never got to go to great parties or meet anyone.

After lunch, we'd go for a walk around the estate like every fine lady in historical movies always did for some reason. All the while, we'd make small talk about topics neither one of us truly cared about and avoided discussing the important event that day by day was inching closer.

Somehow we'd become near perfect strangers to one another. I didn't know if it was my suicide attempt or my father's forcing Ryder to watch me and knowing he was always watching us, but it felt like all the passion we'd shared simply evaporated, leaving the two of us like guests in one another's life.

Each night, we ate dinner in the dining room where a place was always set for my father but he never showed up. Then we'd go up to my room and lay on the bed to watch movies like normal people who liked to spend time together did.

Except we weren't normal in any way. He was my jailer and I was his prisoner, and no matter how much I pretended like this wasn't true, that's what we'd become. We'd loved one another completely, and then we became this. Even worse, the two of us were nothing more than mere pieces my father moved around the board like he did in his favorite game.

Pawns. Expendable for any gain at any time.

I settled in, stretching my legs out in front of me as the movie began, while Ryder kicked off his shoes and stretched his even longer legs down the bed. All day I'd had the sense something had happened with him. He sounded different as we talked on our walk that afternoon. I couldn't place exactly how he seemed different, but I knew.

"Have you ever seen this movie?" I asked as The Sting began. I'd watched it dozens of times growing up because it was one of my father's favorites. Personally, I didn't see the appeal, but maybe having it force fed to you lessened its enjoyment.

Ryder looked at me and shook his head. "Nope. I don't think so. We didn't watch a lot of old movies in my house growing up."

"Lucky you."

"It isn't good?" he asked with a curious look on his face.

Shrugging, I said, "I'm told it's a classic. A lot of people think it's a four-star film. I've seen it so many times that even if it is I don't like it."

"We don't have to watch it then. I'm sure we can find something else," he offered as he reached over me to grab the remote control.

I didn't want to watch anything. What I wanted was Ryder to tell me why he was acting differently tonight.

He flipped through the channels, stopping at each one to ask me if I wanted to watch that movie or show. All I did every time was shrug and wait for him to stop so I could ask what was going on.

Finally, he returned to The Sting and tossed the remote on the bed next to him. "I guess we're going with the four-star movie then."

A strangeness settled in between us from my

unwillingness to give him any help choosing what we'd watch and his indifference. After waiting for a few minutes, I couldn't stand not knowing and turned to face him.

"I know something's happened. Is it something I should know about?"

His expression seemed frozen in place as he stared at me for a long moment. Searching his eyes, I didn't find the answer I wanted in them. They seemed as still as his face.

He finally said in a low voice, "Your father gave me a raise and a bonus today for what I've been doing with you. Seems I'm his new favorite."

Once the words had left his mouth, I finally saw emotion fill his eyes. Not happiness or pride but pain.

"That sounds like something you'd like. Why do you look like he threatened to kill you?"

"No reason."

He winced and then turned to watch the movie, but I wanted to know why he was unhappy. Sitting up, I crossed my legs under me and poked his arm.

"That's not an answer. Why are you so miserable about being paid more and getting a bonus?"

This time he didn't look at me to answer. "It's nothing, Serena. Drop it."

But I couldn't drop it. Something else had happened that he wasn't telling me about. Nudging his arm again, I said, "It's not nothing. I want to know what's going on. Wasn't it enough? Were you hoping for more from this?"

He refused to look at me no matter how many times I pushed on his arm, so I got up off the bed and stood in front of him, blocking the TV. "Why won't you talk to me about this? I know this is your job, but I thought we…"

I couldn't bring myself to talk about how much we loved each other before all this happened and all the plans we'd had, so I said, "You sit in here with me every night until I fall asleep and you can't tell me what's wrong?"

I wasn't sure what part of what I'd said upset him, but his expression contorted into one of disgust and he stood up from the bed. "My job, Serena? When you bumped your wrist against the side of the pool as you were getting out the other day, I was the one who hurried over to make sure you were okay while you sat on the concrete crying."

As he spoke, his voice grew louder and louder until he was practically screaming at me. "When you're going stir crazy because your father won't let you away from this fucking house, I'm the one who sits here and listens to you complain about it, never saying a word about how being the one who has to force you to stay here feels. I've spent every day and night with you for the past three weeks because you chose to try to kill yourself instead of running away with me. This isn't just a job, Serena. Don't ever believe it's just a job. It's never been just a job."

"Then what is it, Ryder? What is this you do with me day in and day out that my father is so handsomely rewarding you for?"

He took a step toward me and then another until I had to tilt my head to look up into his eyes. Rage radiated off him in waves, and for the first time, I worried I'd pushed him too far.

"It's fucking torture, Serena. Do you think I want to keep you locked up here knowing how much you resent me for saving your life? And at the end of this all, I get to watch you marry some other guy. I love you so much it fucking hurts, and you're going to marry someone else. If you think you're the only prisoner here, you're wrong. The only difference is that instead of getting married I get more money from our tormentor. And as for being handsomely rewarded, he could give me millions of dollars and it wouldn't take away the misery every day brings with it having to do this to you."

When he finished, he stared down at me with such pain in his eyes that I had to look away. I'd never considered how doing this to me made him feel. All this time I'd been consumed with my own misery that I hadn't thought of his.

"You can't forgive me for what I did?" I asked,

suspecting I knew the answer already.

"For choosing to check out on everything we were and leave me without even saying goodbye?"

I turned to see him glaring at me. "You don't understand. You can't. As soon as he said he'd hurt my mother, I knew I couldn't leave. But I couldn't bear the idea of marrying another man. I knew what I had to do."

With a sharpness I'd never heard from him, he said, "Kill yourself and leave me behind still in love with you."

His anger hurt, and I looked away so I wouldn't have to see what I'd done to him. "Do you honestly believe I wanted to do that? If only he didn't bring up my mother, I would have left that night with you and gone anywhere."

"You can't even face me when you say that."

As tears filled my eyes, I turned to look at him, not caring that I couldn't hold back my emotions anymore. "I love you, Ryder, but I couldn't live with myself if my father hurt her because of me. I sat right here in this room and tried to convince myself that I could run away with you. You have no idea how much I wanted to, but the thought of him hurting her tore me up inside. What choice did I have then? I didn't want to marry another man. So I decided to do it."

"And leave me alone to live on without you," he

said sadly.

I touched his hand and a rush of memories washed over me. This was Ryder, the man I loved, and I'd hurt him.

"You have to forgive me."

He sighed as he sat down on the edge of the bed. "Like I have a choice, Serena."

Kneeling before him, I took his hands in mine. "You would have gone on and found happiness. Like when I went to Italy, you would have found someone to keep you company."

Ryder shook his head. "Don't. Don't act like this wouldn't have affected me. Don't act like you understand how I feel."

"Do you think I like saying these things? I can't even think about you with someone else without feeling sick. I just didn't have a choice."

"Yes, you did. You just made the wrong one," he said before pulling his hands away.

Hurt by his condemnation of me, I stood up and walked around the bed. "I hear your phone vibrate all the time, Ryder. Something tells me you wouldn't be alone for long if I was gone. Your little Kitty would step in and fill my place like she did last time."

Ryder leveled his stare on me and shook his head. "Don't say another word, Serena. You don't know what you're talking about."

Something snapped inside me, so I rushed over

to where his coat lay on the chair and pulled his phone out. Holding it up in front of me, I swiped the screen and turned it around for him to see.

"What am I going to find if I check your calls and texts, Ryder? You sit here trying to make me the bad guy, but Kitty's just waiting for you to finally say the word. Have you spoken to her? Do you text her back when she sends you a message? What do they say? What do they say, Ryder?"

He jumped up from the bed and lunged at me to wrestle the phone from my hold, but I wouldn't let go. I held on to that phone and screamed, "Why won't you show me? What do they say? Oh Ryder, remember your pretty Kitty so patiently waiting for you. I'm not a problem at all. Not like that Serena. I won't be a hassle or force you to make hard choices. I won't try to kill myself."

Ryder stepped back with a look of horror on his face. "Give me the phone, Serena."

I considered looking at his messages and call logs, but I couldn't bring myself to and have to face the truth that he had spoken to her recently. Tossing the phone on the bed, I walked around to my side and slid under the covers, wishing I hadn't said any of those horrible things to him.

The bed moved when he finally sat down again, but I lay frozen in place lost in my sadness at what I'd done. I waited for him to turn the movie on again, but I heard nothing. After all those weeks together but never feeling him close to me, I yearned for his touch again but couldn't bring myself to turn around to face him.

Not after what I'd just done.

After a few minutes of waiting, I accepted that I'd finally pushed him too far and closed my eyes. As I slowly began to drift off to sleep hating every word I'd said to him, Ryder wrapped his arms around me and pulled me close, enveloping me in his hold.

"I love you, Serena. I don't know how to fix this, and every night as I watch you sleep, I think about the plans we had to leave here and be happy together. Doing this is killing me."

Tears rolled down my face at the sound of those words coming out of his mouth after all I'd done. I wanted so much to go away with him like he wanted, and it broke my heart that I couldn't and would be forced to marry someone else because of it.

"I wish there was something we could do," I said quietly, knowing there wasn't.

He softly kissed my cheek and whispered, "There's nothing we can do. He's got us both right where he wants us."

I brought his hand to my lips and kissed it. "I love you. No matter what happens, no matter what I do, I love you, Ryder."

Not that it mattered. Nothing mattered in this

world he and I were trapped in.

✧ ✧ ✧

JANELLE TWIRLED AROUND my bedroom in her lilac colored matron of honor dress with a smile that looked like she was the one getting married. My only bridesmaid because my father wouldn't let me ask anyone else, she relished the idea of a fancy party where she could get dressed up and be on show.

"How do I look, Serena?" she asked as I walked out of the bathroom from putting on my makeup.

"Like the star of the show. Bridesmaids aren't supposed to upstage the bride, but I think you're going to in that dress. What made you decide on a strapless dress?"

I knew the answer to that question, even if I hadn't had any part in the choice of her gown for my wedding. Janelle liked to show off her good parts, and her shoulders were two of those.

"It's fall, but it had to be strapless. Plus, it matches your dress beautifully," she answered as she walked over to the full length mirror to take another look at herself.

My dress was a white satin strapless dress that I had to admit I liked. It hugged all the right spots on me and made me feel beautiful. Too bad I was wearing it to marry the wrong man.

I looked down my arms to where the scar from

my suicide attempt sat on the inside of my wrist. Wincing, I ran my fingertip over the red mark. "Janelle, can you hand me that bracelet in the box on the bed?"

She tore herself away from her reflection and opened the box. Holding the bracelet up to examine it, she asked, "Is this what Daddy gave you for your wedding present?"

I nodded as she ooohed and ahhhed over the diamond and pearl bracelet just thick enough to conceal the scar on my wrist. "Yes. He brought it up this morning. It's very nice."

Janelle twisted her face into an expression of disgust at how underwhelmed I sounded. Studying it, she sighed. "It's more than nice, Serena. It's stunning. There must be over two carats of diamonds in this."

"I guess. I like the pearls too, though."

Handing it to me, she rolled her eyes at my mention of liking the pearls. I liked them because they didn't hurt when they rubbed against my still tender skin where the razor blade had sliced into me. I didn't bother telling Janelle that, though. We'd never once talked about my suicide attempt, and something told me in her festive mood she wouldn't be much of a shoulder to cry on anyway.

To my sister, the idea of killing herself instead of marrying a wealthy man was such a foreign thought that she couldn't even imagine entertaining it.

"Well, it's almost time. Do you need me to help you get your dress on? I'm happy to help."

I shook my head and pressed a smile onto my face. "No, that's okay. I'm fine with zipping it up in the back, and other than that, I just have to put my shoes on."

It all sounded so perfectly normal, like how two sisters would talk to one another on one of their wedding days. That it was anything but normal escaped my sister, though. My marriage was as much a business transaction as hers was, but since she and Charles seemed to have found some kind of happiness in the months they've been together, I guessed she thought the same would happen for me and Oliver eventually.

But I wasn't my sister. I had a man I loved already.

Lifting my chin with her index finger, she smiled at me. "You look so beautiful, Serena. That Oliver is a very lucky man. Daddy better not let him forget it."

I didn't know what to say to her when she said things like that. Our father didn't give a damn about how Oliver felt about me or vice versa. All he cared about was getting into my soon-to-be husband's business. Nothing more.

Forcing an even bigger smile, I kissed her on the cheek. "You better go. The ceremony is going to start in a few minutes, so my matron of honor needs to be at the altar ready to go."

She bubbled with excitement at that thought. "This is so great! I'm so happy for you. Okay, I'm going to go. See you in a few!"

With a turn, she spun around and headed toward the door. Ryder came in as she left since he had to watch me whenever someone else wasn't around, even on this day. It wouldn't do to get so close to the finish line and have the prize horse come up lame, now would it?

We hadn't spoken more than few vague words since that night I said those terrible things, and now as he closed the door behind him, he didn't even look at me. Sitting down in the chair he spent hour upon hour in, he simply looked down at his black dress shoes and then brushed off a piece of lint from his black suit coat.

I retreated to the bathroom to put on my dress and finish getting ready for the ceremony that was set to begin in only a few minutes. As I did, I looked over at the window that faced out toward a side of the house away from the ceremony and reception area.

No, it was too high. Even if I made it out onto the ledge, I'd never make it down to the ground.

Pushing the last thought of freedom out of my mind, I returned to my room to find Ryder standing just outside the door with a strange look on his face. Without looking at me, he tilted his head and stared past me into the bathroom.

"I was beginning to think I'd have to come in to get you. That seemed to take a long time."

Since there was no reason not to be truthful, I said as I pushed past him, "I was considering trying to escape out the window, but it's too high. You should be thankful. Imagine the hell you'd catch if you let me get away today."

Ryder said nothing, and when I turned around to look at what effect my words had on him, I saw him standing with his arms behind his back and his eyes lowered and firmly set on the floor.

I didn't know how he did it. If someone said those things to me, I'd snap back. I knew I had it coming, but he never said a word in response after that night.

I opened the bedroom door and looked out into the hall. "Time to go, Ryder. Your job is almost done."

Something in me wanted to see a look of pain come over his face or even the tiniest frown turn down the corners of that mouth that made me so happy. He gave me nothing in response to my taunts, though.

Maybe that's what I deserved.

He closed the door behind us and touched my

arm to escort me downstairs. For at least a few moments, I could enjoy being next to him again.

At the top of the stairs, he stopped me and said in a voice full of anguish, "You don't have to do this, Serena. You don't have to marry a man you don't love."

The idea was utterly laughable. Of course I had to. He knew that as well as I did. I couldn't imagine why he'd say something so ridiculous and felt a smile form on my lips, even though inside all I wanted to do was cry.

"You know that's not true. I have to marry Oliver because as long as I'm alive, I don't have a choice. Now unless you have a secret plan to throw me down these stairs and end it all for me…"

I didn't finish my sentence because the agony written all over his face made the words catch in my throat. For the past two days, he'd hardly looked at me, and now those green eyes looked like they were barely holding back tears.

"If you think I'm going to say I'm sorry for saving your life, I'm not. You can hate me all you want, but I wasn't going to let you bleed to death in that bathtub, Serena. I couldn't. And no matter what you say to me, none of it is going to change that I love you."

As I stood there watching the pain and sadness wash over him, I knew he had saved me because he cared. After all we'd endured, he still loved me.

"I don't want an apology, Ryder. What's done is done, and now I have to deal with the consequences."

"I would have made you happy, Serena."

Tears filled my eyes as the dream I'd still held out hope for slowly faded away. "I know."

In the distance, I heard the notes of the wedding march begin outside in the garden. As he continued to look at me like he had more to say, I forced a smile and said what I knew would stop him from speaking.

"This has always been my fate, Ryder. I let myself think it wouldn't be because of you, but that was just a dream."

He gave me that frown I'd wished for and nodded but said nothing more. What else was there to say? In a few minutes, he'd watch me marry Oliver Landon and try to convince himself that my being married to a man I didn't love was better than my being dead.

And I'd try to do the same for the rest of my life.

Chapter Seventeen

Ryder

As THE NOISE of guests celebrating began to die down outside, I sat in my apartment with a bottle of whisky and tried to push the memory of watching Serena marrying another man out of my mind. Every moment of the past week had been torture. Knowing this day would eventually come hadn't stopped me from hoping it wouldn't.

All I wanted to do was protect her, and every single time I'd failed. I'd failed that night when her father found us together and packed her off to Italy. I'd failed when he announced she'd have to marry some guy she never met just to help his business. I'd failed to see how desperate she was and barely saved her life.

And I'd failed to convince her to leave this fucking house.

Robert had happily announced that she and Oliver would live on the estate in their own townhouse he'd had made from a few of the apartments his guards lived in. I'd been spared having to share my rooms with anyone, but the rest of the staff had been doubled up to make sure Serena stayed close and under her father's watchful eye.

I didn't know if he thought she'd try to kill herself again or wanted them to stay for another reason. All I knew was her remaining here felt like the world's worst double-edged sword. If she wasn't nearby, then I wouldn't have to witness the misery of every day the woman I loved with another man she barely knew and didn't love, but to not see her ever again hurt worse than any beating I'd ever taken in a fight.

Tilting the bottle toward my mouth, I took a mouthful of whisky and let it slide down my throat as I closed my eyes and struggled to push the sight of Oliver sliding that ring onto her finger before the priest pronounced them husband and wife. I'd watched from Robert's side with my heart in my throat the entire time, silently praying something would happen to stop the wedding.

But nothing did, and when Serena turned to look at her father as if to show she'd done what he commanded, she looked at me right after with that same awful pained look I'd seen that first night I came here to this place.

It never failed to make my chest ache.

Fuck. Sometimes I wished he'd never brought me here. I could handle the dirty work he made me do. Beating the hell out of people left me cold. I didn't know them, and they didn't know me. I was just the long arm of Robert Erickson's power. Even the people I roughed up knew that.

Serena was different, though. Having to basically keep her imprisoned in the place she called home to satisfy her father's need to have her stay in one piece to marry Landon tore me apart. Unlike the men I hit with my fists, she was someone I knew. Someone I loved.

Someone I never wanted to hurt.

That's exactly what I'd done, though. I'd saved her life only to be forced to make her pay every day since.

Turning the light off on the table beside me, I sat in the darkness wishing it would swallow me up. Only once before in my life had I wished to disappear. Not kill myself or cease to exist but disappear and be somewhere else when the light returned.

My parents had died and my uncle had already begun to fight me to help pay his bills. Fifteen year old boys cost a lot, he said. They had to be fed, clothed, and housed, and none of that came cheap. So instead of sending me out to the mall to get a job selling clothes to teenage girls or hardware to do-it-yourselfers, he put me into fights. And every night after I'd taken the beatings I had to in order to win,

I'd lay in bed in the darkness of my tiny room wishing to disappear.

And every morning, I'd be right there in that bed and in the light of day I'd see the bruises I'd earned the night before when I paid my way.

Now I had bigger rooms and a supposedly better life, but still I wished into the darkness to disappear.

A knock at my door stirred me from my misery, and even though I didn't want to see anyone at that moment, I knew the hell that I'd catch if it was Robert standing on the other side of that door with some job he needed done. Taking another swig of whisky, I headed toward the door still with the bottle in my hand.

Opening it, I saw not Robert but Serena standing there staring back at me. Wearing just a white dress and thin white sweater, she was barefoot, like usual.

"Can I come in?" she asked in a tiny voice that matched the sad look she wore.

I didn't know what to say. I had no idea what she was doing at my door just hours after marrying another man, but I couldn't turn her away, so I stepped back and let her in.

As I closed the door and fumbled to find the light switch on the wall, I heard her say, "I wanted to say I'm sorry for how I've been since that night last week."

Taking another drink, I let her words sink in as

the alcohol headed down toward my stomach. Had something happened with her husband or Robert and one of them had made her come here to apologize to me?

Before I could say anything, she continued. "I've never thanked you for saving my life, Ryder. I've been awful to the one person who deserved my gratitude, and I'm sorry."

I sat back down in the chair and looked up at her, unsure what answer she wanted. My emotions were a fucking mess inside me, so even if I knew what to say it would probably come out all wrong. So I said nothing like I had for days around her.

"It's not so bad, you know? I get to stay in my home and Oliver's not a horrible person, from what I can tell. So it's okay."

"Do you want to sit down?" I asked, really wanting to know why she was there on her wedding night.

She nodded and sat down on the couch next to where I sat. "Can I have a drink?"

I handed her the bottle and watched as she took a mouthful. I'd never seen her drink whisky before and knew even that little amount would likely send her for a loop.

"Be careful with that stuff. If you aren't used to it, it'll fuck you up and tonight's not the night you want that to happen," I said in as casual a voice I could find.

She took a second but smaller swig of whisky and handed me the bottle again. "I've had a drink before."

In just a few seconds, our conversation had wound down to practically nothing, so I asked the question I wanted answered. "Why are you here, Serena? It's your wedding night. Shouldn't you be with your husband?"

Instead of answering me, she stood up and began walking toward the door. Before she reached it, she stopped and slowly turned around, like she wanted to say something, but she just slipped her sweater off her shoulders and hung her head.

"It's my wedding night and the only person I want to be with is you."

"What about your husband?"

"My husband prefers to spend time with his brother at his house instead of being with me."

My chest hurt seeing her like that. First she got forced into marrying someone she doesn't love, and then she got to see that he never cared for her either.

All at once, I hated her fucking husband and thanked God he hadn't touched her. I hadn't let myself go to that place all night, but now that I knew she hadn't been with him, all I felt was relief.

Then I realized the dress she wore wasn't a dress but a nightgown. Unable to stop myself, I asked,

"Did you wear that for him?"

She shook her head. "I didn't know what I was going to do if he wanted to sleep with me. I couldn't, though. I couldn't, Ryder."

I watched as she walked over and stood in front of me before saying in that same tiny voice she'd used to ask if she could come in, "Will you make love to me?"

A few moments ticked by as I thought about how much I'd wanted to touch her for weeks, and then I saw her shake her head.

"Even the person who saved my life doesn't want me. You can't forgive me."

She turned to run away, but I caught her by the hand and held her there. I wasn't the man she deserved, not at that moment or any other time, but I was the man who loved her.

"Let me go. I don't want to hear you tell me things will be okay because they won't. It's just like I thought it would be. I've been traded like a car or some other inanimate object from my father to my husband. It won't be okay. And now you don't want me either. I know that now."

I couldn't stand to hear her say that, so I stood and kissed her like I'd wanted to every day since that night she and I were together in the garden. Desperate for the closeness she offered, I relished the feel of her lips against mine. Soft and eager, her kiss soothed my heart.

As I let myself get lost in her, she pulled away, tearing me out of the moment. I looked down into her eyes and saw she wasn't sure.

"Do you forgive me? I need to know, Ryder."

I nodded my head, knowing only one thing for certain. Nothing she could do would make me stop loving her.

"I'm so sorry," she asked softly.

"I know. None of that matters now. Not that you're married to another man. Not that you tried to kill yourself. All that matters is I love you and you love me."

She took my hands in hers and gently squeezed them. "Whatever happens, you won't suffer because of me. I promise that. Never again."

The touch of her hands on my skin sent ripples of need rolling over my body. I'd waited for what felt like forever to have her next to me like this again.

Pulling her to me, I said in her ear, "I've suffered every night I couldn't touch you, Serena. More suffering couldn't be any worse than what I've already endured."

I kissed her once more, harder this time, and slid that silky white nightgown off her shoulders. It fell to the floor around her feet, leaving her naked for me. Slowly, I let my hands explore her supple body, tenderly running them down her back to cup her ass.

Her fingers quickly unbuttoned my shirt, and she slipped her hands beneath it to touch my chest as she intensified her kiss. Teasing me, she flicked her tongue along the inside of my mouth, and I felt my cock harden.

Backing away for just a moment, I undid my belt and unzipped my pants as she looked up at me wide-eyed. I cupped my hand against the back of her head and pulled her against me, kissing her long and deep.

She felt so incredible next to me, her soft skin touching mine as she trailed her hands across my stomach and down to my hips. My cock ached I wanted her so bad, and when she slid her hand under my boxer briefs to palm it, I groaned into her mouth it felt so good.

"I've needed this, Serena. Needed you. Dreamed about the way you'd feel against me as I fucked you again slow and easy," I whispered against her lips.

As she pushed my shirt off my back, she looked up at me with worry in her eyes. "Even when I was being so horrible to you?"

I cradled her face in my hands and stared down at her. "Always."

"I'm so sorry, Ryder. I didn't mean to be—"

Cutting off her sentence with another kiss, I stopped her from explaining herself because she didn't have to for me. I knew what she was, who she was, and I loved her completely. It wouldn't matter if she spent the rest of her life telling me she hated me. I knew better now.

I led her to the couch and stepped out of my pants before sitting down. The thin piece of cotton was all that separated my cock from her, and I quickly slid out of my boxers before pulling her down onto my lap.

She kissed me and whispered, "Promise me you'll always love me?"

Lifting my hips, I gripped her waist as I slid my cock through her wet pussy. "Always."

Serena pressed her forehead to mine as I slowly pushed her down onto my cock. "I don't want you to get hurt by my father."

The feel of her snug cunt around me made me brave. Or stupid. I wasn't sure which. "I don't care what he does to me if he finds out. Now no more talk about him or anyone else. I want to watch you ride my cock while I fuck you."

Tugging her head back, I kissed her neck like the mere taste of her was all I ever needed in life as she rolled her hips and took every inch of me inside her. Fuck, she felt perfect on my cock. If I died at that very moment, I'd leave this earth a happy and content man.

Tentative and sweet, she responded to me just as she always had. Her movements were slow at first, but gradually she let herself go until she rode me with abandon, her hips bucking wildly as she groaned in the sweetest voice in my ear, "God, you feel so good inside me. Don't stop. Please."

I stuffed my hand into her hair and tugged harder this time to see her wince as her expression showed the sweet mixture of pain and desire. "I won't stop until you come and your legs are so weak you can't stand. Until then, I'm going to fuck you and love every second I get to be inside you."

As much as I wanted to draw out our time together, it was no use. Neither of us could hold back, and when the first sign of her release squeezed my cock, I was lost. Taking every inch of me in, she ground her pussy against me as wave after wave of pleasure raced through her. I thrust as deeply as I could get and let myself come, flooding her cunt with everything I had inside me.

All the need and longing filled her as it had me for so long until there was nothing left between us but the purest satisfaction I'd ever felt with a woman. Serena had given all of herself to me, and I'd given her all of me in return.

Whatever happened, nothing could change that.

Chapter Eighteen

Serena

AFTER MAKING ME come once more on the couch, Ryder carried me to the bedroom and we made love there until there was nothing left of me to give him. He eased out of me and I lay down next to him, exhausted and content. Wrapping his arm around me, he pulled me to him and I laid my head over his heart to hear its strong beat.

Tired but unable to sleep, I ran my fingertips over his skin and felt scars. I'd never noticed them before. How he'd gotten them I had no idea, but I imagined his muscular body taking painful blows to get injuries that would have left scars like the ones that I felt.

Curious, I asked, "What happened to you to get all these?"

He touched a large scar on his right side over his ribs and groaned. "Fighting."

"Who were you fighting?" I asked, wondering what kind of fight would leave such a mark.

"Serena, I was a fighter."

I looked up at him confused. What did that mean? "What kind of fighter? Like a boxer?"

He shook his head. "No. Underground fighting. Street fighting with no gloves and no rules."

Touching a scar near his shoulder, I gently ran my finger along the length of it and imagined what could have injured him like that. "I don't understand. Why would you do that?"

"I didn't have a choice at first. When I was fifteen, my uncle made me fight to pay my way, and then when I got to be eighteen, it was the only way I knew to make money."

"That's terrible. You were only a child. Did you stop because you got hurt?"

He opened his mouth to speak but said hesitated. Finally, he said, "I stopped because your father had me beaten intentionally right after you left."

I sat up, trying to understand what he meant. "Is that why you were in the hospital for weeks right after I went to Italy? My father had someone beat you up?"

Narrowing his eyes, he shook his head. "Your father found me fighting. He bought me, basically, and brought me here that first night. I continued to fight for him and won him a lot of money, but to punish me for what he saw us doing, he set me up with a fight I couldn't win. The other fighter was twice my size and beat the hell out of me. When I got released from the hospital, your father came to me and offered me a job. I didn't have anywhere else to go and no money, so I said yes."

My heart clenched at the idea that my father had punished Ryder like that. "I'm so sorry. I never knew. Why didn't you tell me?"

"I wasn't supposed to tell you or anyone else that I fought for him. He doesn't want you or your sister to know that side of his business."

"He bets on these fights? Is that what you mean?" I asked, shocked that my father could be involved in anything like that.

"He more than bets. He owns the fights, and with me, he owned the fighter."

"You can't own someone, Ryder. Even my father can't do that."

His chuckled, cracking that sexy smile I'd seen so rarely recently. "Really? Because he owned me. I got a nice place to stay and he likes to tell people I'm like his son, but he owned me when I fought for him. I was his property."

My shoulders sagged at this revelation. I'd always known my father had seen me and Janelle as his property to do as he liked with, but Ryder wasn't his flesh and blood. Although I'd never known why he brought him to the house, I never dreamed it was because he basically owned him.

But what was he now if he wasn't fighting anymore?

"He doesn't own you anymore, does he?" I asked, suddenly worried how he could hurt him if he found out about what we'd just done.

Ryder took a deep breath and smiled. "I don't know if I'd call it owning anymore, but it's not like I can go anywhere else without having to pay a pretty steep price if I left."

I didn't want to talk about this anymore. The mere thought of my father owning him in any way made me sick to my stomach.

Placing my head on his chest again, I asked, "If you could go somewhere, where would you go?"

"I don't know. Somewhere quiet, maybe the country. I'd love to buy a little place on some land and leave the world behind."

All I heard was leave me behind because I was stuck in this mad world my father had created in this house. I rolled away from him and pulled the sheet over my naked body, suddenly feeling lonely there with him.

He followed me and kissed me softly on the lips. "What's wrong? Why did you move over here after I told you that?"

I avoided looking at him and stared up at the ceiling. "Because that's not a life I could ever have, so your dream could never include me."

Cradling my cheek, he looked down at me with concern in his eyes. "I didn't mean it that way. It's just what I would do if we ever could leave. Don't you ever think of going away from this house anymore?"

I ran my hand over the scar on my wrist and shook my head. "Not anymore."

Ryder lowered his head and softly kissed where I'd cut into my skin. "I never regretted saving you before this moment."

The sadness in his voice crushed me. He saved my life, and for that, he should have felt like a hero. Instead, I'd blamed him from the moment I opened my eyes, and even now a small part of me deep down wondered if he'd been wrong to rescue me that night.

He looked up from that awful scar that marred my skin and I knew I had to make this right. Pushing his hair off his forehead, I smiled, and for the first time, I said what I should have all this time.

"I've been terrible to you, and you haven't deserved any of it, Ryder. You saved a life. There's nothing more heroic than that, and I've treated you like some criminal for doing the right thing. I'm sorry. My life may not be what I had hoped it would be, but I have a chance every day to make it better. You gave me that chance. I owe my life to you."

My words made him smile, and he wrapped his

arms around me. "I promise to protect you, Serena. It's all I've ever wanted to do. I should have done something that night your father sent you away and then the night he announced you had to marry Oliver. I know you said you couldn't leave, but I should have found a way. If I could have found out where your mother is. Then when I saw you lying in that bathtub…I couldn't let you down again."

"You protected me when I needed you most, Ryder. That's all that matters."

Left unsaid was the obvious truth that now he might not be able to protect me from whatever my husband decided to do. Closing my eyes, I silently prayed I wouldn't need him to ever face that.

"What's wrong?" he asked, kissing the top of my head. "You got quiet there."

So he wouldn't see how much I feared what the future would bring from my husband, I pressed a smile onto my lips and shook my head. "Nothing. I was just thinking about the first night you came here. Janelle was so sure you were meant to be with one of us, and I couldn't imagine that."

"You looked disappointed that night when you came into your father's office and saw me standing there," Ryder said as he twirled a lock of my hair around his finger.

I thought back to that moment when I thought I would see my mother for the first time in so long and instead saw him. I had been disappointed. My father had promised me he would find her that time, but like every other time before, he didn't.

"I was expecting someone else."

"Another stud?" he joked, making me smile.

I looked up to see him grinning that sexy smile of his and rolled my eyes. "No, not another stud. My mother. My father had sworn he would find her and bring her home, but as always, he didn't."

He gently kissed the top of my head again and asked, "Do you really think she's still out there?"

His question made my heart clench. I didn't know if my mother was still alive or if my father had just used the threat of hurting her against me to get his own way when I said I wouldn't marry Oliver. Maybe she was gone and he was just cruel, like always.

Weaving my fingers through Ryder's, I pressed my cheek against our hands. "I want to believe she is. That she never wanted to leave, and when she finds out that I have wanted to see her that she'll come back. But I don't know."

"I wish I knew one way or another so I could at least give you that, but he's never said a word about your mother in front of me. It's like she never existed, to be honest."

"That's how he wants everyone to feel. Janelle acts like we came from him alone, but I can't let myself forget her. It feels like not knowing her is a huge missing piece from my life."

I slid my fingers from his and sat up to get dressed. As much as I could have spent the rest of time right there in his arms talking, I had to go. I didn't have a choice.

He caught me by my wrist, and when I turned to see his face I knew what he was about to say. "Please don't make this harder than it has to be. I don't want to leave. You know that, right?"

Nodding, he lowered his head. "I know. I just don't want you to go already."

I leaned over and kissed him long and deep, only making it harder for me to leave. When I pulled away, he didn't try to stop me a second time.

All the better. There was no point in it. No matter how much I wanted to stay with him, my father had made sure I was another man's wife.

WHEN I WOKE up in my bed in the apartment my father had given Oliver and me as a wedding gift, my husband lay next to me like we were any normal married couple. He'd chosen to go to his brother's on our wedding night instead of staying with his brand new wife, and when he returned sometime during the night, I heard him undress and silently crawl into bed next to me. There were no words said or any gesture of kindness at all.

Just a man getting into bed with a woman and nothing else.

I wasn't emotionally equipped to handle this life. So I turned to the one man who had proven he cared for me. As I lay there watching Oliver's chest rise and fall while he slept, I couldn't say I felt guilty for going to Ryder either. I'd never chosen any of this, so why should I be expected to live without even the slightest caring touch or word?

I got out of bed to begin my day, unsure how to act toward Oliver now that he'd so clearly shown me he had not even the slightest interest in even pretending to care about me. Perhaps he had a woman he cared about on the side, someone like Ryder who made him happy. I couldn't blame him. I wouldn't. It would actually make life much easier if he did.

Day after day, we lived in that apartment but said very little to one another. I offered him coffee in the morning after I'd made some, and he politely declined. He announced every day that he'd be home late because of work, and I genuinely wished him a good day. Then at night, he slept next to me without ever trying to touch me and the next day we'd start over again.

It wasn't good or bad. It was just life.

His absence from my days and nights offered me

the chance to see Ryder, and each night I spent in his arms gave me the strength to face the next day of my messed up life. It wasn't what I'd ever dreamed of for myself, but it was enough.

And then one night everything changed.

Chapter Nineteen

Ryder

T HE KNOCK ON my door made my heart race. Just the thought of Serena in my arms never failed to make everything bad about my life disappear, if only for the time she was next to me.

For three nights, I'd been without her. Secret texts from a phone no one but I knew about told me she was worried Oliver would find out, but today I hadn't gotten any message.

I opened the door to see her standing in front of me in jean shorts and a t-shirt like she used to wear when she'd come to see me in my room over in the main house. Pulling her into my apartment, I quickly closed the door and kissed her, dying to feel her lips against mine.

"I missed you," I said nuzzling her neck to taste her skin.

She squirmed out of my hold and giggled. "Hang on. Let me take these shoes off first."

I looked down and there on her feet were black sandals. Confused, I asked, "Why are you wearing shoes? You never wear shoes."

A sheepish look came over her face. Avoiding my gaze, she shrugged and headed toward the couch. "It's no big deal. They're just shoes."

But they weren't just shoes. In all the time I'd known Serena, she'd hated wearing shoes because of what happened to her as a child. Whenever she was home, she was barefoot. It gave her a natural feel no one I'd ever met possessed. Now she was suddenly wearing shoes and it wasn't a big deal?

Before she could get to the couch, I grabbed her by the arm and spun her around to face me. "You've never worn shoes since the day I met you."

Serena lowered her head to look down at her feet. "It's not a big deal, Ryder. Just drop it."

"Drop what? What's changed?"

Biting her lip, she hesitated before mumbling, "Oliver said I looked like some kind of homeless person walking around barefoot and he doesn't want his wife to look like that. He wants me in shoes now. It's not a big deal."

"Even knowing why you don't want to wear them?"

"I didn't tell him. It's no big deal. Really."

"You keep saying that, but you won't even look at me when you tell me you're okay with this guy saying you look like a homeless woman," I said, my anger rising with every word.

She yanked her arm from my hold and glared up at me. "What am I supposed to do, Ryder? He's my husband! I didn't choose that, but it's the way it is. I can fight him on everything and be completely miserable or I can honor his wishes on some things and not hate my life entirely. What would you have me do?"

My head spun at the idea that now she was honoring his wishes. What did that mean exactly? "What the fuck are you doing to make him happy, Serena?"

A look of horror settled into her face. "What does that mean? Why are you asking me that?"

Something inside me snapped as possessiveness tore through me. I pushed her back against the wall, scaring her. I knew I should stop right there, but I couldn't. Even the mere idea of her trying to please that fuck of a husband made me insane with jealousy.

Her eyes grew wide as I jammed my hand up her shorts to touch her pussy. "So now it's all about making Oliver happy? I guess that means you're sleeping with him. Does he make you feel like I do, Serena? Is his cock bigger than mine? Does he make you come harder? Is that why it's suddenly important to honor his wishes?"

Pushing against my fingers as they slid inside her, she sobbed, "Don't do this, Ryder. Please. You know I don't have a choice. Why are you saying these things to me?"

I held her fast against the wall and answered her even as I began to spin out of control. "Bullshit. There's always a choice."

"How? What choice have I ever had in anything? Did I choose to lose my mother? Did I choose to be sent away from you? Did I choose to be married to a man I don't love? I never have a choice. You know that better than anyone else."

The truth of her words made my heart break, and I let myself collapse against the wall, exhausted from the anger and jealousy coursing through me. I knew how little choice she had in the life her father forced upon her. I just hated the idea that this Oliver guy was changing her.

She began to cry beneath me, making me hate this whole thing even more. "I'm sorry, Serena. I shouldn't have said that. I'm sorry."

Her body heaved against mine as she sobbed, and I took her in my arms as much to make myself feel better as to make her understand how much I regretted what I'd become. Tilting her head back, I kissed her cheek as tears rolled down onto my lips.

"Please don't take these moments away from me, Ryder. You're the only person I can be myself with. Don't push me away because I have to be someone else for him."

My emotions raced from rage to misery and back again as the idea of her changing for Oliver settled into my brain. Backing away, I shook my head, not wanting to accept it.

"I can't do this, Serena. I can't pretend that you doing things to make him happy doesn't kill me inside. I know it shouldn't since you don't love him, but it does."

"No, don't say that!" she cried. Reaching out for me, she took my hands in hers and squeezed them as she stared up into my eyes. "I can't do this without you, Ryder. I spend my days waiting until the moment I can come here to see you. Everything else in my life is a sham. But you, you're real. And what we are is real. I can't believe that you can just walk away from us. I won't believe it."

I looked down at where she and I held hands and wished things were different for us. But they weren't. And they'd never be.

Lifting my head, I watched as tears streamed down her face as she waited for me to say something. I didn't want to say the words I knew I had to, but I didn't have a choice.

"Are we going to do this for the rest of our lives? Are we going to hide out in these rooms and never get to share a day at the beach together? Never get to just go for a walk around the garden ever again? Never lay down and watch TV like we used to? Is this the life you want?"

Serena shook her head sadly. "No, but it's the best of the life I have. Is it that you don't love me anymore? Is that it?"

"No," I answered truthfully, wishing it could be that easy. "I love you more than I thought I could love anyone. You're the first thought on my mind when I open my eyes in the morning and the last when I fall asleep at night. And in between, I can think of little else than when I'll see you next."

Stepping toward me, she cupped my cheek with her palm and smiled. "And I love you. It's not everything we deserve, but it's all we have. Please don't send me away because it isn't perfect."

"Jesus, Serena. Not perfect? You sneak over here at night to be with me after pretending all day to be someone else. Perfect isn't anywhere close to what we are."

"Is it that you have a problem with me not being faithful to my husband? The man who my father traded me to? Is that what this is?" she asked as her eyes pleaded for me to stay with her.

"No. I don't give a fuck about you being faithful to him. It's us that I have the problem with. I want to be able to hold your hand while we walk. I want to sleep with you in my arms all night long and wake up to you next to me. We're never going to be able to do that because I'll always be hiding in the shadows while you work to make Oliver happy."

Hanging her head, Serena said in a tiny voice, "They're only shoes, Ryder."

Her insistence on not seeing how important this was to me made my blood boil. Pushing her away, I barked, "Go home to your husband, Serena. Go make him happy tonight by wearing shoes."

She stood there stunned for a moment as my rejection settled in. I couldn't let this go, no matter how small she wanted to make me think it was.

I turned away from her and walked to my bedroom, exhausted from everything we were and had become. I missed the days when it was just the two of us in that bedroom talking and wishing for a future we'd never have. I even missed the last few weeks we spent together in her room before her wedding. It wasn't perfect and maybe it was more fucked up than even I wanted to admit, but at least it had been just the two of us.

Serena came up behind me and began beating me with her fists. "Don't turn away from me!"

Her punches barely registered against my skin. "Go home, Serena."

"So that's it? You're done with me, so I'm supposed to just go home? I don't get any say in this?"

I turned to see her barely holding it together, but I had nothing more for her. I'd never be done with her, but we couldn't continue on like this. "No, you don't. Go home to your husband."

Her eyes flashed her hatred for me at that moment, and she screamed, "My husband who loves when I fuck him, Ryder? My husband who only asks that I wear shoes in return for buying me anything I want? Is that the man you want me to return to? Maybe I should. I mean, what's wearing shoes when I can have a man who has all the money in the world and doesn't have to be a lapdog for my father?"

Her words cut me to the bone. Even when she'd hated me for saving her, I'd always known deep down she cared. Now as she glared up at me and told me I was nothing compared to Oliver, I saw none of that love I'd believed she felt for me.

"Nothing to say now?" she asked, practically goading me to fight with her.

But fighting isn't what I wanted at that moment. Grabbing her by the waist, I threw her on the bed and covered her body with mine. I pinned her arms above her head and kissed her hard, letting all my rage and jealousy control me.

"You forget I'm not a lapdog, Serena. I'm a junkyard dog, and those bite when provoked."

She struggled against my hold, pushing her wrists against my hands until I released her. Tearing at my shirt, she ripped it off my back and raked her fingernails over my skin.

"Then bite."

I pulled her shorts off and slid my cock out of my pants. With one hard thrust, I pushed into her cunt until I was buried inside her. She bucked against me and wrapped her legs around my waist as I began fucking her with abandon.

She was mine and no man, not even her goddamned husband who could give her the world, could give her this.

Tugging her hair, I pulled hard as my mouth took all I needed from hers. She moaned softly each time my cock filled her, and every time I plunged harder and deeper into that tight cunt than I'd ever before. I wanted to claim her, to make sure anyone who saw her knew she'd been fucked by a man who possessed her body and soul.

Like she possessed me.

"Tell me you don't love him, Serena. Say it."

Her hands clawed at my shoulders as I leaned back to see her face. "I don't. I don't love him. I couldn't love him. I love you. Only you. Tell me you still love me too."

I pushed my hips forward to bury my cock inside her and groaned, "More than you'll ever know."

She was my obsession, and no matter how much I knew it would kill me when she left me in that apartment alone again, I couldn't stop myself. I needed her. I wanted her. And no matter what it did to me, I couldn't stop loving her.

Her release began, and she came hard, tearing her nails down my back as her cunt squeezed my cock. She gave me everything she had and took everything I have to give.

We lay in each other's arms, drenched with the sweat from our lovemaking, and she quietly said, "I'm sorry I said those things before. Do you forgive me?"

As I looked into those deep brown eyes, I would have forgiven her for anything. Kissing her softly, I whispered against her lips, "Always. I don't have a choice."

"Aren't you happy you love me?"

I held her to me and pressed my lips to the scar on the inside of her wrist. "I don't know what I am, but I know this. I love you, and no matter what happens, that won't change."

She told me she loved me and promised someday we'd be together, but I knew better. No matter how much she cared, we were pawns in her father's world and that would never change.

Chapter Twenty

Serena

I RETURNED HOME to find Oliver already back from work earlier than usual. Prepared with a lie I'd concocted before going to see Ryder, I smiled sweetly as I closed the front door and said, "You're home already? If I knew you'd be here, I would have waited for you before I took my walk."

His eyes flashed his clear anger and he asked, "Where were you at this time of night?"

Avoiding his suspicious gaze, I headed toward the kitchen. "Just out for a walk, like I said. It's a beautiful night, so I wanted to enjoy it."

I poured myself some wine and quickly downed half a glass to calm my nerves. I didn't mind lying to Oliver, but I knew by the sharpness of his voice that he suspected me of something. The last thing I could handle now was a fight with him too. My emotions were right below the surface as it was.

With my back to the doorway, I heard him enter the kitchen. My body tensed as I waited for him to say something. When he did, my heart sank.

"Where are your damn shoes?" he asked in a clipped tone.

I looked down at my feet and remembered I'd left them at Ryder's. Scrambling for an answer, I pressed a smile onto my face and turned around to face Oliver.

"My shoes? I must have forgotten them out in the garden. It was so beautiful out, I took them off."

His expression twisted into a look of disgust, and he opened his mouth to scold me, but before he could a knock on the front door interrupted him. Hurrying away to answer it, I prayed to God it was my father to distract Oliver from his rage.

I opened the door and saw Ryder standing there in his suit dangling my shoes off the end of his finger. Terrified he'd say the wrong thing and reveal my lie, I stood frozen to the spot, unable to say a word.

But I saw that gentle look in his eyes that told me everything would be okay if I trusted him. With a smile, he said, "I'm sorry to come here so late, but I found your shoes and wanted to return them to you."

Behind me, Oliver snapped, "What are you doing with my wife's shoes?"

Ryder's gaze slowly left my face to look at the man demanding an answer. "I found them outside and knew she'd want them back, so I'm returning them."

Stopping at my side, my husband asked, "Who are you? Haven't I seen you in her father's office before?"

With a smile I knew would infuriate Oliver, Ryder answered, "I'm her brother, and yes, you've seen me in Robert's office before."

Turning his attention back to me, he handed me my shoes. "Have a good night, and try to remember your shoes from now on."

I quickly took them and thanked him for returning them before slamming the door closed. Avoiding Oliver, I slipped them onto my feet and began walking back to the kitchen, but he grabbed my arm tightly to stop me.

Turning around, I saw the rage in his eyes. "I've never heard of a brother. You only have a sister, so who the fuck is that?"

I tried to pull my arm away from his hold, but he only tightened his grasp on me. "You're hurting my arm."

"Tell me who he is," he demanded, squeezing the skin on my arm even harder.

"He's my brother!"

Oliver glared at me. "No, he's fucking not. He doesn't even look like you or your sister. So who the hell is he?"

Knowing how ridiculous I sounded, I tried to

explain who Ryder was to my father since I couldn't explain who he was to me. "Well, not really, but my father sort of adopted him a few years back, so he sort of is. He's one of his bodyguards."

For a long moment, my husband stood watching me to see if I was telling the truth. I hadn't lied. Ryder was everything I'd said. Just not to me.

To me, he was a lifeline I clung to desperately and couldn't imagine living without. Just knowing I would see him made my days bearable. His touch on my skin ignited the only passion I felt for anything or anyone these days.

And as I stood there facing the man I'd been forced to marry, I wished I could declare my love for Ryder, to be honest to Oliver and the world and say that no matter what my father wanted, I'd found someone who made me want to live.

"I don't want to see him around you anymore. He's got a cheap look about him that I don't want to think about next to you."

Oliver turned to head toward the bedroom as I instinctively defended the man I loved. "That cheap look, as you call it, is from years of fighting for his very existence. Something someone like you could never understand."

Spinning around, my husband narrowed his eyes to angry slits. "What did you say?"

This wasn't a fight I could win, so I merely

shrugged and gave in. "Nothing. Nothing at all."

"That's what I thought. From now on, I don't want you out once it's dark, Serena."

"Why?" This felt like every argument I'd ever had with my father, but unlike him, Oliver wasn't going to control me.

"Because I said so," he snapped sharply. "I'm your husband and that's what I want."

"And what about what I want?" I asked as he walked away.

Oliver didn't answer. He didn't have to. My father had made it perfectly clear how little what I wanted mattered when he offered me up like some thing to be traded between owners.

But I wasn't going to forever be this powerless. I wouldn't let myself be. And when I finally did find a way to control my life, Oliver and my father should worry because I would remember every second of being under their power for the rest of my life.

THE PHONE I kept to communicate with Ryder vibrated against my hip making me smile in anticipation. Eager to have any contact with him after three nights alone, I looked down and saw in his message that he missed me as much as I missed him.

At night I dream about us being far away from this place. In a cabin somewhere in the woods where no one but the two of us exist.

I knew exactly how he felt. Sometimes I dreamed about us running away to some far off place where no one knew who we were and we could just be together and happy.

I miss you. He won't let me out at night anymore. He has someone watching me, I think.

My dear husband had never come out and told me he was having me followed, but I thought I saw someone ducking behind the hedges in the garden earlier that day and again when I went down to my father's office right before dinner. I knew he suspected something, but there was a part of me that didn't care.

What else could he do to me that I hadn't endured before?

There was some strange solace in knowing that whatever Oliver did, I could handle it because I'd had to with my father. So many times in my life I'd doubted I had the strength necessary to withstand what he'd done, but every time I'd come through. Emotionally battered and beaten, but I'd come through.

Almost every time.

I had Ryder to thank for that one time I nearly didn't, and someday when we were free, I'd repay the debt I owed him for saving my life.

Find a way to get to your father's office. I'll be waiting.

My father's office? How would we be together if we met there, of all places? I thought about asking Ryder that very question, but the mere idea that I'd get to feel his body next to mine made any suggestion to see him possible.

Quickly, I grabbed a sweater and opened the front door to my apartment. Looking left and right, I saw no one nearby, but I had a feeling whoever Oliver had watching me wasn't far away. I didn't care. If he or his goon asked where I was going, I'd tell the truth.

My heart raced as I rushed down the stairs toward the main house. Soon I'd see Ryder, and no matter how long I had with him, at least those moments together would be happy.

Barefoot, I ran down the back hallway where I'd made the fateful decision that night to end it all rather than marry a man I didn't love and then turned the corner to see Ryder standing outside my father's office. I slowed down to a walk to catch my breath and smiled, thrilled to finally see him after days apart.

Just as I reached where he stood, my father walked out and stopped when he saw me. "Just who I wanted to see. You must be reading my mind, Serena."

My heart sank. Whatever Ryder had planned had been ruined. "You wanted me for something, Daddy?"

"I did. Ryder here made a wonderful suggestion that I wholeheartedly agree with and I'm sure you will too. As your husband is away so much, he offered to drive you to your sister's since her husband is out of town on business. Isn't that a wonderful idea?"

His words made my spirits soar. Wonderful wasn't the word to describe his idea. Janelle's house was no less than an hour away, more if I could claim beltway rush hour traffic, and that would give us at least a chance to be with each other on the way there and then maybe make a detour on the way back. Whatever way I looked at it, Ryder's plan was perfect.

"I love it! When do we leave?"

My father's eyes opened wide at my enthusiastic answer. "I'm surprised to see you so happy to comply with what I want, Serena. Being married must be doing wonders for you. You two can leave whenever Ryder's ready."

"I'm ready now. Should I take the Mercedes?"

"Fine. And Serena, don't give Ryder a hard time. He's one of my best men."

Standing on my tiptoes, I kissed my father on the cheek. "You can count on me to behave, Daddy. Whatever he says goes. See you later."

Completely surprised by my willingness to do what he wanted, my father sighed contentedly. "I like this new person you are now that you're married. I'll be sure to let Oliver know you'll be back later tonight."

Out of the corner of my eye, I saw Ryder grin in that way that always made me want him. I didn't know how he'd figured out how to outmaneuver my father and I didn't care. All I cared about was the two hours alone we'd have with my father's blessing, and Oliver couldn't say a thing about it.

RYDER PULLED THE car down the long driveway from the main house and through the gates as I sat in the back seat dying to sit up there next to him. A few blocks from the house, I climbed into the passenger seat and turned to see him smiling at me.

"I couldn't let you just sit in that apartment all alone, so I figured I'd kill two birds with one stone."

Moving over to sit beside him, I slid my hand up his muscular thigh covered by the black dress pants he wore. "What two birds would that be?"

He moaned as I palmed his already hard cock

through the thin fabric and winced like he was in pain. "At least let me get a few miles away, Serena."

I pressed my lips to the shell of his ear and whispered, "No need. You drive and tell me about those two birds and I'll do what I've wanted to do all day."

Another moan escaped from his throat when I unzipped his pants and slipped his thick cock out. I'd fantasized about sucking him off, and now that I had the chance, I wasn't going to let it go by without taking advantage of it.

Lowering my head, I wasted no time in taking that beautiful cock into my mouth. Every inch of Ryder was perfect as far as I was concerned, but this part was sublime. Long and thick, his cock was everything a woman could ask for.

I gently sucked the crown between my lips and teased the very tip with my tongue as he buried his right hand in my hair and tugged.

"Fuck, oh God, that feels so good," he said on a moan that hit me deep inside where his cock would later in our drive.

Wrapping my hand around him, I began in earnest to go down on him, slowly easing every delicious inch of him into my mouth until he filled it completely and then ever so slightly faster sliding my lips up his shaft until they reached the head, all the while flicking my tongue over the raised vein that ran the full length of his cock.

"Oh…God…Serena, I'm going to have to pull over," he said in a voice that sounded like he was nearly there.

But I liked the idea of how dangerous this all felt and looked up at him to protest. "No, keep going. I want you to come while you're driving."

Ryder winced and looked back at the road. "You're going to kill both of us."

Taking his cock back into my mouth, I moaned against his silky soft skin and hoped he wouldn't truly kill us over a blowjob. Sliding my hand down his shaft, I cupped his balls and began to suck on the head like I knew he loved. It never failed to make him come hard, and I wanted that.

He yanked my hair with each time I lowered my mouth to the base of his cock, pulling my head up fast so I barely had time to tease him with my tongue. Above me, I heard him groan and he lifted his hips off the seat, making his foot press down on the accelerator and pushing him back against the seat.

Maybe this wasn't the best idea.

I didn't care, though. Sliding my hand up and down his cock, I kept my mouth on the head and sucked hard to get him to that point of no return.

"Right there…fuck…don't stop. Suck it…"

When he said things like that, I couldn't stop

even if I wanted to. Which I didn't. I loved pleasing him, and knowing that I was about to give him pleasure like I'd never given to anyone else made me happier than almost anything else in the world. Only looking into his eyes as I rode his cock was better, but that would come later.

For now, all I wanted was to taste him in my mouth and hear his beautiful moans as he came.

I felt the first twitch of his cock against my tongue and knew he was seconds away. Tightening his hold on my hair, he exhaled deeply and came, spurting cum down my throat. I closed my lips around him so I didn't lose a drop and sucked until nothing was left in him as he groaned with every thrust into my mouth.

The car slowed and I sat up to see him pulling off onto a dirt road in a wooded area I remembered from parties in high school. Barely dusk, we ran the risk of being seen, but neither one of us cared.

He parked the car and pulled me onto his lap to kiss me deep and long like everything he loved about me existed in my lips as he slid my shorts and panties down my left leg. In seconds, his cock was filling me for the second time that trip.

"This is all I could think of all afternoon. I can't stand the idea of you in that apartment waiting for him like he wants you to. I hate it."

Cradling his face, I kissed him and rocked my

hips to take him deeper inside me to touch that spot only he had ever found. "Don't talk about him. Don't talk about that place. All I want to think of is you and me and how you feel when you're inside me like this, Ryder."

He moved his hands to cup my ass, and lifting his hips, thrust hard into me. "I can't help it. You're all I think about. You're my obsession, my addiction, and what he's doing is killing me."

As I rode his cock, loving how he stretched me to take every perfect inch of him into me, I looked into his eyes and knew something would have to change. I couldn't live without being with him like this, and he wasn't going to let another man keep me from him.

Even if he was my husband.

Our hands grasped and clutched at the one another's skin, marking us with the evidence of what we'd done, but I didn't care. I needed him more than I needed safety and security, and if Oliver found out, so be it.

If the choice was Ryder or him, there was no choice. He could do what he liked to me. I wasn't going to give up the only man I'd ever loved completely and without fear.

Sinking his teeth into the soft skin of my shoulder, he thrust his cock into me one last time and I came apart and then seconds later reveled in the feel of him flooding me with his release. It was rough and careless and perfect, and if we didn't get caught, I'd be desperate to feel him just like this again tomorrow.

We sat silently catching our breath, still joined together, and I lay my head on his strong shoulder. Of all the places in the world I could be, none were better than right there in that car with him.

Ryder gently stroked my hair down my back and whispered, "I would do anything to have you away from him. You know that?"

I sat back and looked into his eyes, knowing how much truth there was in his words. He never left any room for doubt, and if I knew a way to make his wish come true, I would have.

"I love you. Nothing will ever change that. Not this sham marriage my father forced on me. Not every horrible thing we've have to endure since the day we met. Nothing will change that I love you."

He closed his eyes and exhaled, knitting his brows. "I think about things sometimes, Serena. Bad things."

A feeling of terror struck me. Bad things? What did he mean?

"What kind of bad things?" I asked, fearing the answer I'd hear. Did he mean that he thought about us not seeing each other?

Slowly, he opened his eyes and stared up at me

with a look so intense it made my breath catch in my chest. Terrified, I waited for him to speak.

But he kissed me instead, a whispersoft kiss that I feared would be followed by the news that he couldn't do this anymore with me. Before I spoke, he said in a faraway voice, "I think about if he just wasn't around anymore."

I knew full well what he meant. Ryder spent his days convincing people to do my father's bidding, and I knew how he did it. I'd never asked if he'd ever done anything more than threaten people, and I didn't want to think of him having to do that just to please my father.

But I didn't want him to be that man for me.

"Don't say that. There will be a way for us to be together. I promise. I don't want your hands dirty when it comes to him."

"I would do anything to be with you, Serena. Do you understand me? Anything."

I shook my head and then kissed him to stop him from talking. No matter what he did for my father, I couldn't bear the thought of tainting what we were, even if it meant I'd be free.

There had to be another way.

Chapter Twenty-One

Ryder

I WATCHED SERENA walk into the main house and back to her life with him, hating how powerless I was to do anything to end our misery. As I pulled the Mercedes into the garage, all I could think about was how shitty he acted when I brought her shoes to her. It wasn't bad enough he forced her to wear things she hated, but then to act like someone being kind to her was some kind of criminal act pissed me off.

Taking a deep breath, I tried to put the thoughts of hurting him out of my mind, but like usual, they returned with a vengeance. I hadn't lied to her when I said I'd do anything to be with her. I would, even if it meant getting rid of him.

My work for her father forced me to do things like that more often than even I wanted to admit, so why would offing her husband be any worse? At least then I'd be making someone's life better.

Two lives, actually. If she wasn't married to Oliver, maybe she and I could be together. Robert seemed to genuinely like me after all this time working for him, so maybe he'd let her be with me.

Not that I had anything like her husband to offer. I had little money, no family to speak of, and no social connections. On second thought, maybe he'd just marry her off to another bastard with cash if I got rid of the first one.

Disgusted at how trapped both Serena and I were in this world of Robert Erickson's, I turned the car off and hung up the keys in the lockbox before heading back into the house. It didn't help to have pipe dreams. They never came true anyway.

I braced myself for whatever might come my way as I stepped into his office, but I found it empty. Since it wasn't even ten yet, he probably hadn't left to see his latest girlfriend. Not really interested in where he might be, I waited around for a minute and left, happy to get a reprieve from him.

My happiness was short lived, though. I hadn't gotten twenty steps away from the office before I heard him bark my name.

"Ryder! Get into my office! Now!"

Quickly, my mind raced to come up with what he could be angry about. I hadn't done anything to piss him off in ages, unless sleeping with his daughter was counted, but he didn't know about that.

Or did he?

It was just like Robert to devise a way to trick

someone into showing what they were up to, and having me drive Serena to her sister's suddenly seemed like far less than a great idea I'd had and more like the way he'd used to find out what we'd been up to. As I hurried to his office, I scrambled to think up a lie that would work, but if he knew about us, there was no lie that could get me out of the trouble I'd be in.

Taking a deep breath, I checked my clothes for any evidence of what Serena and I had done in the car and then told myself to calm the fuck down. If worst came to worst, Robert was old and definitely in worse shape than I was, so I could probably take him, assuming he didn't just blow my head off.

Nothing like that threat hanging over your head as you went to face your boss whose daughter you'd been fucking behind his back.

I took a step into his office and saw him over by the bar pouring himself his favorite drink. I still had no idea what the hell the branch was in his bourbon and branch. Maybe I could distract him by asking about it.

"What's up, boss?" I said as casually as a condemned man would.

"What happened this evening?" he snapped as he turned around so fast an ice cube leaped out of his glass.

So much for trying to distract him with

questions about his drink. "This evening? You mean when I took Serena to Janelle's? Nothing. The car ran fine, we didn't hit much traffic, and we made pretty good time, if I do say so myself."

I was rambling. I knew it, but I couldn't tell if he did. Stopping to take a breath, I waited for him to say something, praying to God his next words didn't involve anything about what we did in the car on the way there and on the way back.

He gulped down a mouthful of his drink and cleared his throat. "Well, her husband is fit to be tied. Something about you holding her shoes the other night and him forbidding her to be around you. Do you know anything about this?"

Feeling like the walls of his office were beginning to close in around me, I took a deep breath and answered, "I did take Serena's shoes to her the other night. I found them outside in the garden and thought she might want them."

Twisting his face into a grimace, Robert said, "And this has that little shit all hot and bothered? You should have heard him. I had to remind him that no matter what he thought he was in this house, nobody raises their voice to me."

"I don't know," I said in my best kiss-ass tone. "I don't interact with him much."

What I wanted to say was that I thought the son of a bitch needed a good beating to teach him how to behave, but I knew better than to do that. Saying anything against Oliver could tip my hand and show how I felt about Serena, and that was the last thing I wanted to do.

"I'm not happy with the idea that he's forbidding my daughter to do anything. I didn't marry her to him to make her some goddamned prisoner."

The irony that Robert ignored or wasn't able to see never ceased to amaze me. It was just a few short months ago that he kept Serena a prisoner for all intents and purposes and had me serve as her jailer. Now her husband doing even less bothered him.

Amazing.

Not that I wanted to defend the little shit. As far as I was concerned, if Robert sent him packing tonight, I'd be the happiest man in the world.

Seated behind his desk, he swirled the ice in his glass for a moment as he thought and then said, "But I have a vested interest in that marriage working, so I guess we have to appease him whenever we can. From now on, you aren't to be around Serena unless you're in this office. Do you understand?"

My chest tightened as his words filtered into my brain. Disrespecting her husband's wishes never gave me a second thought, but now that Robert had decreed I had to stay away from her, I felt like my world was falling away beneath me.

I couldn't show him that, though, so I forced a

stony expression and nodded. "As you wish, boss."

For a few moments, he seemed pleased by the result of our talk, but then he knitted his brows and looked at me and I had a feeling I should have gotten the hell out of there before that.

"That night I found the two of you together right after you moved in here. You know I know what you two were up to."

I couldn't look him in the eyes, so I hung my head and stared down at my shoes. He'd never mentioned that night even once since then, and I'd hoped I'd paid my penance with the beating I took from the behemoth he forced me to fight right after he shipped Serena off to her uncle's in Italy. Now that he'd brought it up finally, I had a feeling I still had more to repent for.

"Yes, sir."

"Look at me, son," he ordered.

Reluctantly, I lifted my head and did as he commanded. I'd expected to see that same surly expression he'd worn when I looked away, but instead he sat there smiling at me. I had no idea what the hell could be so amusing to him, but I had a feeling I'd find out soon enough.

"I told you Serena would take to you like she took to all the strays she brought home. Remember me saying that?"

I did, and being reminded that I was little more

than a stray he'd brought home still stung years after coming to that house.

"Yes, sir."

"Serena is like her mother, Ryder. You see, with Janelle, you know what you get. She's all on the surface. She wants a comfortable life and she's willing to do whatever it takes for that to happen. But Serena, she's not like her sister or me. She and her mother need something more than security. It's never enough with those two. I knew when I married her to Oliver she wouldn't be happy. She thinks marriage and love are synonymous, but you and I know differently, don't we?"

What I knew about marriage could fit on the head of a pin, but I had the sense Robert wasn't asking me for my opinion on that topic. I honestly didn't know where he was going with this conversation, so I did what I usually did with him.

I nodded and tried to make it look like I agreed with him, even if inside I was raging against whatever cruelty he'd decided to impose that day.

"They aren't the same, and I have a sense you're a bright enough guy to know that," he continued. "Marriage is all business. Love, on the other hand, is something rare that needs to be treasured like a fine piece of jewelry."

I'd never heard Robert practically wax poetic like that. The marriage as business idea seemed to be all he considered when it came to love, so his saying it was rare and needed to be treasured made me wonder if, in fact, he'd ever truly loved anyone. I'd assumed he hadn't since he sent Serena's mother away and never let her return, but maybe I was wrong. Maybe he did care about love.

Against my better judgment, I let my curiosity get the better of me and asked, "So do you care if your daughters ever find love, or is the business of marriage more important?"

Without even thinking, he said, "Love will get you nothing but misery. Mark my words, son. I'd be perfectly happy to see Janelle and Serena escape this life without ever having to deal with that. Trust me. Marriage can be negotiated, but love, never. One party always takes all, and the other person is left with nothing."

I still didn't know why Robert wanted to talk to me about this, but his answer unnerved me. If I'd ever truly believed he'd let Serena be with me because she loved me, I now knew that could never happen. I had nothing to negotiate with, so just as she'd been when we were perfect strangers and I was new to this house, she was out of my league.

And no amount of love was going to change that.

Pretending to take his words to heart, I smiled and nodded. "I'll try to remember that."

"I don't think I have to worry about you anyway. I've never seen you with any woman, other than the ones you got at the club those few times, and they don't count. Why don't you have a girlfriend?"

I quickly answered, "Because you told me I needed to stay unattached the first night you brought me here. Remember?"

He thought back to that night and smiled. "You're a smart one, Ryder. I bet you're even smarter than I think. Just be careful. Don't let anything get in the way of thinking straight or you'll find yourself in a place you don't want to be."

I knew a veiled threat when I heard one. He made them dozens of times a day in front of me to business associates and other employees. I just wasn't sure if this one meant he knew what Serena and I were up to or if he was referring to something entirely different that I had no idea about.

Whatever it meant, I did my usual smile and nod routine, and it seemed to make him happy.

Without another word, he picked up his office phone and seeing my cue to leave, I got out of there as quickly as possible before he decided he needed to have another heart-to-heart talk with me about some vague point he wanted me to decipher. Figuring out just what to say to a madman was a never-ending part of my job, but for tonight, I hoped I was done with Robert and his mysteries.

All I wanted to do was get blind drunk and try to forget that I'd just been ordered to stay away from the only person I cared about. I didn't know how I was going to see her, but never seeing Serena again wasn't an option.

No matter what her husband or father thought.

Chapter Twenty-Two

Serena

OLIVER STOMPED AROUND our apartment slamming doors and snapping whenever he passed me as I sat at the kitchen table. I'd lived through years of this kind of behavior from my father, so I knew my best bet was to stay silent and not provoke him any more than my mere presence did.

I didn't have a sense that he knew what Ryder and I had done just a few hours before on that side road surrounded by trees, but just the fact that he'd driven me to Janelle's had made Oliver fly into a rage. I'd barely gotten into the house before he started interrogating me about my whereabouts, and when he heard about who had taken me to my sister's, his face turned beet red and he began to bark about how he'd told me I was never to see Ryder again.

Standing with my back pressed against the apartment front door, I braced myself for him to hit me. That look of rage on his face terrified me, and I stood perfectly still as if I was frozen to the spot while he flailed his hands around and screamed at me about how no wife of his should behave the way I did.

When I didn't say anything in my own defense, he began to storm through the apartment slamming things that got in his way.

I'd never feared my father would hit me because that wasn't who he was, but with Oliver's temper, I knew it was just a matter of time before I angered him enough to make him raise a hand to me. Somewhere deep inside, I wished he would. I knew that was twisted and sad, but maybe if my father saw he was mistreating me he might do something about it.

In truth, I knew what do something about it meant. My father's business dealings involved some very dark areas of the world, and even though I'd never witnessed any of what I was sure went on, Ryder had all but told me that when my father didn't get his way, people suffered.

None of it surprised me. I'd seen it all my life.

"If I ever hear about him near you again, Serena, I swear to fucking God I won't be responsible for what happens to him. I warned your father and I'm warning you. Don't test me!" Oliver bellowed as I sat perfectly still in my chair at the kitchen table.

His voice echoed and made the window behind

me rattle. I wanted to speak up and tell him I didn't care what he did because I was going to see Ryder and nothing was going to stop me. I wanted to stand toe-to-toe with him and stare into his eyes so full of rage when I said, "I am not your property. I will do as I want."

"Do you have anything to say for yourself? I specifically told you not to be around that guy again, and not a few days later you're in a car with him for hours going to visit that sister of yours."

I looked up at him and studied his round face and small eyes for a moment. He really was unappealing, even before he opened his mouth. How my father could have thought I would like him, much less ever love him, baffled me.

He wanted me to apologize for disobeying him. I knew that's what he was waiting to hear. Well, he'd be waiting until hell froze over because I had no intention of apologizing for going to see my sister or who drove me there. Being with Ryder for those few short hours was the only thing that had made the day tolerable. I wouldn't apologize for that or anything else, for that matter.

"My father wanted me to go see Janelle, so I went."

Oliver's face grew even redder. "Even after I expressly forbid you to be around that guy?" he screamed.

"My father chose who would drive me. I had nothing to do with that."

None of my answers were lies, although I didn't care if I had to lie to this son of a bitch. He didn't deserve the respect that came from any truth I could give him about who Ryder was to me. Maybe if he'd ever treated me with even the slightest kindness I may have been willing to show him some in return, but when he wasn't ignoring me completely, he was barking at me like I was a misbehaving child he wanted to beat into submission.

Every night as I lay in bed waiting for sleep to come I wished he would simply go away. I fantasized about waking up one sunny morning and seeing his side of the bed empty. I'd look in the closet we shared and through groggy eyes see none of his clothes there anymore. His shoes wouldn't be scattered around the bedroom floor where I had to navigate around them or risk tripping over them. His toothbrush would be gone, and his razor that he never put away would be absent from the bathroom vanity.

It would be like he never existed in my life, and I couldn't imagine being happier about that.

As he passed by me yet again, he stopped and shook his head violently. "I can't stay here tonight. I can't even look at you. I'm going to my brother's house."

"What's new? You spend more time there than anywhere else. Why don't you pack your things and just move there?" I asked, suddenly feeling braver than I had in months.

Instead of becoming even more enraged, Oliver calmly stepped toward the table and rapped his knuckles off the wood. "He warned me about you, you know that? He warned me that I was marrying below my level."

I'd found few positive things about being born an Erickson, but one of them was the social class I'd been born into. While Oliver and his family were certainly well off, he hadn't married below his level in any way with me.

And he knew it.

"Your brother wishes he was at my family's level, Oliver. Feel free to tell him I said that too."

A stunned look crossed his angry face. I rarely spoke up to defend myself with him, but his attempt at insulting me this way made me want to take a stand.

When he recovered from his surprise, he stood up to his just under six foot height and glared at me. "I know what you and that glorified pool boy are up to. Don't think I don't. I've known all along. So don't think you're fooling anyone, Serena."

I struggled to keep my expression calm as inside I worried that he truly did know about Ryder and me. Maybe all he had were suspicions, but if he voiced them to my father, I had no idea what he'd do to Ryder, and the last thing I wanted was for him to get hurt.

"I told you he's my adopted brother. Ask my father. He'll tell you. And like any other brother and sister, it's not surprising that we'd be around each other sometimes."

Oliver shook his head again. "I should have listened to my brother. He warned me I was marrying a whore. What other reason would your father have to find you a husband unless you were a slut nobody would want?"

His words stung, even if I didn't believe them or care what he thought of me. I wanted to scream that I wasn't a whore. I was just someone trapped in a terrible situation, but I'd be damned if I stayed like this for the rest of my life.

I said nothing, though, and stared into his hateful eyes until he turned around and stormed out of the apartment with a final slam of the front door. When I heard his car squeal out of the driveway, I fished the phone I used to talk to Ryder out of my back pocket and saw a message.

Your father ordered me to not be around you anymore unless he's there.

My heart sank as I read the words he'd sent me.

Now even my father had decided I couldn't be around him. Whatever happened to treating him like family?

My mind whirled as I tried to come up with something that could change his mind. Nothing Oliver had done so far seemed to have angered my father, and I wasn't sure anything he said to me tonight would either.

But I had to try to sway him from his decision. Sneaking around on Oliver was hard enough, but sneaking around on my father too would make it next to impossible for us to ever see each other again.

Quickly, I typed a message to Ryder.

I'm going to see him tonight. Wait for me.

I hurried out of my apartment and down to my father's office in the main house. I found him sitting behind his desk like usual at night, but he already had his suit jacket on, which meant he'd be leaving soon. I'd gotten there just in time.

"Daddy, I need to speak to you."

He lifted his head from whatever had his attention on his laptop and stared at me. No smile or anything for his daughter.

"What is it, Serena? I was just leaving."

Nervous at how disinterested he seemed to even speak to me, I tried to find the right words to say that would make him see that Oliver was being unreasonable about Ryder. The problem was nothing came to mind, and I ended up standing there with my mouth hanging open as he stared angrily at me.

He stood from his desk, a clear sign I was losing my opportunity to have him listen to me, so I blurted out, "Oliver told me his brother thinks I'm a whore. Is that any way for a husband to speak to his wife?"

It sounded childish and ridiculous to say that to him, but he'd been the one to force me to marry Oliver in the first place. Unfortunately, even hearing his daughter referred to as a whore didn't seem to matter to him.

"Serena, married people have arguments and sometimes they say things they don't mean. I'm sure Oliver was just upset about the fact that you weren't there when he got home today. I take the blame for that since I was the one who sent you to your sister's, but I think you're getting upset about nothing. I'm sure if you go back and talk to him, you two will be able to smooth things over."

His dismissal only made me more desperate, so I stopped him as he began to walk out. Looking up into his dark eyes, I pleaded with him. "He isn't there. He decided to go to his brother's again. He does that all the time, Daddy. And just how am I supposed to smooth over his calling me a whore who isn't even at his social level?"

My father bristled at the mention of our family existing beneath the Landons on the social ladder, but still he refused to support me. Patting me on the arm like I was a puppy, he said, "Serena, I'm sure that was taken out of context. Give him a chance. Do it for me, okay?"

And with that he left me standing in his office before I could remind him my entire marriage was for him. But what was for me?

After both Oliver and my father basically treated me like a second-class citizen, I didn't care who saw me go to Ryder's apartment. When he opened the door, my emotions overwhelmed me and I barely got inside before I began to cry.

"What happened? Did he do something to you?" he asked in a protective voice I so desperately needed at that moment.

Shaking my head, I dried under my eyes. "No. I don't know why I'm crying. I guess I just feel like every day gets worse and worse. First, I'm forced to marry a man I don't love so my father can be happy, and then he forbids me from seeing you and my father says the same thing to you. It's like the whole world is against us, Ryder. I don't know how much more I can take."

He put his arms around me and held me to him,

and it was the best feeling in the world. After hours of dealing with men who didn't care, he showed me with that one simple gesture that he cared for me.

That I meant something.

"Don't think about them now. Here in this place it's just you and me. Ryder and Serena. Nobody else."

I looked up at him as my anger and stress began to melt away under his protective gaze. Someone just seeing him on the outside would only see the hardness that had settled into his face after years of working for my father. He hadn't aged much from that handsome teenager with the stunning green eyes and chiseled features, but I saw the differences in him after all he'd done.

In those first days after he came to the house, I'd marveled at how beautiful he was. Even beaten up he had a sweetness that came through. A lightness that drew me to him.

Now I only saw that in his eyes when we were alone.

"What are we going to do, Ryder? Sometimes I feel like it's a hopeless cause."

He shook his head and frowned. "We are not a hopeless cause. It's not us. The problem isn't with us." Pointing to his front door, he continued, "It's out there with them. With people who only care about others when they can get something from

291

them. We don't belong with them, but we don't have any choice. For now, this is where we are. What matters is that we have each other."

When he talked like that, I believed that sometime in the future, somehow we'd be free of all the terrible things we had to live with now.

"I won't let them stop me from seeing you, Ryder. I won't. I don't care what they do to me. I'll find a way to always be here with you."

He cradled my face in his hands and kissed me long and deep until nothing existed but him and me in the center of that room. The rest of the world fell away, leaving only us.

"I love you, Serena," he whispered against my lips. "You're the only good thing in my life. The only thing that makes me want to keep going on. If it wasn't for you, there'd be nothing for me."

I knew just how he felt. I'd never tried to kill myself again only because of him. If Ryder wasn't in my life, all I'd have was a father who saw me as a commodity to trade and sell and a husband who had not a shred of caring for me. I'd have no reason to not finish the job I started that night in my bathtub.

Sliding his hands down my face, he encircled my neck and gently tilted my chin up. "How long do you have tonight?"

I smiled up at him. "He's gone to his brother's tonight and my father is at his girlfriend's, so he'll be gone for at least a couple hours."

"Good. I can take my time then."

Ryder lifted my t-shirt over my head and buried his face in the space between my shoulder and my neck, peppering kisses along my collarbone as he unhooked my bra. My nipples hardened to excited peaks at his touch, and when he lowered his head to suck one into his mouth, my body practically melted.

Gently, he bit down on me, sending a jolt of desire to between my legs. I loved when he was like this. Unhurried. Playful. So incredibly sexy.

Burying my hands in his hair, I held him to me and moaned, "Harder...mmmm..."

He did as I asked and bit down harder on my nipple while his hand pinched the other one, doubling my excitement. Need pooled in my belly, making me wet and wishing he would move lower with that beautiful mouth of his.

As if he read my mind, he slid my nipple out between his lips and knelt in front of me to remove my shorts and panties. I stood before him naked and needy for his touch, but he simply sat back on his heels and stared up at me like I was something beautiful he had to adore before having me.

"I love it when you look at me like you are now," he said in a voice edged with need that hit me deep inside.

"What kind of look is that?"

"Like everything you need is in me."

Although I didn't know what he saw in my face, that was exactly how I felt when I looked down at him. Ryder offered me refuge from the world of my father and Oliver. In him, I found love and caring I'd never found in any other man.

"Everything I need is in you, Ryder," I explained, loving how he smiled when I said that.

Leaning forward, he kissed a path down over my stomach to my hip, making me tremble with each time he pressed his lips to my skin. His touch was reverent, adoring me more than merely fucking me.

His hands trailed down over my hips and squeezed for a moment before he spread me wide with his thumbs. Open and vulnerable, I stood watching as a look of desire washed over his face, and then I felt the most exquisite sensations as his mouth began its work on my pussy.

The tongue that thrilled me when he kissed me just minutes earlier now teased my needy clit with careful and measured movements that made me weak in the knees. I adored that mouth and its ability to deliver such perfect sensations.

And then when I was sure the next flick of his tongue over my tender clit would send me over the edge, he stopped and moved his mouth to the inside of my thigh. Desperate to come, I whined, "Why did you stop? I was so close."

Looking up at me, he smiled. "That's why I stopped."

My mouth turned down in a pout even though I couldn't say I was angry with him. I knew how much he loved to get me to that point where I was practically begging for him to let me come, and in truth, I loved it too. He read my body perfectly, knowing how to push me to the verge and then how to hold me there, edging me closer and closer to release until my orgasm exploded through me.

He returned to kissing my leg, concentrating on the tender area near where it met my body and teasing me by being so close to where I so desperately wished he'd go with that beautiful mouth of his. I touched his soft hair, longer now than when I first met him, and delighted at the feel of its silkiness against my fingers. I loved when his hair would touch my cheek on those nights when we'd lay on his bed and talk before I was sent off to Italy. It was a part of him I could have even if the rest of him was out of reach.

As I remembered those nights, I looked down and saw him watching me as he slowly eased one finger and then two up inside me. Hands that had pummeled opponents and these days took care of my father's enemies and those who stood in his way gently caressed me in a way I wouldn't have thought possible. Those fingers that directed such anger and aggression to others worshipped my body, bringing it to the point of no return.

"Yes...don't stop, Ryder," I whispered as he gently thrust two long fingers inside me.

"I can feel you're close. Tell me how close you are."

I bit my lip knowing that as soon as I told him he'd stop and answered truthfully, "I'm right there. Please don't stop."

But I knew he would. He wanted to make our time last, and a quick fuck like we'd had earlier in the car wouldn't be enough for either of us. Like me, he wanted to feel that refuge he found in what we were for more than a few seconds.

Slowly, he slid his fingers out of my body and took them into his mouth, sensually sucking my juices off them. "You taste so fucking good. I can't wait to bury my face in that pretty cunt of yours. But first, I want to tease you a little more."

Tilting my head, I looked down at him as he licked his lips and pouted again. "You're mean, you know that?"

"No, I'm not. Not with you."

I cupped his cheek and smiled, knowing how much it meant that with me he could be someone other than that brutal man he had to be in every other part of his life.

Taking my hand, he weaved his fingers through

mine and leaned forward to press his lips to me, sending shockwaves through my body. This time, he didn't want to merely tease me. With his free hand, he slid two fingers into me and began fucking me hard as his mouth sucked and nipped at my clit.

My legs buckled as my orgasm began to wind through me, and then with one last flick of his tongue over my swollen clit, I came apart and nearly fell back as my head swam from the sensations he expertly produced in me. His hand squeezed mine as the other one stopped me from falling, but he didn't move his mouth away until the last of those sweet tremors dissipated.

Sitting back on his heels, he looked up at me like a man satisfied with what he'd done. "That was payback for what you did in the car. And, by the way, you're lucky I didn't drive off the road from what you did."

Crouching down, I kissed him on the lips and tasted myself on them. "Death by blowjob. Not exactly what most people want written on their headstone."

He smiled one of those rare broad smiles he gave me when he was truly happy. "Speak for yourself. I think going out that way would be the best way I could imagine."

"Mangled in a car wreck just as you came? I don't think so."

Twisting his face into a grimace, he shrugged. "Okay, maybe that part wouldn't be so great, but the blowjob part is still one of the best ways to go. Especially from you."

I rolled my eyes at his praise and knelt before him. "I love when we get to be like this. No one makes me feel like this but you."

Pulling me to him, he kissed me. "It must be real love then."

I looked into his eyes and saw the gentleness I'd searched for all my life. "Must be."

Whatever this was, it was as real as anything I'd ever felt. As real as the fear I'd lived with every day since I realized what my father was and what he could do to me. As real as the hope that one day I'd escape this world and find what everyone else seemed to take for granted.

Love, security, and freedom.

Taking my hand, Ryder stood from the floor and lifted me up. "Time to move this to somewhere more comfortable. Floor sex is great, but my body's taken too many beatings to do it for too long."

As I followed him to his bedroom, I thought about how hard his life had always been. Bringing his hand to my mouth, I pressed a kiss into his palm. He stopped and looked down at me, and I did it again.

"I thought you should feel kindness to help you

forget everything you've had done to you."

Shaking his head, he said, "I don't want to forget the beatings. They make the time I get to spend with you even more special. If I forget the beatings, I might take this for granted, and I never want to do that."

I unbuttoned his shirt and slipped it off his body, seeing firsthand the evidence of the life he didn't want to forget. Unable to tear my gaze from the scars from those beatings, even hidden in the tattoos that covered his arms, I ran my fingertips over the one near his left shoulder as he stepped out of his pants and tried to imagine the pain that left that mark.

He pulled me down onto the bed and kissed away my sadness from seeing his pain displayed so clearly on his body. I wanted to tell him I was sorry, even though I hadn't caused any of it, but with the first slow thrust of his cock into me, all that disappeared, replaced by the sweetest and purest happiness I'd ever felt.

Only Ryder, a scarred and broken human being like me, could give me that. I couldn't risk losing him or all he gave me. I wouldn't.

Chapter Twenty-Three

Ryder

ROBERT'S OFFICE BUZZED with activity when I walked in at nine sharp. He didn't tolerate lateness, so often his employees arrived early, but after spending much of the night holding Serena in my arms and talking about the day the two of us would finally get away from this place, I barely got a shower and dressed in time to make it to work as Robert's massive grandfather clock struck the hour.

Looking up from his laptop, he shot me a look that told me he knew exactly how close I'd cut it. "Sleep in this morning, son?"

For a moment, the fear that he knew what I'd spent last night actually doing raced through me, but when he punctuated his question with a smile that didn't resemble his usual crocodile grin, I pushed that thought out of my mind. I doubted he'd be able to joke so casually with me if he knew about Serena and me.

"Rough night. Too much whisky and not enough sleep, to be honest," I said as I took a seat in one of the red leather chairs he'd recently bought for right in front of his desk.

"Well, I need you on your game today, so get some coffee in the kitchen and wake yourself up. It's an all-hands-on-deck kind of day."

Looking around for some clue as to what he meant, I saw the other men he usually kept around shrug as if to say, "We have no fucking clue either."

"Okay, boss. I'll be right back. Can I bring you one too?"

Robert shook his head, already engrossed in something on his laptop screen, so I headed out to the kitchen and grabbed a cup of coffee. Always unusually strong on Robert's orders, it never took more than a few gulps to snap my brain out of whatever morning funk affected it.

Not that I really wanted the caffeine to rouse me from the haze still clouding my brain. My time with Serena softened the hardened edges, making me not so much dulled as kinder. I liked that she brought that out in me, but I knew that Ryder wouldn't be very good at the jobs her father needed me to do.

The work version of me had to be part junkyard dog, part professional ambassador for his business dealings. Neither of those allowed for my kinder side.

By the time I returned to his office a few minutes later, everyone else had left on their assignments for the day. I stood at the door watching Robert as he frantically typed away on his computer and then scowled at what appeared in front of him. Over and over, he repeated this until something finally made him smile, but I knew it couldn't be anything good.

Whenever that crocodile smile spread across his face, nothing good ever came from it. That was the sign that someone was in for a world of pain.

I just hoped it wasn't Serena or me.

Still fixated on whatever he was reading on his laptop, he said, "Ryder, sit down. You're making me uncomfortable in my own damn office standing at the door like some goddamned sentry. I don't need a bodyguard in my own home."

Taking a seat in one of those red leather chairs again, I said, "Sorry. I didn't want to interrupt. You look like you're engrossed in something."

He looked up and nodded, his mouth turning down in a frown. "I am. In fact, what I'm looking into involves you today."

Another spike of fear tore through me. As calmly as possible, I asked, "Me?"

My question hung heavy in the air as he didn't answer for a few torturous moments, but then he looked up and nodded in a matter-of-fact way. "Yes, you. I'm going to have you do something for me today. Nothing out of the ordinary. Well, a little, but I have no doubt you'll be able to handle it."

I knew what that meant. I'd be acting as one of his henchmen today, as Serena liked to call those of us whose job was to convince people to see things as Robert wanted them to.

"Okay. I'm on it."

My answer sounded far more enthusiastic than I truly felt. While I didn't mind roughing people up, I just wasn't in the mood for putting a beat down on some guy today. Maybe that was because I'd spent the night happily fantasizing with Serena about the future and how someday we'd go far away and begin a brand new life for just the two of us. A dream so full of promise and love, it made me wish for the softer things in life, not the reality of busting some guy's nose so he'd realize paying Robert was in his best interests.

As I reminisced about my time with her, Robert continued pounding on the keys, likely writing some nasty email that wouldn't elicit the right response, which would then lead to me having to do my job. Who would it be today? One of the club owners who never seemed to be able to understand paying the boss wasn't optional or maybe Floyd over at the Pit?

Part of me wished it wouldn't be Floyd. I'd rarely seen him since I stopped fighting, but I held no ill will toward him. He had more sense than most of Robert's business contacts and paid his money on time. But maybe he'd gotten greedy lately and started skimming off the top again. I knew he'd done it once or twice while I was fighting for him.

I wouldn't beat up Floyd, though. I wouldn't have to. Half my size and nearly double my age, he knew better. He'd spent enough time around fighters to know even those out of the game for a while could still hurt him more than he could handle.

Finally, Robert closed his laptop and sat back in his chair, a sign he was ready to begin. I sat up in my chair and finished the last of my coffee, wide awake for whatever he planned to have me do.

"I heard something unsettling last night, but I needed to investigate a number of issues before I did anything in response. I know you and Serena are close, so I want your input on this and then I'll decide what to do."

His mention of Serena made me sure I didn't want to know the next words to come out of his mouth, but I still forced myself to smile and nod like everything in the world was okay. "I'll do whatever you need me to do."

Knitting his eyebrows, he grimaced. "I'm afraid my daughter isn't happy with her marriage to Oliver. I'd hoped they'd grow to care for one another, but that hasn't happened. He clearly likes her. That show of jealousy over you driving her to her sister's proves that. But he doesn't seem to understand that all whip and no stroking isn't going to make that mare do what he wants."

I tried to control my face as my expression threatened to morph into something full of disgust at his comparison of Serena to a horse. Thankfully, he appeared too involved in his own thoughts to notice my reaction.

"That he's not very good with her disappointed me, but last night pushed it too far. She told me he said his brother told him she was a whore and he was marrying down. I defended him to her because the last thing I need is her getting the idea I don't support that union, but the more I thought about it, the more it ate at me. Oliver's brother rubbed me the wrong way the first time I met him, but since he wasn't marrying Serena, I didn't let it get in the way of the marriage, but that kind of insult can't go unanswered."

Serena had told me everything Oliver had said to her, including his brother's claim that she was a whore and that was why no one wanted her. If I could have without risking hurting her, I would have gone over to that fucker's house and beat the hell out of him when she told me. She'd also told me about her father's reaction to what her brother-in-law said, and I hadn't been surprised.

Nothing mattered as much to Robert as much as business. Not even his daughter's honor. He wanted part of the Landons' company, and if that meant he tolerated some shitty talk about Serena, he'd take it because in the long run, he'd get what he wanted.

That he planned to have me do something in response to these insults surprised me. However, I knew if he intended to have me retaliate for him, it meant he had some trick up his sleeve that would make the Landon brothers understand who they were dealing with in Robert Erickson.

"So I think it's time to make a statement, don't you?" he said, less as a true question than a statement of fact he expected me to agree with.

"Absolutely."

I agreed with him and looked forward to smacking Oliver's brother around. Hell, if Oliver was still at his house, maybe I'd give him a few shots just because the fuck deserved it.

"Then take care of him tonight. I've found out he usually spends a half-hour or so in his hot tub on the back deck of his estate around eight o'clock, and I'll make sure his brother doesn't go anywhere near there tonight. The rest is up to you. Don't let me down, son."

My mouth dropped open in shock. I'd expected Robert to tell me to teach the guy a lesson, not give me the order to get rid of him. Robert never said to take care of someone unless he wanted them dead. I'd only heard that order four or five times in the entire time I worked for him. Fuck, as vicious as he was, ordering someone to be killed wasn't something even he did every day.

Killing Oliver's brother didn't bother me so much as surprise me. That was his son-in-law's family. Striking like that meant Robert wanted to make a real statement to him.

A statement he wouldn't misconstrue. Keep mistreating Serena and the next person to go would be him.

Without another word, Robert opened his laptop and began typing feverishly again. Clearly, he didn't see any need to elaborate on what he wanted, and I didn't need to be told twice. I knew my role, and tonight it meant getting rid of the brother of the man I hated more than anyone else in the world.

I should have felt bad knowing what I had to do. But I didn't. If anything, I relished the idea. I knew he wasn't paying for what he'd said about Serena so much as for stepping out of line with Robert, but it didn't matter all the same.

I knew what had to be done and I'd do it, just like always.

IGNORING HOW MUCH I wanted to message Serena and tell her I loved her before I did what I'd been ordered to, I left the house just before eight and took the Mercedes she and I had used just days before. Even though I made sure to get it detailed afterward, as soon as I closed the door I smelled the scent of her vanilla shampoo. Struck by how that could be the only scent left over from our time together, I passed through the estate's front gate and began my trip to Jacob Landon's home.

I drove the roads there in a daze, my mind filled with thoughts of what Serena and I had talked about the night before. A time when we'd live together and spend each day making one another happy. Nobody to order me to be a killer, and nobody to demand she accept the role of property to be traded from one person to another.

We knew for now it was more dream than even possibility. Her marriage to Oliver, as much as it was a sham, kept her tied to the estate, but I knew even without him in the picture, she'd still have to overcome incredible odds to get away. Robert had gone from simply being cruel to her to being obsessed with controlling her life, and even if Oliver disappeared, he likely would simply replace him with another man whose business connections offered Robert a chance to improve his own wealth and power.

But we still dreamed of a day when neither of us were shackled to him or that place anymore.

I turned the car onto the street leading to Jacob Landon's estate and turned off the headlights to park. For a moment, I sat with the car running, making a mental note that I needed to start squirreling away money for that time when our dream came true. I needed to make sure I could take care of Serena if we got away.

Taking a deep breath, I turned the car off and silently began making my way toward my job that night. That's what it was. A job. Nothing more, nothing less.

Jacob Landon had made the mistake of crossing the wrong man, and now he had to pay.

The act itself felt like it had every other time I'd done it, just with the slight variation of the method. Landon sat relaxing in his luxurious hot tub like some fucking movie star with a glass of champagne in his right hand and his eyes closed. All he was missing was the big fat cigar dangling from his mouth.

He never heard me coming, probably because of the sound of those jets making all the fucking bubbles around him. Alone for the night, he made himself easy prey. I had no idea where his security was, but if he was like Robert, they were safely somewhere else enjoying a night off while the boss soaked his wealthy ass in a tub.

I pushed up my sleeves and snuck up behind him. I pushed hard on the top of his head, stuffing him under the water. Holding him even as he kicked his legs and flailed his arms, I waited until his limbs slowly stopped moving and then finally he fell still.

And whatever Jacob Landon had been other than the man Robert Erickson wanted gone, he was no more.

❖   ❖   ❖

BRIGHT AND EARLY the next morning, I stood against the wall in Robert's office as Oliver and Serena sat in the two red leather chairs in front of her father's desk listening to him profess his sympathy for the loss of Jacob Landon. Each word rang hollow because they were nothing more than meaningless sounds coming from his mouth.

Then he smiled one of those crocodile smiles and said, "This thrusts you into the CEO chair at your company, Oliver. I hope you remember our agreement. If anything were to happen to you, God forbid, Serena here would then step into the position you find yourself in right now. Of course, none of us wish to see that, but accidents do happen."

Robert's not-so-subtle reminder to Oliver of who possessed the power wasn't lost on him. One look at the grieving man's expression told me he understood if he stepped out of line, Robert would punish him. I couldn't tell if he suspected his father-in-law of having anything to do with his brother's death, but it didn't matter if he did.

A power shift had occurred, and whatever

control Oliver had thought he possessed no longer existed. He was living in the enemy's house now, and Robert had all but told him if he screwed up with Serena one more time, he'd pay a steep price.

His warning issued, Robert again expressed his condolences on the untimely and premature passing of Jacob before Oliver excused himself in order to deal with the funeral arrangements for his brother. Serena stayed behind looking like she wanted to say something, but Robert cut her off before she had the chance to.

"I'm looking forward to hearing nothing but marital bliss exists between you two from this point on, Serena."

Just as he'd warned Oliver, this was his warning to Serena that he didn't want any more problems coming from her house. She opened her mouth to speak but then pressed her lips together as if whatever she wanted to say was pointless.

I knew what she wanted to say. I wanted to say it too. Eliminating Jacob may have helped Robert's control over Oliver concerning business, but it did nothing to improve Serena's marriage to him. If anything, it damaged it even more because if he had even a hint of suspicion that her father had killed his brother, anything or anyone connected to Robert would be nothing but a hated reminder of Jacob's death.

Waving his hand to dismiss us, Robert said, "I need the two of you to leave. Ryder, take the day off. You deserve it."

We filed out into the main hall and walked silently beside one another until we reached the back hallway that led to the other parts of the house. Serena swiveled her head to see who was nearby and put her hand on my chest to stop me.

She looked up at me with fear in her eyes, and I knew what she planned to say. "Did you do this?"

I could have lied to her, but that wasn't something we did with one another. I'd lied so many times in my life that it was practically second nature, but I didn't want to do that with her.

So I told the truth, knowing that she may hate to hear that part of me truly existed.

"Yes."

Her expression turned to sadness. "Just yes? You kill someone and your answer is a simple yes?"

"Serena, your father wanted him taken care of because of what you told him he said about you," I answered flatly, still feeling nothing about what I'd done.

She looked away and sighed. "Tell me you aren't just that man. Tell me who you are with me is the real man you are."

"Why does it matter? You've known who I was for months. Why does this bother you?" I asked, truly confused as to why Jacob Landon's death mattered. "He wasn't the first and he won't be the last, Serena. You know your father better than anyone."

Shaking her head, she struggled not to cry as she said loudly, "It's not my father I care about! I don't care what he does. I care what you do, Ryder. I care that you don't become him."

I pushed her down the hall away from the main hall and her father's office to one of the utility rooms at the back of the house and closed the door behind us. She stood looking up at me with hurt in her eyes, and for a moment I wondered if there was a possibility she did care about Oliver.

"Why are you asking me about this, Serena? You act like I had a choice here, not that I would have done anything differently if I did. That's my job. Who I am with you has nothing to do with that."

"How can you say that? How can you act like you're two entirely different people, one who does these horrible things for my father and doesn't bat an eyelash or feel any guilt at all, and another who says he loves me more than anything else in the world and swears he'll protect me like some honorable knight in shining armor? Don't you feel anything about what you did?"

I looked into those gentle brown eyes so full of sadness staring up at me as she waited for my answer and told her the truth. "It's the man who loves you more than life itself who wanted to kill Jacob Landon last night, Serena. He called you a whore. You're the woman I love. The woman I'd give my life for, and he and that fuck of a brother of his called you a whore."

The tears that had been welling in her eyes rolled down her cheeks as I spoke, and she buried her face in her hands. "What are we going to do, Ryder? My father thinks my marriage is going to be all sweetness and light now. How can that be now?"

Pulling her close, I held her to me as sobs shook her body. I may not have felt any guilt over what I'd done to Jacob Landon, but seeing her sad over who I had to be to do that ripped me apart.

"We're going to do what we've always done. We keep looking forward to a future when this isn't our life and spend whatever time we can together."

She looked up at me, her beautiful face tearstained, and as I dried her cheeks, she whispered barely loud enough for me to hear, "I found out this morning I'm pregnant. When he finds out, he's going to know what we've been doing, Ryder."

Stunned, I struggled to find the words. "Pregnant? When?"

"My wedding night, I'm guessing."

"How far along are you?"

"Just about three months."

I took a step back and shook my head, still trying to get my brain around what she'd just told me. "Why didn't you say anything all this time?"

"I didn't know until this week. I thought I missed a couple months because of all the stress of having to marry him, and then I took a test and found out."

As much as I didn't want to question her, I had to. "Is there any chance it's his, Serena?"

She backed away from me like I disgusted her and her face twisted into a look of pain. "How could you ask me that? You know how I feel about him. I hate him!"

"But you slept with him at least a few times, didn't you?" I asked, my jealousy rearing its ugly head as I thought about him raising my child.

Serena hit my chest with her fist and then hit me again as hard as she could, crying out, "You bastard! I tell you I'm going to have your child and this is what you say? You are that terrible man who does my father's bidding! How can there be any hope for this child with a father like you?"

Her words cut me to the quick, and even though I barely felt her punches against my skin, I grabbed her wrists and held her arms still in front of me as my emotions warred inside my brain. Part of me rejoiced at the thought that Serena could be carrying my child, but another knew what she said was true.

What kind of father could a killer be?

"Don't say that. Whatever this child is, they'll be loved. I promise."

She closed her eyes and sagged against my body as she began to cry again. "I'm sorry. I don't mean that. I know you're not that man who does those horrible things. I believe that, Ryder."

Stroking her soft hair, I reveled in the feel of her against me. I was that man who did more than horrible things, but I was also the man who loved her and wanted to be more than I was at that moment.

I didn't know what the future held for us or our child. Married to another man, she would have to pretend it was his, but I'd know the truth.

And that's what mattered most until that day we could escape this place and find that life we dreamed of.

Chapter Twenty-Four

Serena

F OR NEARLY TWO months, I hid my pregnancy from Oliver behind baggy sweaters perfect for the winter weather that had settled into the Chesapeake region, and every day I tried to come up with a plan to get away from this life before I had to tell him.

And every day I came to the same sickening conclusion. In a few short months, I'd give birth to Ryder's child and be forced to pretend Oliver was his or her father. Every moment that ticked by and I hadn't escaped him and this place became a painful reminder that what should have been the happiest time of my life was simply a horrible extension of every other day I'd lived here.

The moments I got to spend with Ryder remained the happiest of my life, even if they were fleeting and too rare. Oliver worked late almost constantly after his brother's death, so whenever I could, I snuck down to Ryder's apartment. Part of me secretly hoped I'd get caught because then at least I'd be able to stop living the lie that my life had become.

Then one night, a fight between Oliver and me laid bare everything I'd hidden.

As usual, he returned home at nearly midnight and proceeded to throw himself onto the bed next to me. Still suffering from nausea from morning sickness that didn't seem to know the time, I nearly vomited there in the bed and quickly ran to the bathroom to throw up the tiny bit of toast I'd had for dinner hours before.

From the bedroom, I heard him complain about something involving work, and by the time I returned to bed, he had moved on from being unhappy about the art auction business to being miserable about his life with me.

"So now my own wife can't even be around me without throwing up? Nice," he snapped as he sneered at me.

"It's late, Oliver. I'd like to go to sleep."

I turned away from him and closed my eyes, but he wasn't finished. "What kind of man has no control over whether his wife loves him or not, where he lives, what he does…or any part of his life, for that matter?"

Not answering because I knew he wouldn't like what I had to say, I lay there wishing for sleep and knowing it wouldn't come anytime soon. Oliver had been unhappy from the beginning of our marriage, and his brother's death had only intensified his feelings about our life together and me, but now it all seemed to come to a head.

"I hate living here, Serena. We have no life here because of your father. He's like an overseer."

I couldn't disagree with that, but his complaint made me chuckle. He'd lived under my father's rule for less than a year. I'd lived under it my entire life. He'd get no sympathy from me.

Rolling over, I looked up to see him sitting on his side of the bed, his arms folded across his chest like a petulant child. "You knew what you were getting into when you agreed to this marriage, Oliver. You and your brother got something, I'm guessing money that you needed for the company, and in return my father got what he wanted, which when it comes to most things in his life is complete control. And I got nothing I wanted. As far as I see, you came out ahead."

He sneered at me again. "By getting a wife who never loved me? Never even wanted to love me? Yeah, that's definitely coming out ahead."

Behind his anger, I sensed real unhappiness, and for the first time, I pitied him. Maybe he had thought we could be happy in some way in the beginning, although leaving me on our wedding night to go to his brother's was a strange way of showing it.

I rolled over again and prayed he'd grow tired of talking about things that couldn't be changed. The problem was whatever had set him off tonight had brought everything to the surface, and nothing was going to stop him now.

"So you don't love me at all, do you?"

Despite knowing I shouldn't feed into his anger, I sat up and stared at him in disbelief at how clueless he truly was. "You have never shown me the tiniest kindness. You left me alone on our wedding night to go spend time with your brother, and you've trapped me in this apartment to keep me from seeing other people while you're away all day, every day. And now you're surprised I don't love you?"

His eyes opened wide as my words hurt him as much as his had hurt me all those times before, and he angrily said, "I regret ever saying yes to my brother when your father came sniffing around. He told me what you were but said if I simply waited it out, your father would eventually leave his businesses to me. I should have never believed that. My brother was wrong about Robert. So wrong."

"That you thought marrying me would get you my father's businesses shows me exactly what you always thought of me. And by the way, if you think being my husband is the golden ticket to getting things from him, you're sadly mistaken. He'd no sooner leave you anything more than he'd leave me,

320

and I'll be lucky to have a home when he goes. I'm the wrong sex, and you're not his son."

Oliver stood from the bed and pointed his finger at me. "You're just like him. You know that? Just like him. This whole family disgusts me."

"Well, it seems that we're all you have now that Jacob isn't around for you to go running to every time."

Oliver stormed out of the bedroom, slamming the door, and as my stomach roiled from the stress of fighting him, I tried to simply breathe and keep calm. My heart slammed in my chest as my nerves began to fray while he stomped around the apartment mumbling to himself.

I didn't want to fight with him. In truth, I didn't want to do anything with him. No fighting, no love, no anything. But I sensed he hadn't finished saying what was on his mind.

He flung open the bedroom door and screamed, "Your father killed Jacob! I know it! Did he do it because you told him to?"

Laughing at the very idea that my father would do anything like that for me, I shook my head. "I had nothing to do with what happened to your brother. I don't know what you're talking about, but I just want to go to sleep, Oliver, so why don't you go out so I can go to bed?"

"This isn't over, Serena!" he yelled and then

slammed the door again.

Unsure what he might do, I got out of bed and changed out of my baggy sweatshirt and shorts into a pair of jeans and an even baggier sweater just in case I had to get away from him in a hurry. I'd barely dressed when he returned to the room with a glass in his hand. From the smell coming off it, he'd started with the gin, his drink of choice.

"I think it's time we finally had it out, Serena. Why aren't you even trying in this marriage? I want to know what's wrong with you."

His words struck me like a bolt of lightning. What was wrong with me? Why did he get to say there was something wrong with me simply because I didn't love him like he thought I should? All my life I'd had people around me who thought there was something wrong with me because I didn't think like they did. All my life I'd been convinced I wasn't right.

Until Ryder. And now Oliver thought he could question what was wrong with me?

Pushing past him, I walked out to the kitchen to get a drink of water before I vomited again, this time from my nerves, and tried to keep my mouth closed as I knew I should. But then he repeated his question, and all of a sudden, all I wanted to do was tell the truth.

Every last bit of it.

I spun around as the room began to swim in front of me, but I couldn't hold back the words any longer. He wanted to know why I wasn't trying to make our marriage work? Then I'd tell him.

"What's wrong with me? Nothing!" I screamed, making him take a step back in surprise. Usually so docile, now I was anything but.

"I have a father who trades me like I'm livestock to the highest bidder, your brother and you. I begged my father to not make me marry you. Begged! There was nothing wrong with you, but I didn't want to be married. I wanted to go to school and get my degree, and then I wanted to move away and live my life. A boring life, but it would be all mine. But I wasn't given a choice. Did you know I tried to kill myself when I found out my father was going to force me to marry you?"

Oliver stared at me in horror, but I wasn't finished. Not by a longshot.

I held out my left wrist and pointed at the faint scar where the blade had cut into my skin. "I slit my wrist because I didn't want to be handed over to another man! I wanted to die, but I couldn't. Someone saved me, and what did I get for it? I got to be married to you, a man who only married me because it was a good business deal for you and your brother. And now you think you should ask me why I'm not trying to make our marriage a success?"

He shook his head in disgust, my admission only serving to make him more confident in his belief that everything was my fault. "I knew there was something wrong with you. Is that what you're doing with all this sickness lately? Are you trying to kill yourself to get away from me?"

"Don't flatter yourself, Oliver. I don't have to get away from you. You're never around anyway."

"Then what is with all the throwing up? Do you have something else wrong with you other than being a head case?" he snapped.

I looked into his eyes as he stood there so sure I was defective and that he had good reason to deny me the basic respect even strangers received from him and decided I didn't want to pretend anymore. Lifting up my sweater, I showed him my slightly swollen belly and answered, "There's nothing wrong with me. Pregnant women often have morning sickness."

His eyes narrowed to angry slits. "That can't be mine, so whose is it, you whore? The two times we've had sex couldn't have resulted in that, so who's the guy you've been with, Serena? Tell me!"

"Never!" I screamed as I ran away to the bedroom, locking the door behind me.

Oliver followed me, banging his fists against the door when he found it locked. Terrified what he might do if he got in, I rushed to get the phone I used for Ryder and called him, but he didn't answer. I quickly typed out a text to tell him I needed him right now and sent it off.

"Open this door, Serena! I want to know who you've been whoring around with! Tell me or I swear to God I'm going to bust down this door!"

Cowering in the corner as I clutched the phone in my hand, I desperately waited for Ryder to call or text back, but he never did. With each minute that passed, I grew more and more terrified as Oliver continued to threaten me through the door for nearly a half hour.

Finally, I heard the front door slam and waited with bated breath to hear Ryder's voice as he argued with Oliver to see me, but all I heard was silence. I waited for a few minutes, but there was no sound at all.

Convinced Oliver had left, probably to go find my father, I walked out to the kitchen. Parched from fear, I poured myself another glass of water and prayed to God this night would end with me still alive.

From behind me, Oliver said in a low voice, "You really aren't too hard to fool, are you, Serena? Now tell me who the father of that bastard is or I swear I won't be responsible for what I do next."

My hands shook from fear and rage. The child I carried wasn't a bastard but one created from love, something he had not a single clue about.

Slowly, I placed the glass on the counter and turned around to see him standing there with pure rage in his eyes and for a moment I wasn't sure I could say what I wanted to. But if I was going to die right there tonight, I wasn't going to die a coward.

I'd been one nearly all my life, terrorized by my father and his demands on who he expected me to be. I wouldn't give Oliver that power too.

"You can do whatever you want to me, but I won't tell you who the father is. I will say this, though. He's a real man. He's loved me as completely as one person can love another, and I love him. I always have. So do your worst, but I won't put him in harm's way."

Oliver's eyes flashed such anger I stepped back in fear that at any moment he'd hit me. "A real man? You mean like the type that knows how sad and pathetic you are with your poor little rich girl act and your attempted suicide for attention act? That type of real man?"

Inside me something snapped, and I reached around and grabbed the glass to throw it. It sailed from my hand toward his head but instead of hitting him, it smashed off the wall behind him, sending a thousand shards of splintered glass through the air. He lunged at me, encircling his hands around my neck. Shaking me like an old ragdoll, he screamed,

"I'll kill you before I let you have this baby, you whore!"

"Let me go!" I barely croaked out as I frantically tried to peel his hands away from the hold they had on my neck.

With his face so close I could feel his hot breath on my cheek, he yelled, "Tell me! Who's the father of this fucking kid?"

I wouldn't tell him, even if it meant I had to die to protect my secret. Ryder had protected me, loved me, and I wouldn't repay those gifts with a betrayal merely because I stood there terrified Oliver would eventually kill me if I refused to give him his name.

Shaking me even harder, he stared at me with those wild eyes so filled with hate as his face grew redder and redder by the second. I wasn't sure which of us would die first. Me from his choking me or him from a stroke he was so furious.

And then suddenly, he dropped his hands from my neck. I fell to the floor gasping for air and in agony each time I swallowed from the pain of being nearly strangled. He stood over me saying nothing for a few moments, and then walked away, leaving me in an exhausted heap on the kitchen tile.

I had no idea why he let me go, but he'd given me a chance to get away and there was no way I wasn't going to take it. Pulling myself to my feet, I stumbled to the bedroom and grabbed my purse. I didn't know where I'd go. Maybe to see my father. Maybe to my old bedroom in the main house.

Maybe to Ryder's apartment. Maybe it was time to stop lying about us and let my father and the whole world know we loved each other and were having a child.

It didn't matter where I went as long as I wasn't in that apartment with Oliver for another second of my life.

He was nowhere to be found when I walked out of the bedroom, and I breathed a sigh of relief that the worst of it had passed. He'd bellowed and barked in my face, threatened and choked me, but I was free now and I wouldn't be staying around for any more.

I just hoped my father would now finally see by the hand marks on my neck that Oliver and the deal for his company wasn't worth it. If not, I knew he'd use the threat of hurting my mother against me, and I didn't know if I could live with myself if my stand for independence led to him hurting her.

All I knew was never again would I live another day in fear.

Looking around at the rooms Oliver and I had shared, I saw nothing familiar, nothing welcoming. This had been an apartment I'd been sent to after being forced to marry a man I didn't love. This was never home.

I walked toward the front door tired but happy

that I'd finally stood up for myself. Never again would I let a man use his hands to hurt me. Never again would I be yelled at and treated like a possession.

Pressing my palm to my belly, I knew I couldn't let that happen again. This child needed me to be strong, and even if I'd never been strong a day in my life before today, I'd be strong from this point on.

From behind me, I felt something brush against my shoulder, and I turned around to see Oliver standing there, his hands ready to choke me again. I ran toward the back door, but he caught up with me just as I reached the stairs, and then all I felt were those hands pushing hard against my back and I fell.

When I opened my eyes, I saw him standing over me looking down like he couldn't believe he'd actually done it. I didn't know if any of my bones were broken or even if what was happening was real. I only knew he stood there glaring down at me for a long time without saying a word. It was almost like he didn't know I could see him standing there.

And then he lifted his foot and kicked me. The toe of his dress shoe jabbed into my belly, sending pain so sharp through my body that it took my breath away. Then he kicked me again, and the pain overwhelmed me. I couldn't keep my eyes open anymore. I closed them as everything went dark.

Chapter Twenty-Five

Ryder

THE DRINK IN my glass gone, I sat up and grabbed the neck of the whisky bottle and considered whether it would just be easier to skip the middleman. Who needed ice anyway?

Tipping it up to my mouth, I downed a big gulp of whisky and felt it warm my insides as it traveled down to my stomach. It must have hit my bloodstream almost instantaneously because it didn't take long for it to affect me and I sat back in the chair as thoughts of Serena flooded my mind.

Even stone drunk, I couldn't get her out of my head. Not that I wanted to forget her. How did you forget the only part of your existence that made you happy?

No, I didn't want to completely forget her. After what she told me hours earlier, all I could think about was how she was carrying my child.

My child. Even the sound of those words echoing in my head sounded strange. I'd never truly thought about being a father. Maybe if my parents hadn't died and I hadn't been sent to live with my uncle I might have. Maybe if I wasn't still a kid myself when he sent me to fight and I didn't have to grow up right then and there I might have someday thought having a child would a nice thing.

But none of that happened. I'd been made an orphan and thrown into fighting to earn my keep before I could even get a driver's license, and even though I had to grow up overnight or suffer at the hands of the real adults around me, I never truly felt like an adult until I came to this place.

My drunken brain full of thoughts about Serena travelled back to one night a couple months after Serena was shipped off to Italy. I sat in that very room missing her and drinking just like I had for the past few hours because it hurt so fucking much to be away from her. I had no way to contact her and even though I checked every day, she never sent even a postcard to say hi all those months.

And for the first time in my life, I felt like an adult. I didn't know why because I'd lost people in my life before, but that night missing her made me feel older than I'd ever felt before. Even getting beaten to a pulp and barely being able to move in the hospital hadn't made me feel as bad as missing her did.

And that missing her made me feel like I'd spent years without what she gave me. I wasn't sure I'd known how alive she made me feel until she was ripped from my life.

I swigged another gulp of whisky and thought about how much I missed her even though she wasn't even a hundred yards away. How strange that someone could miss another person with them so close.

Not that it ever mattered how much distance anyone put between us. Her bastard husband could order her to never see me again, and her father could say I was only allowed to be around her in his presence and still we found a way to one another.

And in a few months, she'd give birth to my baby, a child that would live in her house with her husband acting like their father and I'd have nothing to say about it. Just the thought made my chest hurt.

There had to be some way to get her away from this place. Some way we could escape and live together where no one dictated the terms of our lives to us. Somewhere it didn't matter who she was or who I was, and all that mattered was we loved each other and the child we created from that love.

I'd leave this place and never look back as long as I had her with me, but never without her. She needed me to protect her, and I needed her for so much more.

I placed the bottle down on the table, drunk enough that I didn't want any more. As I drifted off with thoughts of that perfect day when she and I would run away and never look back, my phone vibrated against the whisky bottle. I'd had enough that even if it was Robert calling I didn't care, but then the reality of what would happen if I didn't answer him flashed through my mind.

Nothing like the threat of a tyrant's temper to make you do something you didn't want to do.

Grabbing the phone from the table, I tried to figure out who was texting me, but everything looked blurry. I shook my head to gather some semblance of sobriety and focused hard on the letters floating across the screen.

Jesse had texted me about some girl he wanted me to meet at his favorite bar a few hours ago. Delete. I didn't care to meet whoever she was.

Then he'd sent a second text telling me how much fun I was missing out on. Delete again.

Kitty had sent her almost daily text begging to know why I didn't come around anymore. Delete.

I kept scrolling and saw a call from Serena and then a message a little while later. My eyes grew wide as I tried hard to read each word. Oliver came home furious and they were fighting. She was afraid he'd do something to her.

Adrenaline coursed through my body, yanking me into sobriety in seconds. My heart slammed into my ribs as thoughts of him laying a hand on her tore through my mind, and I stood up and threw on a shirt to race over there.

With each step, I thought about what would happen if I burst into her apartment and she didn't need me to save her from Oliver hurting her. He'd know for certain she'd been with me, and Robert would know too.

But I couldn't worry about that. She'd never sent me a text saying she needed me to help her, and I had to make sure she was okay.

I looked outside for Oliver's car and saw he was gone. Relief washed over me as I stared down at that empty spot. Maybe he'd just left and hadn't done anything stupid. Hurrying to her apartment, I pounded on the front door but got no answer. It had been left unlocked, so I walked inside and began looking for her.

"Serena! Where are you? Are you hurt? Can you hear me?" I called out but heard nothing.

Checking each room, I found them empty but in the kitchen I saw broken glass scattered all over the floor. I didn't see any blood, but the fear that Serena had done something horrible to herself settled into my brain and took my breath away for a moment.

"Serena! Answer me! Where are you?" I yelled and again heard nothing back.

Panic tore through me with each time my pleas were met with silence. I finished searching every room and turned toward the stairs leading to the basement door for some clue that might tell me where she went to. Looking to see if the door had been left open, I saw a figure lying at the bottom of the stairs.

Racing down the steps, I took them by threes and in seconds, I stood above her staring down in horror. She lay in a pool of blood and her neck had marks where someone's hands had choked her. My heart in my throat, I crouched down beside her to check if she was still breathing, and when I placed my hand in front of her mouth, I felt a light touch of air hit my skin.

"Serena, wake up, baby. I'm here. You're not alone. I'm going to stay with you," I said, rejoicing that she was still alive.

I dialed 911 and in seconds had the ambulance on the way. I knew I should call Robert too, but he could wait. For now, she needed me more.

Stroking her cheek, I sat down on the floor next to her and whispered to her the words I hoped she could somehow hear. "The ambulance will be here in a few minutes and we'll get you to the hospital. You're going to be okay. I promise. You're not leaving me. I got to you in time before and this time is no different."

Her face looked so pale, like all the blood had drained away. Suddenly, I looked down at where the pool of blood came from and knew what Oliver had done. He'd found out about the baby and pushed her down the stairs to get rid of it and her.

Taking Serena in my arms, I held her to my chest and prayed to God they both would survive. Her body stayed limp against me, and with each second that ticked by, I feared the worst.

Like the last time when I'd found her nearly dead in that bathtub, everything seemed to move in slow motion after the ambulance arrived. They took her from me as the cops asked me question after question about what happened, assuming I'd done that horrible thing to her.

I answered each one with what I knew and left my suspicions out of it, knowing that's what I had to do. Without any proof, I couldn't accuse Oliver of trying to hurt Serena, even if that's exactly what I wanted to do every time they pressed me for who could have done this to her.

Finally, they left and I called Robert to tell him once again Serena had been taken to the hospital and I was on my way there. Unlike the first time, he didn't sound worried or surprised this time. He just said he'd meet me there and ended the call.

As I ran to the garage, a terrible thought settled into my mind. Had Robert been so calm when he found out she was found unconscious and bloody because he had sent one of his men to do this to her?

Was I wrong about Oliver being the one who hurt her? Was this the doing of her father instead?

ROBERT GRABBED ME by the shoulders to stop me as I walked through the ER doors, and I couldn't help but be struck by the anger I saw in his eyes. Had something happened? Was she dead?

"What is it, Robert? What happened?" I asked, desperate to hear anything but that Serena hadn't made it.

"She's in surgery now. They tell me she lost a lot of blood when she fell down the stairs. How could that happen, Ryder? How could she fall down stairs like that and get injured so badly?"

I didn't know what to say. I wanted to scream at the top of my lungs that she didn't fall. She was pushed and by the man he'd forced her to marry. A son of a bitch who beat up on women. A fucking coward I would make pay for this if it was the last thing I did.

I wanted to ask about the baby. Had she lost it? Remembering all that blood on the floor beneath her made my heart clench.

Our baby. The child I was sure Oliver had found out about and intentionally tried to get rid of.

But I said nothing about any of that, instead trying to keep my emotions from unraveling in front of Robert who wouldn't understand why I cared so much.

"I don't know how that could happen. When I found her, she was at the bottom of the stairs unconscious. I tried to get her to talk to me, but she never woke up."

He listened to me, but nothing I said made him feel better. Walking away, he began pacing back and forth across the waiting room until he stopped in front of me a few minutes later.

"How did you come to find her?"

The look in his eyes was one of suspicion. Did he think I did this to her?

I couldn't tell him she'd messaged me that she was afraid Oliver would hurt her. Even though I could prove it with the text she'd sent, that would only make him question why she and I had been communicating that way at all. He may have thought of me as his son in some respect, but he'd ordered me to stay away from her and the two of us texting back and forth meant I'd disobeyed him.

So I lied once again.

"I was outside and heard a noise near the back door of the house. That's how I found her at the bottom of the steps."

He thought about my answer for a moment and then shook his head. "Where is that husband of hers? Why isn't he here?"

"No idea. He wasn't home when I got there," I

answered truthfully, wishing I could tell Robert what I really thought.

"I better call him. He should be here when she wakes up."

Robert began pacing again as I thought about how little her husband deserved to be anywhere near Serena. I wasn't sure I'd be able to stop myself from ripping the fucker apart if I got stuck anywhere near him either.

But I couldn't leave her here with just her father and him. Neither one of them gave a real damn about her. Part of me wondered if Robert only came to the hospital because it would be what he was expected to do because of who he was.

It wouldn't do for Robert Erickson, wealthy and influential businessman, to have his daughter lying in a hospital bed near death and him to be nowhere nearby. What would his friends in high places think?

Robert stopped his pacing in front of me again and returned his phone to his jacket pocket. His eyes narrowed to slits, he made a growling sound and said, "He's on his way. Says he was at his brother's house because of work."

I opened my mouth to say that claim would be easy enough to check but instead just nodded. With security cameras trained on all the outside spaces and a guard at the estate's front gate, there would be no way for Oliver to not have been seen if he'd been home at any time that night. I saw in Robert's suspicious look that he knew that too.

As we waited, my rage toward Oliver grew until my hands stayed in constant fists at my sides. I'd beaten the hell out of dozens of people as a fighter and then for Robert, but I'd never hit a woman. Hell, even Robert had never asked me to do that.

To many people, we'd be villains, for sure, but even we didn't lay a finger on women that way. Only fucking cowards hurt a woman.

Robert continued to talk in spurts when a thought entered his head as he passed by me sitting in one of the plastic waiting room chairs until a doctor came out to speak to him about Serena's condition. Tired looking with grey peppered through his dark hair, his face seemed to be in a permanent frown, probably due to what he usually had to say to people when he told them the news about their loved ones.

"Mr. Erickson, your daughter's out of surgery and in recovery. She'll be taken to a room as soon as she can be."

"I want a private room for her. And I want to know what's going on. What happened to her?"

The doctor nodded solemnly, like Robert impressed him with his demand, and answered, "She doesn't have any broken bones, thankfully. She has a bruised kidney and a few bruised ribs. A fall down a flight of stairs can be quite bad, but thankfully, she's young so she should be fine after some rest. I'm sorry to say she lost the baby, though. However, she's lucky to be alive since whoever attacked her tried to strangle her before they pushed her down those stairs."

Robert's mouth hung open for a moment before he said, "Attacked! Did she say she was attacked? And what baby are you talking about?"

The doctor looked confused and shook his head. "Your daughter hasn't said anything, Mr. Erickson. The marks on her neck tell us she was nearly choked to death. And your daughter was very definitely pregnant. We stopped the hemorrhaging, but we couldn't save the fetus. I'm sorry. We'll take you to her as soon as we get her into a room."

He walked away as the news that our child was dead settled into my brain. That fucker Oliver had done what he set out to do. There was no way with the marks on her neck and the text she sent me that it was anyone other than him who was responsible for this.

The urge to find him and pound my fists into his face until all that was left was a bloody mess of flesh and bone nearly overwhelmed me, and I stumbled back into one of the waiting room chairs. He'd tried to choke her to death, and when that didn't work, he pushed her down a flight of stairs and killed my child.

As Robert paced again, mumbling about how he didn't even know she was pregnant and questioning how an intruder had gotten onto the estate to hurt her, I pushed my hate for Oliver down into my gut and swore that no matter what, he'd pay for what he did to Serena and our baby.

RYDER AND SERENA'S STORY CONTINUES IN IF YOU FIGHT (CORRUPTED LOVE #2)

About the Author

K.M. Scott writes contemporary romance stories of sexy, intense, and unforgettable love. A New York Times and USA Today bestselling author, she's been in love with romance since reading her first romance novel in junior high (she was a very curious girl!). Under her Gabrielle Bisset name, she writes erotic paranormal and historical romance. She lives in Pennsylvania with a herd of animals and when she's not writing can be found reading or feeding her TV addiction.

Be sure to visit K.M.'s Facebook page at **facebook. com/kmscottauthor** for all the latest on her books, along with giveaways and other goodies! And to hear all the news on K.M. Scott books first, sign up for her newsletter today and be sure to visit her website at **www.kmscottbooks.com**.

Books by K.M. Scott:

The Heart of Stone Series
Crash Into Me (Heart of Stone #1)
Fall Into Me (Heart of Stone #2)
Give In To Me (Heart of Stone #3)
Heart of Stone Volume One Box Set
Ever After (Heart of Stone #4)
A Heart of Stone Christmas (Heart of Stone #5)
Unforgettable (Heart of Stone #6)
Unbreakable (Heart of Stone #7)
Heart of Stone Volume Two Box Set

The Club X Series
Temptation (Club X #1)
Surrender (Club X #2)
Possession (Club X #3)
Satisfaction (Club X #4)
Acceptance (Club X #5)
The Complete Club X Series Box Set

The SILK Series
SILK (Volume One)
SILK (Volume Two)
SILK (Volume Three)
SILK (Volume Four)
The SILK Box Set

K.M.'S BOOKS ARE IN AUDIOBOOK TOO!

Books by Gabrielle Bisset:

The Sons of Navarus Series
Vampire Dreams Revamped (A Sons of Navarus Prequel)
Blood Avenged (Sons of Navarus #1)
Blood Betrayed (Sons of Navarus #2)
Longing (A Sons of Navarus Short Story)
Blood Spirit (Sons of Navarus #3)
The Deepest Cut (A Sons of Navarus Short Story)
Blood Prophecy (Sons of Navarus #4)
Blood Craving (Sons of Navarus #5)
Blood Eclipse (Sons of Navarus #6)
The Sons of Navarus Box Set #1
The Sons of Navarus Box Set #2

The Destined Ones Duology
Stolen Destiny (Destined Ones Duology #1)
Destiny Redeemed (Destined Ones Duology #2)

The Victorian Erotic Romances
Love's Master
Masquerade
The Victorian Erotic Romance Trilogy

Printed in Great Britain
by Amazon

16445672R00203